Deliverance

Jennie Marsland

Dedication

To the Korol family, for their warm hospitality under prairie skies.

Acknowledgements

My fourth novel. Writing has become a way of life for me, and a lot of people have helped make that life richer.

My editor and friend, Pat Thomas, helps me see my stories from a reader's point of view. Kim Killion at Hot Damn Designs applied her artist's touch to create my cover, as she did with my last novel, Shattered. My fellow members of Romance Writers of Atlantic Canada are a continuing source of knowledge and inspiration. My partner Everett and my parents never stop supporting me and believing in me. And then there are the readers whose encouragement keeps me going when the going gets tough.

Thank you all.

Other Books by Jennie Marsland:

McShannon's Chance

Trey McShannon survived the carnage of the Civil War, only to discover that the deepest wounds are those to the heart. A traitor to his home state of Georgia, Trey has built a new life for himself in the untamed Colorado Territory. Now it's time to find a wife to share the future he's worked so hard for – but can he free himself from his past?

McShannon's Heart

When Rochelle McShannon accompanies her father to his old home in Yorkshire after her mother's death, she thinks she's leaving everything that matters behind her – including the man she expected to marry. When tested by the divided loyalties of the looming Civil War, she can't choose love over her bond to her family. Chelle wonders if she's even capable of the kind of love that can overcome bitterness and grief, the kind of love that lasts a lifetime.

Shattered

Liam Cochrane no longer belongs. He lost his youth and his brother on the battlefields of Europe. Now he's home in Halifax, Nova Scotia, trying to dull his pain with liquor and the occasional willing woman. He's become a stranger in the North End neighbourhood where he grew up.

Alice O'Neill has never belonged. Able to read notes, but not words, she dreams of teaching music – and of Liam, who has held her heart for years and never known. But Liam has shadowy ties in England that he's revealed to no one, and in that fall of 1917, Halifax is on a collision course with fate. On December 6, a horrific accident of war will devastate the city's North End. What will be left for Liam and Alice when their world is shattered?

Chapter 1

Naomi Franklin paused above the steps of the Pullman car to let her eyes adjust to the bright autumn sunlight. When the familiar outlines of the station came into focus, she breathed a sigh of relief and stepped down to the platform. Home. A short walk, and at last she could shut her door against the world.

No one else got off the train except a man with the mail. On the empty platform, Naomi set her valise down and stretched her back, easing muscles cramped from sitting for so long – nothing more. She'd stayed in Winnipeg long enough for the physical reminders of her procedure to fade. 'A month-long visit with an old friend she hadn't seen since before the war,' was what she'd told everyone, even her father and Laura.

A chill breeze plucked at her skirt. Winter had crept closer while she was away. Naomi picked up her valise and took a couple of steps, then had to halt when two porters struggled out of the car behind hers, carrying a man between them.

They tried to set him on his feet, but his legs buckled. The older of the porters, a thin, stringy, middle-aged man, swore as he struggled with their burden. When his gaze met Naomi's, he flushed with embarrassment.

"Pardon my language, miss. Is there a jail in town?"

"It's on Railway, five minutes from here. There's a sign. Turn right in front of the station." Naomi took a step closer. Her stomach rolled at the reek of stale alcohol coming from the derelict. The middle-aged porter grimaced as he got a fresh grip on the dead weight of the semi-conscious man.

"Thanks, miss. Come on, Frank. We'd better be going."

On closer inspection, the man's grey wool jacket, jeans and only slightly scuffed boots seemed a bit too new for a derelict, and he looked like he might be ill as well as drunk. Naomi's mind clicked into triage mode. Breathing a little shallow, face a little flushed, with a few fading bruises. He'd been in a fight, and likely had a cold or the flu now. Not her concern, but still Naomi stopped the porters before they could carry the stranger off.

"What's he done?"

"Public intoxication should do it. We knew yesterday that he was drinking on the sly, but he wasn't bothering anyone so we left him alone. This morning we found him like this. Looks like he might be sick, too. We aren't going to have the other passengers complaining, miss."

The drunken man's eyes were closed, but with his black hair and fair skin, Naomi guessed they'd be blue. Scottish or Irish descent, probably. A few days' growth of stubble darkened his jaw. His face had a pared-down look, stripped of youth and innocence, but he couldn't be more than twenty-five or twenty-six. Maybe she should have the porters bring him to her house so her father could check him over and... No. If she did, her father would insist on looking after him, and she would have to nurse him. The thought of touching any man, let alone a roughneck like this, made Naomi nauseous.

"What's his name?"

The middle-aged porter shrugged. "He never said. He made it clear he wanted to be left alone."

"Where did he get on the train?"

"Don't know. He was aboard when we got on in Montreal."

"Did he have any luggage?"

The younger porter looked down at the Army kit bag slung over his shoulder. "Just this. Not much in it, I'd say."

Naomi stifled a pang of pity. She'd been told very early on in the field hospital that her feelings were a liability, not an asset. "My father is the doctor here, and I nursed overseas for two years. He doesn't look very ill to me. If he is, Constable Walters will send for my father. Good luck."

She left the porters behind, walked through the station and out onto Railway. The savoury smell of meatloaf floating from the open door of the restaurant across the street mingled with the smell of blackstrap molasses from the general store next door, along with the familiar odors of horse and dust. The store doubled as the post office and filling station. The only other businesses in town were her father's practice and the harness shop. Add the school and the Catholic and Presbyterian churches, and that was Mackenzie.

Half a mile to the east or west, the street gave way to open prairie. If a person on horseback looked back after a fifteen-minute ride, they'd see no trace of the town. The browns and whites, yellows and greys of the buildings had bleached or darkened with the years, until they were as subtle as the colours of dry grass and shorn wheat fields.

All were of wood. The soft prairie soil wouldn't support brick or stone. To Naomi, after seeing London and Paris, the place seemed poised to disappear, to be swept away as easily as smoke on the constant wind. Her love for her hometown had blended with a subtle kind of mourning – not as much for the changes war had brought to Mackenzie as for the changes in herself.

Home was a rambling, yellow-shingled, two-story house, larger than most in town, but as faded as all the others. The front door always stuck, so not even her father's patients used it. Naomi entered through the back door and set her valise down in the kitchen.

Nothing important had changed here since Naomi's childhood. The same round, spindle-legged ash table and matching pantry cupboard, the same scarred pine floor, the same creamy yellow walls and white muslin curtains at the windows. Not very modern, but no one wanted to change it, even after all these years. It held too many memories of her mother.

"Dad? Laura? I'm home."

Laura bustled in from her bedroom off the kitchen. "Naomi! You're back. Why didn't you wire? We weren't expecting you 'til later in the week. Your father is out at the Johnson place. Little Ethan managed to scald himself this morning."

With her wiry salt-and-pepper hair pulled back in a bun that emphasized her narrow face, Laura Thompson looked much as she had when she'd come to the Franklins as their housekeeper fifteen years ago, and would probably look the same fifteen years from now. Tall and thin, with more angles than curves, Laura's severe features and snapping dark eyes gave her the air of a strict schoolmistress, but she had a mother's heart where the doctor and his daughter were concerned.

Laura folded Naomi in a hug, then held her off. "You look well. Your father was right. You needed a change of scene."

"Yes, I did." And if Naomi had her way, her father and Laura would never know that her trip had been anything more than a chance to get away. They'd suffered more than enough for her since the summer. "I'm going upstairs to unpack and clean up."

She put her clothes away, ran a bath and soaked away the grime and fatigue of her journey. As she lay in the soothing hot water, her conscience twinged at the thought of the man from the train. Had the porters managed to deliver him to the jail? If not, there'd been nothing to stop them from just dumping him in the street and leaving him there.

While she was dressing, the phone in the kitchen rang. Laura picked it up. Naomi ran down, praying it wasn't something urgent. The last thing she needed today was a visit to one of the outlying farms.

Laura hung up as Naomi walked in. "Jen Davis is in labour. I'll make a call to your father. Looks like it'll be just the two of us for supper."

Laura's call caught the doctor just as he was leaving the Johnson farm. Naomi settled on the sitting room sofa with a book to pass the afternoon. She kept an ear open for the phone. Her father would call if he expected to be late. Jen Davis was healthy and only a year or two older than Naomi, but with a first baby anything could happen.

Dark came. Over supper, Naomi told Laura the carefully evasive story of her trip that she'd thought out on the journey home. They cleared the table and did the dishes, and still they got no word. At seven o'clock, the phone finally rang.

"Naomi, you're home. Jack Walters here. Is the doctor in?"

Naomi's heart sank. She hadn't thought of the man from the train since she'd finished her bath earlier. He must be sicker than she'd thought.

"No, Dad's out on a call. What's the matter, Constable Walters?"

"I have a man locked up here who's pretty sick. He was put off the train drunk this afternoon. Didn't look like there was much else wrong with him, but now he's got a fever and he's having trouble breathing."

So he was ill after all. Naomi pictured the stranger's tough-looking face. Nothing about him invited trust, but she could have shown him some compassion.

"I don't know when Dad will be back, but I'll be there in fifteen minutes."

"You don't want to come down here, Naomi. It's no place for a lady. I'll run over to the store and get someone to help me bring him to you. Won't be long."

Naomi hung up. If she'd had the sick man brought here this afternoon, would it have made a difference? Maybe not, but another time she'd go with her instincts. Now she'd be stuck with him anyway, until he could go on his way or back to jail. She wasn't going to like this, and neither would Laura.

"Laura, we're going to have a patient. He might have pneumonia. Jack Walters will be here with him before long. We'd better get busy."

Laura's hands flew to her nearly non-existent hips. "Jack Walters? Is this man in the jail?"

"Yes. He fell ill on the train. I saw him when I arrived this afternoon. The porters didn't know where else to take him, so they took him to the jail. I should have had him brought here, but he didn't look very ill then. Besides, he'd been drinking and…"

And if he hadn't been, that might have made the difference.

Laura's mouth set in a harsh line. She had little patience for drinkers.

"Then the jail is just where he belongs."

"Laura, from what Mr. Walters said, the man is really ill."

"Then leave him where he is and let your father go see him tomorrow. We've no room for drunkards in this house."

"You know that if Dad were home, he'd have him brought here right away."

Laura huffed. "Probably. Your father is too soft-hearted, but it isn't his job to take in tramps off the train."

"Maybe not, but it's too late now. They're on their way. Will you crush some ice, please? He has a fever. I'll get a fire going in the spare room."

Naomi ran upstairs, kindled a fire in the spare room fireplace, stripped the bed and brought the bedding down to warm by the stove. Laura filled a basin with crushed ice. Then they sat at the table to wait.

"Don't look so grim, Laura. He'll be harmless enough in his condition, and I've probably seen almost as many cases of pneumonia as Dad has." Naomi spoke to reassure herself more than Laura. Many of those patients hadn't survived, but others – sometimes the sickest – had pulled through. As for this drifter, Naomi might hate the thought of touching him, but if he died she'd feel guilty for weeks. She'd just have to put her fears aside.

Twenty minutes later, Constable Walters arrived with Mr. Anderson from the store. "We've got him in the car. I hope moving him won't make him worse."

"You couldn't look after him at the jail. Bring him in."

Laura hurried upstairs with the warm bedding. Mr. Walters and Mr. Anderson carried the stranger in, wrapped in a couple of car blankets, and took him up to the spare room. Naomi added water to the bowl of ice and followed. The men laid the patient on the bed, took off his jacket and unbuttoned his shirt.

Naomi sucked in a breath. His ribs were bandaged, a professional job by the look of it. The remains of heavy bruising showed along his clavicle, and he had what looked like a scar from a bullet wound on his right shoulder. Mr. Anderson let out a low whistle.

"Looks like he was in quite a scrap not too long ago. I'd say he's been overseas, too."

"So would I." Naomi fetched a pair of scissors from the drawer of the desk and cut away the wrappings on the stranger's torso. More deep bruises. A scrap? Someone – or several someones – had beaten the tar out of him. He must have seen a doctor afterward. Why on earth had he been travelling when he belonged in hospital?

He smelled, and the smell of a drunk now had a new element. This man sweated in a fever. He was too thin, but his body looked solid – not the body of an alcoholic vagrant. A criminal? A deserter? His bruises were just starting to fade to yellow. The beating couldn't have happened more than a couple of weeks ago.

"Will you get him undressed and into bed for me? Just leave the covers down. Then you might as well go back to town. There's nothing more you can do."

As the men removed the stranger's shirt and jeans, he muttered a few foreign words. Naomi's face burned. She'd learned those words overseas, and she wouldn't repeat them in any language. As soon as Mr. Anderson and Constable Walters left, Laura took Naomi by the arm, marched her out into the hall and shut the bedroom door.

"Have you taken leave of your senses? That man could be a spy! Your father will—"

"Calm down, Laura. Most soldiers pick up a few words of German and French overseas, and I'm sure he's been a soldier."

Laura glanced over her shoulder as if the stranger might have his ear to the door. "Perhaps, but he still reeks of liquor. As for you, you've had enough to deal with since you got home from Europe last winter. You haven't been yourself for months. Your father is worried about you. So am I."

A chill settled in the pit of Naomi's stomach. Did her father have an inkling of the real reason she'd gone to Winnipeg? God, she hoped not. He'd aged enough during the two years she was overseas, without him knowing about that.

"I'm all right, Laura. I'm going down to find a thermometer."

The sound of the sick man's laboured breathing filled the spare room when Naomi stepped back in. She pulled a couple of extra pillows from the closet and eased her arm behind his shoulders. It was all she could do to lift him. He might be thin, but he was all bone and muscle. She tucked the pillows behind him and a couple of towels on either side of him, pulled the desk chair to the side of the bed and slipped the thermometer into his mouth.

A hundred and four.

Her heart started racing. She laid a hand over his ribs and pressed firmly. Bone shifted. One broken rib, possibly two. No doubt he'd been drinking to dull his pain. He must have hidden the bottle well, or he would have been put off the train before this.

The stranger groaned and opened his eyes. As Naomi expected, they were deep Celtic blue, dark and glassy with fever. His gaze met hers and slid past with no sign of awareness. She touched his cheek to get him to focus on her.

"I'm sorry. I had to find out if your ribs were broken."

A gleam of irony cut through the glaze in his eyes. "Could have told you."

His voice was hoarse and gritty with pain. Naomi sat in the desk chair and hid her compassion behind a professional mask as she'd learned to do overseas. "You weren't awake to tell me. What's your name?"

He seemed to have to make an effort to remember. "Ben. Ben MacNeil."

"Mine's Naomi Franklin. Mr. MacNeil, you have pneumonia. You shouldn't have gotten on the train in your condition."

He coughed, then winced as the movement jarred his ribs. "You sound like my mother."

Naomi almost rolled her eyes. A hardhead, like some of her patients overseas. The kind who couldn't or wouldn't admit to pain. "Probably. What happened to you?"

"Long story."

"I'm sure. It can wait 'til you're feeling better. We have to try to get your temperature down."

She wrung out the cloth Laura had put in the basin and ran it lightly over MacNeil's bruised chest and ribs while she kept her gaze fixed on his shoulder. He didn't react to the icy water, but Naomi shivered, repulsed by the feel of his skin, the smell of liquor, male sweat.

Stop. You've done this so many times before.

She wet the cloth again and washed MacNeil's face. It looked as if he'd been punched to the ground and then kicked. A fading ring of yellow and purple circled one of his deep-set eyes, his lower lip had been split and was still a little swollen…and another healing cut ran across his left cheekbone. With those prominent brows and that aggressive slant to his nose, Ben MacNeil looked like a bare-knuckle boxer – a very sick bare-knuckle boxer. His palms showed traces of calluses, as if he'd worked hard in the not-too-distant past, but hadn't done much for a while. Likely he hadn't been back from overseas long.

He'd drifted back into a doze. Naomi dropped the washcloth in the basin and laid her fingers against his wrist to check his pulse. Thready and way too fast, but something else, a roughness to his skin, made her look down.

More scars. They looked like burn marks rather than cuts, so faded they were barely visible. She checked his other wrist and found similar marks there as well. It looked as if at some point, not very recently, his wrists had been bound.

"Laura, look at this."

Laura looked. "Well now. How do you suppose he got those?"

"I don't know, unless he was taken prisoner overseas. He might have had his hands tied then." Naomi shrank from the ugly possibilities that came to mind. She'd treated one or two soldiers who'd been prisoners of war, managed to escape and were sent back into battle. They'd told her they hadn't been mistreated by the enemy. If MacNeil had been a prisoner, he must have had a harsher experience. Naomi pulled his covers up and rose. "A fighter, are you? Well, you've got another fight ahead of you now."

Mr. Walters had dropped MacNeil's kit bag on the floor in front of the oak highboy. Surely there'd be something in it to help Naomi place him. Laura joined her as she lifted it to the desk. "I hope there's something in here with an address on it. We'll have to try to contact his family."

Naomi undid the buckles and looked inside. "There's nothing here but a couple of changes of clothes." She laid them on the desk. Laura took the bag and turned it inside out. With a resigned sigh, she tucked it in a dresser drawer.

"He would have been easy enough to rob, I suppose."

Naomi returned to the bed and gently shook MacNeil's shoulder. "Mr. MacNeil, where are you from? We want to contact someone for you."

With a flicker of black lashes, those intense blue eyes looked into hers again. "Wire Dennis. Good one on him." His eyes closed and his head rolled to one side. Naomi straightened up, rubbing at the knot in the back of her neck as she pictured MacNeil's worried family.

"We'll just have to wait. You might as well go downstairs where it's warmer, Laura. I'll stay with him 'til Dad gets home."

Naomi settled into the bedside chair, tilted her head back and rolled her shoulders to work out some tension. MacNeil stirred, drawing her gaze. She studied his flushed, hard-featured face. He looked rough enough, but not vicious. Still, the man must be running from trouble of some kind. Not that it mattered. He'd be gone as soon as he had the strength to leave.

Downstairs, the kitchen door opened and shut with a bang. *Dad.* On a rush of relief, Naomi hurried out to the head of the stairs. She heard Laura filling him in on their patient, then his footsteps in the hall. Naomi watched him as he came up the stairs. A chill touched her heart. Had her father really aged visibly in the month she'd been in Winnipeg, or was it her imagination that his face looked thinner and the lines around his eyes more pronounced?

He dropped his medical bag on the hall table and wrapped Naomi in a hug. "Welcome home, dear. Did you have a good visit with Barb?"

She held him closer, breathing in his familiar scent. "Yes. It was good to see her again. Dad, are you all right? You look tired."

He held her off and smiled. "I am a bit tired. I've had a couple of late nights this week."

"It's time you slowed down." Naomi regretted the words as soon as she'd spoken. As the only doctor in a hundred square miles, the only way her father could slow down was to turn away patients, which he'd never do. He didn't need the extra burden of her worry for him. "Did Jen have a boy or a girl? And how is Ethan?"

"Jen had a little girl. She and the baby are both fine. As for Ethan, he has a bad scald. I don't know how they're going to keep it from getting infected in that barn of a house, but his father wouldn't hear of my bringing him here. Says any help is charity. The stubborn goat." His slanting brows drew together in an impatient frown. "But from what Laura told me, that might be for the best. It sounds like we're going to have our hands full with this man from the train."

"Yes, it does. He must have pneumonia. He has a temperature of a hundred and four, and he can hardly breathe. His heart is working double time."

Naomi's father picked up his bag and put an arm around her shoulders. "Let's see what we've got."

They found MacNeil in an uneasy sleep, broken now and then by a tight cough. Naomi's father rummaged for his stethoscope and handed it to her. "Tell me what you hear."

She put the instrument on and placed the chest piece over MacNeil's lungs. The knot of apprehension in her stomach tightened. "A lot of liquid."

Naomi handed the stethoscope back. Her father sat in the bedside chair to listen, then straightened up and gave her a grim nod. "You're right, and you're also right about his heart straining. That scar on his shoulder...a bullet?"

"Yes." When Naomi showed her father the burn marks on MacNeil's wrists, he shook his head. "He's survived worse than pneumonia, I'd say. Where is he from?"

"He hasn't been coherent enough to tell us."

"That's a shame. We could very well lose him."

A painful lump rose in Naomi's throat as MacNeil's face blended with hundreds of others in her memory. When his glassy eyes opened, she leaned over him to hide the mist in hers from her father. She didn't want to have to close the eyes of another young man whose life had ended far too soon.

"You're going to get through this."

MacNeil looked over Naomi's shoulder, as if someone stood behind her. "Don't waste...time on me, Alice. You never did before. No reason to now."

Alice. His girl? Sister? Friend? It didn't matter. She was someone he'd cared for. Naomi leaned closer and took his hand.

"I'm not going anywhere, Ben. Now you rest."

"You never were very smart, were you?"

The words sounded as regretful as they did insulting. MacNeil's eyes closed as he faded out again. Naomi gently released his hand. At least he knew he wasn't alone.

Her father rose and circled the bed to stand beside her. His smile made the lines around his eyes seem even more pronounced. Where had the last three years gone?

"You know that with pneumonia, it's a matter of luck and a strong constitution. I'd say he has the constitution. As for the luck, the next day or two should tell." He squeezed her lightly. "I'm glad you're home. I've missed you."

Naomi leaned against him, wishing she could stay there with his arm around her, wishing she could tell him everything the way she had when she was a little girl. "I've missed you, too."

Naomi and Laura took turns watching MacNeil through the afternoon. By dawn his breathing had worsened, and his fever continued to rage. Naomi thanked heaven she'd arrived home in time to ease the burden for her father and Laura.

MacNeil didn't have the strength to move or talk much in his delirium, but Naomi guessed from the little he said that most of the time, his mind was back overseas. Only once or twice did he seem to be visiting better times. Then, he smiled, and it made him look so much younger and more human Naomi forgot to be afraid of him.

Just after sunrise, his breathing grew very shallow, so that he was hardly getting any air at all. Naomi propped him up on pillows and it seemed to help a little, but only a little. Her father had said the next day or two would be critical, but it was starting to look like MacNeil wouldn't last that long. He looked up at Naomi, and again she sensed he was seeing someone else, someone who mattered.

"I wish..."

As she'd done before, Naomi took his hand. At times like this there were always wishes and regrets. She'd heard them often, and they always tore at her heart. The fingers of her other hand slid into his hair.

"What do you wish?"

In a moment of clarity, he focused on her. Naomi saw his guard go up when he recognized her as a stranger.

"Nothing."

"Everyone has wishes, Ben."

Without answering, he closed his eyes. Naomi pulled up his covers and watched him drift off. Perhaps Ben's denial of his wishes hurt her because she'd denied too many of her own.

Chapter 2

Still and quiet. Too still and quiet without the rocking rhythm and steady rumble of the train. He opened his eyes to a dimly lit, chilly bedroom that smelled faintly of beeswax. When he took a breath, pain stabbed him in the ribs, but the heavy pressure on his chest was gone. He tried to sit up and found he barely had the strength to prop himself on an elbow.

Shit.

The muted hiss of rain against the roof and window filled the room. This place reminded him of the spare room at home, with solid dark furniture and thick, heavy ivory drapes at the window. Hadn't Alice been here? Or was it his mother?

No. The feminine voice he'd heard belonged to someone else, a young woman with a heart-shaped face and serious grey eyes. Unless he'd conjured her up in his fever, she must live here – wherever here was. Somewhere in Manitoba or Saskatchewan. Just after the train had crossed the Ontario border he'd finished his last bottle of whiskey, and it had dulled the pain in his ribs enough for him to fall asleep. He didn't remember anything clearly after that.

The clothes he'd been wearing lay neatly folded on the desk across the room. His duffle bag was nowhere in sight. He prayed that they'd found his wallet in his bag. These people would expect to be paid, he'd need another train ticket, and the only other money he had was banked in Halifax, where he didn't dare return.

They'd removed the bandages on his ribs, and he vaguely recalled the chill of a stethoscope against his chest. So they'd called a doctor. Another bill to pay. *Forget it. They can't get blood from a stone.* He settled back on his pillow and stared at the ceiling. Pneumonia, he thought the girl had said. If so, he was damned lucky to be alive.

Light footsteps sounded in the hall, his door creaked open and the girl with the heart-shaped face peered around it. So she was real.

The word 'wholesome' came to mind, perhaps because of the sprinkling of freckles on her pert nose. A dimple in her pointed chin, a generous, soft-lipped mouth, and delicate dark lashes fringing her luminous eyes. Not a type he usually fancied, but all in all a very pretty country girl.

"Good morning. I hoped you'd be awake. How are you feeling?"

Her quiet, reserved voice suited her face. He rose on his elbow again and gritted his teeth as his ribs protested.

"Lousy."

The girl's eyes lit up with a smile like the flare of summer lightning across a stormy sky. It vanished just as quickly. She came in, sat in the chair by the bed and crossed slender legs under her dark green skirt.

"That's not surprising. You've had a rough three days."

He muttered a curse. Nothing had ever scared him like this weakness did. "I've been here three days?"

The girl's rain-grey gaze held his briefly, then slid away. She crossed her arms, an oddly defensive stance when he was flat on his back. "Yes. They put you off the train just in time."

"Did you find my wallet? It was in my duffle bag."

A shake of her head set her shoulder-length cloud of fine, nut-brown hair swinging. "No. There was nothing in your bag but some extra clothes. They're in the top drawer of the dresser."

His hands clenched into fists. So he was broke as well as helpless. "Damn. There goes a hundred dollars."

"I'm sorry."

The girl's chin lifted, as if she expected him to accuse her of stealing his cash. He swore again, under his breath this time. It didn't matter who'd stolen his money. He was stranded just the same.

"Will you do me a favour? Tell the doctor who saw me I've been robbed. I'll pay him as soon as I can."

Her chin lifted a notch higher. "The doctor who saw you is my father, and you're in his house. He's willing to wait awhile to be paid. Besides, I was there when they put you off the train. If I'd had you brought here right away instead of letting them take you to the jail, you mightn't have gotten so ill. So, don't worry about money for now."

"I was in jail?" It wouldn't be the first time, but he had no memory of it at all.

"Only for a few hours."

This girl had a way of holding her head that accentuated her trim figure. Not that he could afford to be thinking below the waist when he had secrets to keep. He needed to watch his tongue, and he needed to know what he'd already told her.

"Tell your father I appreciate that, miss... I'm sorry, I don't know your name."

"Naomi Franklin. You can call me Naomi if I can call you Ben, Mr. MacNeil."

A memory of overseas touched him like a cold hand. He shook it off. *Smart man.* So he hadn't let his real name slip. Ben MacNeil had been an easy-going sort, the joker among his men. If he were alive, he wouldn't object to a comrade borrowing his name in a pinch. Ben MacNeil, Carl O'Neill. Close enough to be easy.

"Sure." As for Naomi, her dignified, old-fashioned name suited her, but Carl hesitated to use it. Being on a first-name basis would make it just a little bit more difficult to maintain the distance he needed. "So where is here?"

"Mackenzie, Saskatchewan. If you're not local, you probably won't have heard of it. It's a small town."

A medical bag sat on top of the dresser. Naomi reached into it, slung a stethoscope around her neck and pulled out a thermometer. Really? She hardly looked old enough to be in her first year of university, let alone in medical school. "I thought your father was the doctor."

Her cheeks coloured. "I nursed overseas for two years. Red Cross." When he parted his lips in surprise, she slipped the thermometer in his mouth, sat and focused on her watch. After what felt like a long pause, she looked up. "Normal."

That's surprising, with you here. He almost spoke the thought, just to make her blush. Something about her crisp manner made Carl want to tease her, get under her skin, but right now he just wasn't up to it. Her attractiveness only made this whole mess more galling. "Miss Franklin, I guess I owe you, too."

"Now for your pulse." She pressed her fingers to his wrist. Her touch was soft, her hand a bit large for her build, feminine but strong-looking. "You can pay me by telling me something about yourself. All I know is your name."

So now would come the questions. It made sense to assume Ben MacNeil's background, as far as Carl knew it, as well as his name. "I'm from Newcastle, New Brunswick. It's a lumber town on the Miramichi River."

"I know. I passed though there on my way west when I got back from overseas." Naomi released his wrist, but the warmth of her touch lingered. "Where were you headed?"

"I was on my way to Vancouver to look for work."

"Do you have family back East?"

"No." Not any longer. The way he'd left had cut those ties for good. His mother and Alice would miss him for a while, he supposed, but they'd get over it soon enough. His other sister, Georgie, was probably too disgusted with him to care what became of him, and his father had never given a damn.

Naomi's gaze slid from Carl's face to his torso and back again. "Who strapped your ribs? If it was a doctor, he should have put you in hospital. It's obvious you took quite a beating. What happened?"

The truth could do no harm there. "I got into a fight trying to help out a friend. I was in the hospital, but I felt well enough to leave, so I did." She didn't need to know that his 'friend' was a bootlegger who owed the wrong people money.

"That wasn't smart. Neither was drinking on the train, but you must have been in a lot of pain. As for your bullet scar, I guess you got that overseas?"

"Yeah." She didn't need to know he was officially still in the service, either.

Naomi leaned over him. "I need to listen to your heart and lungs. Breathe in as deeply as you can."

When he did, her clean, subtle scent filled his senses. Carl closed his eyes and breathed when she told him to, while she moved the chest piece of the stethoscope over his torso. His skin heated as if it were her fingers touching him instead of chilly metal. He didn't open his eyes until she finished. When he did, she sat straight in her chair, brisk and professional.

"Your lungs are clearing quickly now that they aren't constricted by strapping, but you've had a very close call. You're going to have to be careful for a few weeks. You need to rest and let yourself heal."

Weeks? With no money, dependent on strangers? *Yeah, right.* "Whatever you say, Doc."

Naomi's gaze cooled and her brows lifted. She really did that expression well. "If you need to hear it from my father, you will. He'll be in to check on you soon, but I was here when you very nearly died the other night. If you want to stay alive, you can forget about travelling for a while."

Carl glared at her until she lowered her gaze. If only it were that simple. "And where am I supposed to stay?"

She looked up, eyes sparkling… So, Miss Franklin had a temper. "Here. I told you we aren't in a rush to be paid, but if that worries you, I can contact whoever you'd like. Alice, perhaps. You mentioned her. Who is she?"

"Someone I knew a long time ago. There's no point in contacting her." No lie, when you got right down to it. He and Alice and Georgie had been close enough as children, relying on each other when they couldn't rely on anyone else, but that closeness had died quickly as they grew up.

Naomi's gaze softened. She really had beautiful eyes, but having her look at him that way made Carl more uncomfortable than the throbbing in his ribs. "What about Dennis? You mentioned him, too. Is he a friend?"

Yeah. Dennis should be the one to get him out of this mess. The man bloody well owed him. If not for good old Dennis welshing on his debts, and then running away when the going got tough, Carl wouldn't be lying here helpless now. "That's a good idea. I'll get you to wire him for me."

Naomi took the stethoscope from around her neck, coiled it and set it in her lap. "There's no rush. We're not going to put you out on the street."

The door opened again, and a stocky man who looked to be about sixty joined Naomi by the bed. They didn't look a lot alike, but a subtle resemblance about the eyes and mouth marked them as father and daughter, as did the affection in the smile she gave him.

"Morning, Dad. Mr. MacNeil, this is my father, Doctor Kenneth Franklin. Dad, meet Ben MacNeil from Newcastle, New Brunswick."

The doctor held out a hand. Carl shook it and found the older man's hand surprisingly rough, like that of a labourer. Of course, Doctor Franklin's life in a place like this would be very different from a city doctor's. "Pleased to meet you. I owe you and Miss Franklin thanks for saving my life."

Perhaps Doctor Franklin was closer to fifty than sixty, after all. A fair bit of brown still showed in his greying hair, and the lines on his tanned face looked like they came as much from weather as from age. Naomi rose and handed her father the stethoscope.

"Dad, his temperature's normal now, and his lungs sound a lot better. I'm going to get you some breakfast, Mr. MacNeil."

Doctor Franklin took her place in the bedside chair as Naomi left the room. "Your ribs must be painful. Your cough has kept them from beginning to heal. I'll give you something to make you more comfortable if you like."

"Maybe after I eat." Carl held the doctor's gaze. Naomi's father's eyes were dark brown, not grey, but they were shaped like his daughter's. "I'm sure Miss Franklin told you I don't have any money with me, but I promise I'll pay you as soon as I can."

"Don't worry over that, Ben. We haven't spent anything on you but time."

"You can't treat patients for nothing."

Doctor Franklin put on a frown. "You sound like the father of a young patient of mine. Too proud to let me bring the boy here and look after him properly. In a week you'll be wanting to walk out of here rather than take my 'charity.' That's your choice – you're a grown man – but you won't get far before you'll be sick again, and you aren't likely to pull through a second time."

Feeling cheap, Carl looked away. "So your daughter said. Look, don't think I'm not grateful, but I don't like owing people money. Usually leads to trouble one way or another. I was on my way to the coast to look for work. What are the chances of my finding a job here in Mackenzie?"

"This time of year, they're nil. The few businesses here are small and don't need help. The farmers won't be hiring until spring." The doctor looked him up and down, his gaze appraising but not unfriendly. "What did you do for work before you enlisted?"

"Whatever I could find. I'm not trained to do anything but labour work." A poor accounting for the son of a successful businessman at twenty-four. That had never bothered Carl before, so why did it now? Naomi's father seemed to pick up on his embarrassment.

"You aren't alone in that these days, Ben. Ah… Here's your breakfast."

Naomi was back, carrying a tray with two mugs of coffee and a plate of scrambled eggs. "Dad, yours is in the kitchen."

Her father stood. "Thanks. I'll leave you to Naomi, Ben, but remember what I said. You do what she tells you and you'll be on your feet that much sooner. Naomi, I'll leave a dose of laudanum in the office if he wants it. I'll see you tonight."

He gave her a peck on the cheek. Her brow furrowed with concern as she watched him leave, then she resumed her crisp professional expression, set the breakfast tray on Carl's lap and tucked an extra pillow behind him.

"Can you manage?"

"Of course I can manage." The aromas coming from the tray made his empty stomach rumble. To Carl's shock, when he lifted his mug his hand shook so that he almost spilled the coffee. When he took a swallow, it nearly came back up again.

Stupid. You know better. You've been hungry before. He followed the coffee with a forkful of scrambled eggs. The concerned furrow appeared in Naomi's brow again.

"You should have started with the eggs."

" I know." Thankfully, Carl's stomach quieted when he took another forkful. "How long has it been since I've eaten?"

"As far as I know, you haven't had anything solid to eat since you got off the train. I don't think you were fed at the jail, and you've had nothing but some broth here."

"I don't usually like eggs, but these taste fine."

"I'll tell Laura you enjoyed them." Naomi's gaze shifted from Carl's face to the scar on his shoulder. "When did you get back from overseas?"

"September. You?"

She sat, picked up the other mug of coffee and sipped, her grey eyes watching him over the rim. Her tall, slender figure reminded Carl of Alice, but Naomi had an air of strength his sister had never possessed. Yet this woman seemed fragile, too. The way she moved so carefully around him… Did he frighten her?

"January." Naomi set her mug on the nightstand and folded her hands in her lap. A quiet posture, but Carl sensed that beneath it she was poised to move. "Where were you wounded?"

"Guillemont."

"Is that when you were captured?"

How had she figured that out? Her gaze followed his hand as he took another forkful of eggs, and Carl knew. Of course she'd seen the rope burns on his wrists. They couldn't be gone soon enough, and he didn't need the compassion that showed on her face. He'd earned those marks though his own stupidity.

"Don't look at me like that. I survived."

Naomi still held his gaze, looking deep. "I'm not sure I'd like to know exactly what you survived. That battle happened over a year ago."

Yes, and he'd said all he was going to say about it. "Like I said, 'I survived.' Escaped eventually and got shipped home." Time for some questions of his own. "What about you? Where did you do your nursing training?"

"McGill. I finished just after the war started and then I signed up to go overseas."

Carl swallowed his last forkful of eggs and tried to picture Naomi in the organized chaos of a front-line hospital. That explained her air of strength, and perhaps her fragility, too. "Why? With university training, you could have gone into any military hospital in Canada."

She looked away, and Carl realized he'd been more or less staring at her. "The honest truth? Because the opportunity came up, and after living in Montreal and seeing part of the bigger world I didn't feel ready to come back to Mackenzie."

Her chin lifted and she met his gaze again with a hint of a challenge, ready to defend her reasons. As if he had a right to question them, when the only reason he'd enlisted was because his parents threatened to throw him out.

"You have backbone, I'll give you that."

Naomi shrugged off the compliment and reached for the breakfast tray. "You've talked enough for now. I'm going to give you your dose of laudanum, and you're going to rest."

She left the room and returned with a glass. Carl drank the bitter medicine, chased it down with a glass of water and settled back on his pillow. Sleep. He could use a week of it. It surprised him when Naomi sat down beside him again.

"You don't need to wait. I'll be out in a minute or so."

"I haven't got anything pressing to do."

Too tired to argue, he closed his eyes. Before the drug had time to ease the pain in his ribs he faded out, to the soothing sound of Naomi's regular breathing.

Chapter 3

Naomi set MacNeil's breakfast dishes in the sink and filled a plate with the toast and eggs waiting in the warming oven. Before the war they'd thought to convert the old Enterprise Range to oil, but with prices soaring it made no sense, and Laura insisted wood worked better for baking. Naomi just liked the cosiness of a wood fire. She stood by the stove for a moment, soaking up its warmth. Today felt more like mid-November than October.

At the table, Laura sat dicing apples and tossing them into a saucepan with unnecessary vigour. "Your father's already gone." She dropped her paring knife and glanced up at the ceiling. "Is he asleep?"

"Yes."

"So what does he have to say for himself? The doctor didn't tell me anything."

Naomi brought her plate to the table and took the chair her father had left pulled out. The information MacNeil had given her seemed even sketchier as she passed it on to Laura. "He says he's from New Brunswick. He got home from overseas last month and he was on his way to Vancouver to look for work."

Laura grabbed another apple and sliced it in half with one cut. "All the way across the country? What about his family?"

"He says he doesn't have any family."

"None that will own him, probably."

Naomi tried her eggs and found she didn't have much appetite. Her doubts about MacNeil fed off Laura's. "If he has no ties back East, maybe he just wanted to start over somewhere new."

The paring knife hit the cutting board in a staccato rhythm, reducing the cored apple to small cubes. "Maybe, but that doesn't explain his broken ribs and bruises. He didn't get those at any church tea."

"He told me he got into a fight trying to help out a friend." Naomi forced down another forkful of eggs and pushed her coffee away. It wasn't sitting well this morning. "He also told me he was captured at Guillemont last fall."

Laura looked a little shamefaced. "Well, he's got the scars to back that up, but I still don't trust him."

"I don't trust him either, Laura. He's too close-mouthed. Even when he was delirious he said next to nothing, but he has a look I've seen before. He's been back in Canada a few weeks. It's as if he hasn't really come home yet."

Laura gathered the cubed apple in her hand, dumped it in the saucepan and wiped her hands with the tea towel she'd draped over her shoulder. "You may be right, but he has no claim on us, Naomi. He's a drinker, and you know too well what comes of that."

Naomi's palms turned to ice. The feel of the rough grass beneath her back, searing pain – but the memory didn't connect itself to MacNeil. "I can picture him as a bootlegger or a thief, but somehow I can't see him doing anything really cruel or hateful. Remember what he said that first day about Alice? He told me just now that she was someone he knew a long time ago. I think he really cared about her."

"It's a rare person, good or bad, who hasn't cared for someone." Laura's gaze met Naomi's. "Right now, it's you I care about."

Naomi reached across the table and touched Laura's hand. "I know, and I love you for it. I'm sure he'll be on his way as soon as it's safe for him to travel, if not before. There's nothing to hold him here." Before she turned to go, she lowered her voice. "Laura, was Dad sick while I was away? He looks tired."

Laura looked away. "If he was, he wouldn't admit it. I think he just forgets that he isn't a young man anymore."

Naomi lost what little appetite she had as fear settled lower in the pit of her stomach. "He's only fifty-five. Laura, you're worried about him, too. I can tell."

Laura leaned on her elbows and pushed some stray strands of hair back from her face. She looked tired herself. She must be a few years older than Naomi's father, and she worked as hard as he did. She'd never allowed Naomi to do any of the rougher chores around the house.

'Your mother wanted you to grow up a lady,' she'd always said. 'You pay attention to your books and your looks. There'll be nothing and no one for you in Mackenzie when you're older, unless you want to marry a farmer.' And so Naomi had studied hard and gone away. Only now, she no longer felt she belonged here – or anywhere. Without her father and Laura, she'd be as anchorless as the man sleeping upstairs.

"I expect your father's just tired," Laura said. "You know he's always pushed himself too hard. After your mother passed away, he worked himself into exhaustion to deal with his grief, and over the years it's become a habit."

"I know. Now that I'm back from my trip, I'm going to do all I can to spare him. I'll sit down with him tonight and find out who he's got on his books. I'm sure there's a few I can take over for him."

"I'm sure there are. Now finish your breakfast and let's not borrow trouble."

Under Laura's watchful eye, Naomi finished her eggs. Rainy mornings like this always took her back to her childhood, before she'd started school. On days too wet to play outside, she and her mother would spend the morning in the kitchen. Naomi clung to those memories, tried hard to keep them from fading.

After breakfast, Naomi did some mending and tried to write letters to a couple of friends who still served overseas, but she couldn't write well with half her mind on the man sleeping upstairs. When she checked on MacNeil at noon, he looked so peaceful she almost let him sleep through lunch, but remembering how hungry he'd been at breakfast, she decided to wake him.

She sat by his bed, trying to understand the hold he'd taken on her imagination. All morning, she'd tried to push him to the back of her mind – and failed. She'd pictured him wounded and in enemy hands. She'd thought about his parents and wondered how long he'd been alone.

With his deep blue eyes and fighter's face, a lot of women would likely find him attractive. His body matched his face, strong looking without being bulky. She'd become familiar with it over the last few days of caring for him.

For shame, Naomi. He's a patient. But something primal spoke to her through the shame.

Three months ago, you might have found him attractive yourself.

Perhaps. Or maybe it was just his vulnerability that appealed to her. Asleep, lips slightly parted, dark hair rumpled... The hair on the back of her neck prickled. Now that he was out of danger, MacNeil —she didn't really think of him as Ben — would likely recover as fast as any other normal young man. Another day or two, and he'd no longer be helpless, but even so, there'd be no question of him travelling for a couple of weeks or more. Looked like Naomi would have to deal with him as a man, not just as a patient.

A shiver ran along her spine. *Not for any longer than necessary.* She rose and touched MacNeil's shoulder. Still a little groggy from laudanum, he looked up at her, blinking. Then, as the fog cleared, a light kindled briefly in his eyes. Naomi couldn't mistake it for anything but pleasure at seeing her. She kept her gaze down as she set the lunch tray on his lap.

"You've had a good sleep."

"Yeah. What time is it?"

"Just past noon. I hated to wake you, but I thought you'd be hungry again."

With most of its hoarseness gone, his voice had a pleasant timbre, with a touch of roughness and a slight East Coast accent. He stretched and ran a hand through his hair. Naomi imagined the soft feel of it between her fingers. Thankfully, *his* attention was on his lunch.

"I am. That smells good."

MacNeil couldn't possibly have gained a noticeable amount of weight in such a short time, but somehow he looked bigger to Naomi than when he'd arrived. More intimidating. She took a slow, calming breath and sat again. "Beef stew. I've never tasted any better than Laura's."

MacNeil looked up briefly between mouthfuls. "Who's Laura?"

"Our housekeeper. She's been with us since my mother died, years ago. How long have your parents been gone?"

"Quite a while." And he obviously didn't like talking about them. He couldn't be much older than her. How young had he been when he lost them?

Naomi sat in silence while MacNeil finished his meal. When he handed the tray back to her, his fingers brushed hers. The fork rattled in the empty bowl as she flinched. Dark brows drew together and blue eyes shot her a swift look.

"What's the matter, Naomi? Are you afraid of me?"

"Of course not." But her heart galloped and her stomach knotted. Could he tell she was lying? "You startled me, that's all."

"I'm jumpy, too, sometimes." The knot in her stomach tightened when his gaze locked on hers. "I'll bet you got a lot more than you bargained for overseas. It takes a tough woman to survive in one of those hospitals."

She held her head high and sent his challenge right back. "Yes, I did get more than I bargained for. Didn't you?"

He read her perfectly. A hint of a grin tugged at his lips. "I suppose so. Two years. You were over there as long as I was."

The only thing they had in common. Maybe that explained why she told him what she'd never admitted to anyone but her father. "Sometimes I feel like I'm not really back yet."

A swift glance, an instant of connection, then he looked away. "I know what you mean. So do I."

That feeling of displacement showed in a dozen small ways, ways Naomi wouldn't have recognized if she hadn't seen signs of it so often before, in so many other men. No doubt he'd be annoyed if he knew she read him that well. "I should introduce you to a friend of mine, Barry Foley. I went to school with him and his wife. They're my closest friends. Barry was lucky. He was wounded at Vimy, just badly enough to be sent home. He and Corinne married before he enlisted, and now they're on his father's farm outside of town."

MacNeil settled back against his pillows with a shrug. A barrier rose between them. That moment of connection must have disturbed him, too.

"I appreciate the thought, but I won't be here long enough to make an introduction worth his time or yours. Which reminds me. If you'll bring me a pen and paper, I'll write out a wire for you to send."

Naomi took the dishes from the lunch tray, gave it back to him and brought pen, paper and ink from the desk. He scribbled a brief message, folded the paper and handed it to her. "This is for Dennis. You should get a reply in a day or two. I'll write a letter later. Is there a bank in Mackenzie?"

"No, the nearest bank is in Donwell, twenty miles from here."

"I thought as much, so I asked him to send cash."

Ben's eyelids drooped. He'd spent his energy for now. Naomi tucked the note in her skirt pocket and stood. "You need more rest. Dad left instructions to give you another dose of laudanum if you wanted it."

"No. I'll sleep without it." Naomi didn't argue. His cough had eased, so his pain would have lessened as well. He fell asleep as soon as he closed his eyes.

Down in the kitchen, Naomi pulled the note from her pocket. Ben had penned his message in large script with an aggressive slant.

Am sick. Was robbed on train. Need money. Send cash care of Dr. K. Franklin, Mackenzie, Sask. Writing. Rabbit.

She jumped when Laura came in from the porch and spoke from behind her. "Rabbit? What do you suppose that means? And I thought he said he was from New Brunswick, not Nova Scotia."

Naomi glanced at the Halifax address on the note. "That's no reason why he couldn't have a friend in Halifax. Rabbit. There must be a story behind that." Thinking about it, she saw where the nickname might possibly have come from. Ben had a watchful quality about him, and no doubt he'd be quick-moving enough when he was on his feet. "Maybe I'll ask him about it when he's feeling better."

Laura raised an eyebrow. "No doubt he'll have a story ready. Naomi, Corinne called while you were upstairs. She asked you to call back. Sounded like she had news. Or maybe she's just curious."

Of course. Naomi knew her best friend well enough to be sure of that. Corinne would be wondering about Doctor Franklin's patient from nowhere, just like everyone else in Mackenzie, but not in a malicious way. Not that Naomi could tell her friend much. Ben was still an enigma, just as he'd been when he'd arrived.

"I'm going into town to send this telegram."

Laura peered out at the sheets of rain sweeping by the kitchen window. "In this weather?"

"The sooner it's sent, the sooner he'll get an answer. I'll call Corinne when I get back."

Naomi bundled up and ran to the train station. The stationmaster's brows lifted when she walked in with water streaming from her oilskin slicker.

"Not much of a day, Naomi."

"This is important." She handed over Ben's message and shrugged when the man's brows quirked higher. "I don't know any more than you do, Tom. He's been too sick to talk until this morning."

Tom put on a grave face. "This is a bit of a riddle. Might be hiding something bad. You and the doctor keep your eyes on him. The shape he was in, he must have had a good reason for being on that train heading out of Dodge."

Like Mrs. MacPherson at the restaurant, Tom Findlay lived for gossip, and he relished being the first person in Mackenzie to get any news from the outside world. Naomi liked him, but she had no inclination to satisfy his curiosity today. "We will. You'll send that right away, won't you?"

The wind fairly blew her home. She hung her wet coat in the back porch and pushed away the thought of her father making his rounds with the rain seeping in around the windows of his third-hand Model T. In fine weather he preferred to hitch the buggy to Hannah, their black mare, but today he'd left her in the comfort of the stable. Once the snow came, he'd have to rely on her again.

When she called Corinne, a couple of muted clicks told Naomi interested ears were listening on the party line. Inevitable. Corinne answered with a smile in her voice that Naomi easily pictured on her friend's freckle-dusted face.

"So you finally decided to call! It's been forever."

The stove's heat began to warm away the chill from her walk, just as her friend's voice warmed away the chill on her spirits. She'd grown apart from almost all her other schoolmates when each had settled into the farming life Naomi had never wanted. Corinne was the exception. "It has been a while. I've been meaning to call you since I got back from Winnipeg, but you've likely heard we have a patient here."

"Yes, I heard. How is he?"

"He's getting better. He'll be on his feet in a day or two. What's new at your place? Have you heard from Garnett?" Corinne's husband Barry's older brother was still overseas and hadn't been heard from for a while, but at least there'd been no telegram. No news was good news.

"Yes. We got a letter yesterday. It's two months old, but Garnett was all right then. I can't believe it's almost time for Christmas boxes." Corinne paused, signalling Naomi that she had other, more private news. "I'm going to take the truck and come into town. I've missed you. It's been over a month."

"I've missed you, too, and your timing couldn't be better. Laura used most of our week's sugar on cinnamon buns yesterday." Through the receiver, Naomi heard a single clear chime. The clock by the hall door struck one an instant later. Barry and Corrine's kitchen clock had been broken for months. She couldn't resist. "Corinne, did you get your clock fixed? If so, I think it's a little fast."

Corinne giggled. "No, it's still broken. Are you sure yours isn't slow?"

"It might be. Laura's not as particular about time as some people."

A receiver dropped into its cradle with a vicious click. Probably Mrs. George Parker. Everyone in Mackenzie knew Mrs. George made a hobby of eavesdropping on the phone, and as for time, she threw a fit if the doctor kept her waiting five minutes for an appointment. Naomi and Corinne shared another giggle before saying goodbye. Half an hour later, the Foleys' truck pulled into the yard.

Corinne whirled through the kitchen door, brightening the grey day with her bright blue coat and strawberry-blond curls. She shed her wet things and wrapped Naomi in a hug, then stepped back and looked her over.

"Naomi, what have you been doing with yourself? You're thinner than you were when I saw you last. I should be so lucky."

"Thank you – I think." Naomi laughed and looked her friend over in turn. "You have filled out a little, haven't you? And…" And the glow on Corinne's face could only mean one thing. "Corinne! You're expecting, aren't you? I know you've been trying."

Corinne's eyes lit up like candles. "I'm two months late as of yesterday. I haven't told Barry yet, but I'm as sure as I can be."

Naomi folded her in another, fiercer hug. "I'm so happy for you." But beneath the joy, a cold spring of loneliness bubbled up to chill her. She ignored it and focused on her friend. Corinne deserved some happiness. She'd looked so stressed before Barry came home from overseas. "All the worry while Barry was away must seem worth it now. He's going to be thrilled."

Laura demanded a hug as well. Corinne obliged and wiped away happy tears. "I still hate to think of those weeks after we got notice he'd been wounded, before his first letter came. I can't wait to tell him. Now that you have my news, it's your turn. Tell me more about this man from the train."

They moved to the table. Laura cut cinnamon buns and filled the teapot. Naomi hesitated. Was Ben asleep? Sound carried easily through the heating grate in the ceiling. She kept her voice low.

"His name's Ben MacNeil. He gave us a good scare. We almost lost him the first night. He was as sick as anyone I saw overseas, but he's getting better fast. I expect he'll be downstairs in a couple of days."

Corinne took Naomi's cue and lowered her voice as well. "What's he like? From what I heard in town, he might be trouble."

"I can believe that, but I think he's just at loose ends. He's been back from overseas for less than two months, and I think he had a rotten go of it over there. He says he doesn't have any family. I think he's been drinking a fair bit and living pretty rough, but why wouldn't he? Of course, we don't really know anything about him. He hasn't been well enough to say much."

"What does he look like?"

"Dark hair, blue eyes. He looks tough, but of course, he hasn't shaved or anything."

A slow grin spread across Corinne's face. "I think you like his looks."

Naomi rolled her eyes and grinned back. She'd get no peace if Corinne got a whiff of how much Ben unsettled her. "I haven't had time to think about his looks. When he's on his feet, I'll have you and Barry over for dinner to meet him. I think it would do Ben good to talk to another man who's been overseas, and of course he knows no one out here."

"We'd like to meet him, too."

They talked about Naomi's trip to Winnipeg for a few minutes. She told Corinne the same stories she'd concocted for her father and Laura. They didn't come any more easily the second time. How long would it be until she no longer needed lies?

After Corinne left for home, Naomi ran upstairs to check on Ben. She found him still asleep, his breathing slow and even. To be able to sleep like that with painful ribs, showed how depleted his body must be. He needed as much rest as he could get.

She'd told Laura she'd be right down to peel the vegetables for supper, but Naomi lingered, watching Ben's face. Why? Maybe she did like his looks, but that didn't explain this confusing push and pull of attraction and repulsion.

Overseas, there'd been no time to get to know her patients. You did what you could do and tried to accept that it was never enough, but she'd spent the better part of three days with Ben, as he fought for his life. Perhaps that was why he drew her as much as he frightened her. Whatever the reason, that moment at lunchtime when their gazes connected had touched something in her heart.

Downstairs, the porch door slammed in the wind. Naomi put aside her unsettling thoughts and ran down to meet her father. She reached the kitchen as he finished hanging up his coat and hat in the porch. When he turned to face her, her heart jumped into her throat. His face looked grey – he seemed to have aged ten years in a day.

Chapter 4

"Dad, what's the matter?"

Laura and Naomi reached him at the same time. He let out a long breath and took Naomi's hand.

"I'm all right, Naomi, but I'm afraid I have sad news." He led her through the kitchen and sat her down on the sitting room sofa. "I ran into Reverend Mitchell coming back through town. He was on his way to the Pheeney place."

"Gordon—"

Her father nodded slowly. "He's been killed in action."

Gordon Pheeney, with his brown eyes and crooked smile. Gordon and Naomi had teased and bantered their way through school together, the best of friends, with never a thought of anything more. Now he was gone and she'd never laugh with him again.

Laura followed them into the room, ready to comfort as always, but she looked in need of comfort herself. Gordon had been a favourite of hers among Naomi's friends.

"His poor parents. Is this ever going to end?"

"I know, Laura." Naomi's father put an arm around her. "And we worried about Naomi, working overseas… At times like this, I'm thankful I don't have a son. As selfish as that sounds, it's the truth."

Naomi leaned against him while waves of grief rolled over her. Then came guilt. "You aren't selfish, Dad. If they'd agreed to take you, I know you'd be over there now, just as I should be."

Her father's voice turned stern. "Naomi, I won't have you talking that way. You served your country. You came home because it was time. You were exhausted and you were burning out. You did all you could, and I couldn't be prouder of you."

Logic told Naomi he was right. She'd recognized the signs of burnout in herself, but right now her heart didn't want to listen. For her father's and Laura's sake, she put tears aside until later.

"I'll call on the Pheeneys tomorrow. Dad, you must be hungry."

"Of course he is. Both of you come and eat." Laura shooed them back to the kitchen. Thank God for Laura, in a world turned upside down.

When she'd finished her plate of baked beans and scalloped potatoes, Naomi took a plate up to Ben. She didn't linger to talk, just woke him and left him to his supper. He was too observant, and she didn't feel up to answering questions. Later, after her father and Laura had gone to bed, Naomi stoked the sitting room fire and curled up on the sofa, dreading the thought of climbing into her cold bed.

But when she did go to bed, she found it warmed by a hot water bottle – Laura again. Naomi curled her toes into the flannel-wrapped warmth. Rather than think of Gordon, she focused on Ben, comfortably asleep across the hall. One soldier who'd survived, one who might not be alive now if not for her. The thought of him softened her grief enough to let her fall asleep.

The next thing she knew, the water bottle had gone cold and a cloud-swept moon was shining its fitful light on her bed. Naomi sat up and curled her arms around her knees. *Gordon.* Had she been dreaming? Gordon couldn't really be dead. Not her old friend. The swiftly changing pattern of light and dark conjured up the memory of the night Gordon had run away from home, and come to get her to go with him – as far as the knoll behind the Franklin lot. Two seven-year-olds in a tent made from the quilt off Naomi's bed, with a summer moon shining through it.

The tears came. Tomorrow she'd have to be strong for her father and Laura, but right now, Naomi had no strength for herself.

Carl woke shaking and drenched with cold sweat. He recalled nothing of his dream but its terror. It often happened that way.

He curled into himself and took slow, deep breaths to calm his racing heart. This was the first time it had happened here, and he had nothing to drink, nothing to ease him back to sleep. A different kind of fear gripped him at the thought.

It's still a choice. You can take it or leave it, Carl. Dad stopped drinking. Eventually.

But right now, he'd consider a bottle of whiskey his best friend.

He swore at the fierce pain in his ribs. He should have stayed in the veteran's hospital in Halifax until he was well enough to leave, but he'd been sick of being cooped up, and ashamed to see the bruises on Alice's face when she came to visit him. Bruises he'd given her in one of his rages. And she the only one in the family who'd come to see him in the hospital after the fight – and the only one who'd spared Carl a tear when he enlisted a few years earlier. The night before he shipped out, he'd wakened and heard her sobbing quietly in her room.

Yeah, right. She was probably crying over some beau. She'd had a couple by then.

Then, like an echo from the past, Carl heard it. A woman's restrained weeping. Only it didn't fade when he sat up and opened his eyes. The sound came from down the hall.

Naomi?

His hands curled into tight fists. Did night terrors wake her like they did him? She'd seen her share of the ugly realities of war. How did a woman react to that? Did she have moments of anger like he did, anger that blotted out everything else? Why didn't her father or the housekeeper go to her? It didn't seem right that she had to bear the bad hours alone.

Come on, O'Neill. We all do. But when ten, fifteen, twenty minutes went by and no one went to comfort her, Carl couldn't wait any longer. He swung his feet to the cold floor, gripped the bed-post and stood.

His legs wobbled a little, but they held him. He hadn't yet walked as far as the bathroom without help, but he was damn well going to now. Staying close to the bed in case he fell, Carl eased his arms into the robe Doctor Franklin had lent him. Then he took a couple of careful steps and opened his door.

She was crying so softly her father must not have heard her. With a hand on the wall for support, Carl crept down the hall to the door he assumed was Naomi's. His heart thumped in his chest when he stopped with his hand on the doorknob.

Stupid. You'll only frighten her. He didn't know what to say, hadn't the faintest idea how to comfort any woman, let alone one he barely knew. He should go wake the doctor, but instead he knocked softly.

"Naomi, it's Ben. What's the matter? Do you want me to get your father?"

"No. Just go back to bed. I'll be all right."

"You don't sound all right."

"Please, Ben, there's nothing you can do. Just go back to bed."

Perhaps he would have gone if her voice hadn't sounded so shaky, but it did. He opened the door. Naomi sat up in bed with her arms around her knees, moonlight shining on her tear-streaked face.

"You can't come in here."

Carl stepped in and shut the door behind him. "I just did."

He took another step. Naomi turned to the nightstand on the other side of her bed. When she faced him again, she held something in her hand that gleamed metallic black against her white nightgown.

"Get out."

Carl froze. To survive two years of war and bring home a Military Cross, only to be shot by a hysterical woman who'd probably never fired a revolver before – how ironic would that be? And why the hell did she have a gun in her room?

"Shit, Naomi, calm down. I'm not going to hurt you. I just thought I might be able to help. Do you know how to use that?"

She glared at him, but her eyes held more fear than anger. So much fear he could smell it. "Yes. Very well. My father taught me to shoot years ago."

Good. She wasn't likely to pull the trigger by accident. "Why do you keep it in your nightstand?"

"That's none of your business."

None at all, but the tears on her face kept Carl from backing away. How deeply shaken would a girl like Naomi have to be, to feel the need to sleep with a gun close by in her own home? He took another slow step forward...stopped when she levelled the revolver at his chest.

"Will you use your head? I can barely stay on my feet. You know you could puncture my lungs with a punch right now. Either shoot me or let me sit down before my legs give out. Scream for your father if you want to."

She didn't scream. Clutching her covers in her free hand, she kept her gaze locked on Carl's as he took the last few steps to her bed. When he sat down, his head swam. Yeah, he was a real danger to defenceless females in this condition.

The revolver was a 1911 Colt New Service, the same model he'd carried himself. After a few seconds Naomi lowered it to her lap. Chin up, shoulders stiff, she sat watching him – as high-strung as they came.

"Now tell me why you're crying. I'm not going to go away until you do."

Naomi's reply came out laced with anger. "We found out last night that a good friend of mine has been killed in action. Now leave me alone."

Pain knifed Carl in the chest, a kind of pain he'd never known before. The pain of so many memories, and of being helpless to help.

"Naomi, I'm sorry."

She frowned, but her eyes still looked wide and fearful. "I'm sure you've lost friends yourself."

Friends? No. Overseas, Carl had been promoted too quickly to make real friends along the way. Comrades, yes, but that was different, especially if you were in charge.

A cool head under fire – or recklessness, whichever you wanted to call it – tended to draw attention from the brass, but he'd lost enough of his men. He'd been as powerless to save them as Naomi had been to save many of her patients.

"No one who meant as much to me as this friend meant to you. What was his name?"

Naomi relaxed her rigid posture, just a fraction, but she kept a firm grip on her gun. "Gordon. We were friends from our first day of school. He was always laughing, always playing practical jokes. He never took anything seriously." She let out a deep sigh. "We corresponded after he enlisted. His last few letters didn't sound like the old Gordon. He sounded like he didn't even care if he came home anymore."

Maybe he hadn't. Carl remembered some of his own men who'd stopped caring, men from close families in small places like Mackenzie. Human nature at its worst was more than they could handle.

"I've known a few men like that. Sometimes it's the ones with the most to go home to who give up."

Naomi held his gaze. "You didn't have much to go home to, did you, Ben?"

The question raised too many regrets. Besides, this was about Naomi, not him. "Maybe that was an advantage. Naomi, does your father know that you keep a gun in your room?"

"No. I don't think he even knows I own one. I brought it home from overseas."

"Then unless you tell me why you keep it in your room, I'm going to tell him."

Her eyes spit sparks at him. "I told you that was none of your business."

"Fine, have it your way."

"You think you're really something, don't you? Look, it makes me feel safer, that's all."

"Safer from what?"

"Nothing in particular. Just safer. Go ahead and tell my father if you feel you have to."

And Carl would bet his bottom dollar that if he did, he'd get the cold shoulder from Naomi for the rest of his time here. Whatever her reason, she wasn't going to tell him now. "Naomi, do you ever wake up in the night confused, thinking you're still overseas? If you do, it isn't safe for you to have a gun in your room. What if Laura or your father came in at the wrong moment?"

"No. I have nightmares now and then, but they aren't like that. Are yours?"

"Sometimes."

The tears had dried on Naomi's cheeks. Her grey eyes looked dark and soft in the moonlight, as soft as her lips – a hell of a time for him to be noticing that. If Carl stayed here any longer he'd do something stupid, like try to kiss her and get himself shot. "All right, it's none of my business. I'm going back to bed."

He got to his feet a little too quickly and had to take a moment to steady himself. Naomi set her revolver on the nightstand. "Are you all right?"

"I will be."

Carl turned to leave, but she stopped him. "Thank you for coming to check on me."

Maybe it was because he'd spent his waking hours today thinking about her. Maybe it was her tone, but Carl spoke without thinking. "It was the least I could do. You saved my life. Naomi, when I leave here I won't forget you."

A sweet, fragile smile. "I won't forget you either."

He got himself out of the room and back to his own bed, where he lay caught between his concern for Naomi, the fear in her eyes as she pointed her revolver at him, and the softness of her voice.

The least I could do. Since when had other people's problems become his business? But Naomi's problems were starting to feel like his problems, and that couldn't be good.

Dennis, you'd damn well better come through. I have to get out of here. Fast.

Chapter 5

Carl woke just after sunrise, to sounds of Laura moving around the kitchen. The rattle of a stove grate told him she was starting the kitchen fire. He didn't feel like waiting for its warmth to filter upstairs. Or lying there longer, waiting to find out how Naomi was feeling now.

He got out of bed slowly and found his legs steadier than they'd been last night. The sting of the cold floor on his bare feet helped wake him up. In his thick robe, Carl padded down the hall to the bathroom and found an extra razor and shaving soap laid out for him, next to the doctor's. Thoughtful of them. He hadn't shaved since he'd gotten on the train.

He eyed the bathtub, wondering if he should use enough hot water to take a bath. The plumbing looked as if the Franklins had a small, coal-fired water heater in the cellar, like his family did at home. Might as well chance it. He didn't feel fit to see Naomi as he was. Carl shaved while the tub filled, then eased himself down into the warm water. After his bath, he felt more human than he had since the fight.

Back in his room, he rummaged in the desk for paper, pen and ink. It was high time he wrote to Dennis, with a few specific threats to back up his telegram. The sooner Carl got out of here, away from Naomi's influence, the better.

Dear Dennis,

You will have already gotten my wire, telling you the mess I'm in. I was put off the train with pneumonia in this town in the middle of nowhere, and if one of the locals hadn't taken me in, I'd be on my way to Hell now. To top things off, my wallet was stolen on the train. I haven't got a cent to my name, and there's no work here, even if I wasn't laid up.

Of course, I wouldn't be laid up if I hadn't gotten pneumonia. And I wouldn't have gotten pneumonia if I hadn't gotten my ribs broken. And I wouldn't have gotten my ribs broken if you hadn't lied to me about how much trouble you were really in, then run out on me when the going got tough. So, the way I see it, you owe me and you're going to pay, one way or another.

Here are your choices. If I receive a hundred dollars from you by November 15th, we're square. If I don't, I'll write to Austen Oickle and tell him all I know about your suppliers and runners – who they are and where they live. I don't imagine having his cousins beat me up was enough to satisfy Austen, but shutting you down likely would be.

I don't have any identification to cash a cheque and I don't want anyone to know where I am. Send the money in cash, in a letter addressed to Ben MacNeil. He was a friend of mine overseas – a friend with a backbone. You don't need to take that as an insult. It got him killed. You were never that stupid, so don't be stupid now. I'll be expecting a letter.
Carl

That ought to do it. He'd seen Dennis before leaving Halifax, and made it clear there would be a reckoning somewhere down the line. The man was no fool.

Dressed in jeans and his extra shirt, a warm one of blue flannel, Carl headed downstairs with his sealed letter in hand. He found the kitchen empty, with the fragrance of baking bread wafting from the oven.

He peered out the window and saw the Franklins' car parked by the small stable out back. The doctor must still be in bed. Naomi, in a black skirt and a shapeless coat the same dull brown as the grass, walked past the window leading a shaggy black mare from the paddock.

The horse placidly followed her into the stable. Carl turned from the window. Everything here looked older and more worn than in the kitchen at home. The floor needed refinishing and the furniture had its share of nicks and scratches. Altogether more like a farm kitchen than what he'd expect in a doctor's home, but a small-town practice like this likely didn't provide the income for anything fancier.

"Naomi, is that you?" Laura called from the sitting room. She'd popped into Carl's room once or twice, but he hadn't made her acquaintance properly yet, and didn't feel like making it now. He stepped into the back porch, grabbed a cap and one of Doctor Franklin's jackets and slipped his arms into the sleeves on his way to the stable.

He stood in the doorway and buttoned the jacket while his eyes adjusted to the dim light. A roomy stall took up most of the building. The mare rattled a bucket as she munched her breakfast. Naomi's voice rose above the noise, gently scolding.

"Don't eat it too fast, Hannah."

The scent of molasses-rich winter feed mingled with the smell of horse. Carl had never been fond of animals, but from her tone, Naomi was. When she heard Carl's boot-heels on the floor, she came out from behind Hannah and leaned on the half-door of the stall.

"I'm not sure you should be outside yet."

The brisk morning air had put colour in her cheeks, but her eyes had dark smudges beneath them. She should still be in bed herself. Carl's chest tightened and ached with an urge to comfort her again.

"I was going stir crazy, and I wanted to see how you were feeling. Did you get some sleep last night?"

"Yes. Did you?"

"Some."

When Carl moved toward her he saw Naomi's body tense. Even after last night she was nervous around him – or was it *because* of last night? He turned away to hide his irritation. It might be natural for her to be wary of him, but he didn't like it.

"I'm going to take a walk and see where I've landed."

She straightened up, the professional nurse again. "Not alone, you aren't. Last night you didn't look like you could walk ten yards on your own." Naomi slipped out of the stall but still kept a safe distance from him. The coat she wore must be her father's. It dwarfed her, but it didn't keep Carl from imagining the slim curves underneath. The ache in his chest intensified. Why couldn't she have been plain, so both of them could focus on their problems without the distraction of this pull between them? Oh, he knew she felt it, too, even if it scared her.

"I'm feeling better today. I have to start moving around."

She sidled past him a little too quickly, stopped in the yard and looked over her shoulder. "Follow me."

He did, along a path that wound behind the stable and up a gentle slope. At the top, Naomi stopped and waited. Short of breath, Carl came up beside her. He needed this all right. He'd never take easy breathing for granted again.

They stood looking out over miles of dun-coloured prairie, featureless except for two or three dark objects in the distance that might be buildings or copses of trees. The wind rushed to meet them, carrying the scent of the dry grass that rippled under its touch. Surrounded by so much space, something inside Carl opened and expanded. He didn't feel restless here.

Naomi gave him a moment before meeting his gaze. Her lips curved in a subtle smile, as if she saw the change in him. "What do you think?"

"It reminds me of the ocean." Nothing else in Carl's experience compared. Nothing else changed so constantly while remaining essentially the same.

"Me, too." Naomi tucked a few strands of wind-blown hair behind her ear. "The wind never stops. Some days, it's gentle, like today, and some days it's rough, but it's always there."

She sat on the grass, long legs folded to the side. Carl breathed a sigh of relief and sat beside her. Had she noticed that his energy was ebbing?

"You love it here, don't you?"

"Yes, I do."

Carl leaned back on his hands and inhaled as deeply as his sore ribs would allow. Overseas, he'd seen men hurry to hide tears of homesickness when mail from home arrived – or didn't arrive. It had always left him at a loss. The few letters he'd received from his mother and Alice had gone without reply.

If you'd written, would it have changed anything? Not likely. If it ever occurred to him to love a place, it wouldn't be one like this, even if there were something soothing about its emptiness. "Some of the men overseas talked about home like you do. I never knew whether I envied them or not."

Naomi pulled her knees up and curled her arms around them, another reminder of last night. "It's strange. Growing up, all I wanted was to get away from here, to see something of the world. Like I told you, that's one of the reasons I went overseas. I couldn't imagine coming back here to stay. Now I know I may not stay here forever, but it will always be a part of me, wherever I go."

For a minute or two they sat in silence, looking out over the prairie. Carl stole glances at Naomi out of the corner of his eye. What was it about her that brought all his regrets to the forefront of his mind?

"Naomi, I'm still curious about why you keep a revolver in your room."

"And what I keep in my room is still none of your business."

"Of course… Have you always wanted to be a nurse?"

She grinned at him. "No. When I was little, I wanted to be a railroad engineer."

"Really?"

"Yes. I was a tomboy, Ben. I was eight when Mother died, and Dad treated me like the son he never had. He never told me I could only do certain things, just because I was a girl."

A picture flashed into Carl's mind of a pigtailed little girl watching the trains that passed through Mackenzie. He'd liked trains as a kid, too. They'd represented freedom and escape, the wider world with all its possibilities.

"When did you change your mind?"

Her grin became a reflective smile. "By the time I was thirteen, Dad had remembered that I was a girl and Laura had made up her mind there would never be anyone good enough for me here in Mackenzie. I liked school, and they both encouraged me to study hard. I had no interest in teaching or office work, and I enjoyed helping Dad in the practice. So, I chose nursing, and I was right. It suited me. What did you want to be as a kid?"

"Something different every week. Before I enlisted I worked on construction crews mostly. Casual jobs whenever I could pick them up." The truth was Carl had forgotten his childhood dreams, if he'd had any. Things like that faded early when you made no effort to remember. "If you could go anywhere you wanted to go and do anything you wanted to do, what would it be?"

Naomi huddled deeper into her coat, an unconscious gesture of self-protection. "I don't know. All I know is I've seen enough trauma cases. I want to focus on something else, something happier. Maybe obstetric nursing. Maybe something completely different from nursing. I've been waiting for it to come to me." She turned to face him. "What about you?"

"I'm waiting for it to come to me, too."

Sitting here with her brought too many half-formed longings to the surface. Time to go in, but before Carl could move, Naomi got up and dusted off her skirt. "You've been out long enough, and Laura will have breakfast ready. Come on."

They found Naomi's father at the kitchen table and Laura ready to serve up porridge and toast. The doctor's eyes lit up with a smile as they came in.

"Morning, Naomi. Ben, it's good to see you on your feet."

Carl nodded a greeting. "Feels good, too."

Naomi slipped off her coat. The dark crimson sweater she wore underneath brought out the colour in her cheeks. She washed her hands at the sink, then wrapped an arm around her father's shoulders. "Dad, who do you have to see today?"

The doctor pulled out her chair and added cream to the coffee Laura set in front of her. Had Carl's father ever done that for his mother or the girls at home? Not that he could remember. "Only Ethan Johnson, to change the dressing on his arm. Then there's office hours this afternoon."

"Good. After breakfast I'll ride out to the Johnson place and tend to Ethan. You can have a lazy morning."

"Sounds good to me."

Carl focused on the bowl of creamy porridge Laura put in front of him. Growing up, mornings had always been hectic, with him and the girls scrambling to find misplaced schoolbooks and his father in a rush to leave for work. As often as not, there'd be a school crisis of some sort thrown in for good measure. Carl had made passing grades without really trying, but he'd had a knack for rubbing his teachers the wrong way, and Alice was a poor student. Even when things went smoothly, there was never this kind of easy companionship at the breakfast table.

The doctor glanced at Carl as he spread jam on a triangle of toast. "Ben, do you play chess?"

"Yes, but badly. I haven't played in years." He'd never had the patience for it. The doctor responded with a smile that reminded Carl of Naomi's.

"We'll be well-matched then, if you feel up to a game after breakfast."

"Sure."

Carl couldn't help thinking that Naomi's father didn't look like a doctor. He had the face of a man who'd spent much of his life outdoors. Of course he spent his days riding or driving from house to house in his scattered practice, but he gave the impression that he'd lived a different kind of life, a rougher life in his younger years.

After helping Laura clear the table, Naomi put on riding clothes and left for the Johnson farm. She rode past the kitchen window, looking very much at ease on horseback. Carl followed the doctor into the sitting room.

It had a little more elegance than the kitchen. There, Laura ruled, but Carl suspected that in this room, Naomi's mother's taste still held sway. Lace curtains, muted wallpaper with a gold leaf pattern, a comfortable-looking, overstuffed sofa and armchair in dark gold, a couple of glass-shaded floor lamps. A room Carl's mother would have appreciated.

The sofa faced the fireplace, with a coffee table between. They set up the chessboard there and added wood to the fire. It took ten minutes for Carl to see that the doctor was right about them being well-matched. Neither of them took the game seriously.

Carl's mind drifted to the image of Naomi riding off earlier. "Naomi must be a big help with your patients. She's a good nurse."

"Yes, she is. She's a smart girl, and she isn't afraid of work. She's got a career waiting for her."

"Until she marries." The thought didn't warm Carl's heart at all. How would Naomi feel about giving up her work to keep house and raise babies for some man? The doctor gave him a level glance.

"She might choose to keep working. It isn't unheard of now."

"I think it would be a shame if she didn't."

Hand on one of his knights, Doctor Franklin paused. "What's troubling you, Ben? I can see there's something."

"I'm thinking of myself. When I think of a career, not just a job, nothing really appeals. Not that it matters. I'll take what work I can find and go from there."

Doctor Franklin moved his piece, sat back and looked Carl up and down – an appraising look that make him sit straighter. Silly. Who was he trying to impress?

"How old are you?"

"Almost twenty-five."

"What did your father do?"

"He was a financial manager in a manufacturing plant."

"On the Miramichi? It must have been a paper mill."

"Yeah." Carl forced himself to hold the doctor's gaze. Lying to him felt as cheap as lying to Naomi.

"That's a big responsibility. He likely expected as much from you."

Carl made a careless move with a pawn. "I couldn't say."

"But you expect as much from yourself?" Doctor Franklin took Carl's piece, then looked into his eyes. "It took me a while to find my way, too. I had itchy feet as a kid, so I spent a few years drifting. Worked at a lot of different jobs, here and across the border. A ranch in Montana, the docks in Vancouver, even tried my hand at mining up North. Then, at twenty-four, I decided I wanted to study medicine. When I told my parents they laughed at me, but eventually they saw that I was serious. I met Suzanne – Naomi's mother – while I was in university. When I graduated, we married and settled here. I've never regretted it. It doesn't matter so much what you do, Ben, it's what you put into whatever you choose that counts."

Carl saw the satisfaction in the man's eyes, heard it in his voice. The satisfaction of a life well lived. It made Carl feel as cheap as his lies did.

"I suppose so. Well, I'm not afraid of work either. As for Naomi, I'm sure she'll do well."

A touch of sadness crept into the doctor's expression. He covered it quickly. "Yes, and I hope she'll take as much satisfaction in her work as I have in mine, but even more, I hope she'll have a happy marriage like I did. There's nothing better in life."

Probably not, for the lucky few who had one. "Naomi's an attractive girl. I'm sure she could marry whenever she wants to."

"Naomi looks like her mother. As for marriage, there's no one in Mackenzie for her. All the decent young men around here are already married. That's why I encouraged her to go away and get her training, and then of course the war interfered." Doctor Franklin spoke with a touch of regret. "I know she's lonely here now. All her friends have settled down."

Carl pictured Naomi sitting with him out on that knoll earlier, heard her words again. She had choices to make, as he did, but she valued something he'd chosen to give up. Roots. "I think she likes the life here."

"She does. Naomi's a country girl, and without her mother, she grew up a bit of a tomboy. I taught her to shoot when she was fourteen, and she took to it." Her father grinned. "When the boys at school found out, they started teasing her about it, so she challenged them to a contest. She won."

Lucky for you, O'Neill. If she hadn't been taught how to handle a gun, you might be dead right now. How angry would Naomi's father be if he knew Carl had been in her bedroom last night? "Remind me to stay out of her bad books."

They shared a laugh before Carl moved his queen and put it in jeopardy. "Doctor Franklin, I've noticed that Naomi seems a bit nervous around me. Is she usually like that? I don't like to think she's afraid of me."

All the humour left the doctor's eyes. "Naomi doesn't have a nervous disposition, but it doesn't surprise me that she's a bit wary around you. Being overseas shook her more than she'll admit."

Maybe, but instinct told Carl there was more. He'd seen raw terror in her eyes last night, but if Doctor Franklin knew why, he wasn't sharing the information. Carl already knew the man well enough to be sure of that, and he could hardly ask Naomi. Far too personal.

Carl shrugged off the thought. Another couple of weeks and he be out of the Franklins' lives for good. It was just as well for all concerned that Naomi shied away from him. That meant he couldn't hurt her, and he'd left enough hurt behind him already.

Chapter 6

As she stopped by the paddock, Hannah gave a half-hearted jump sideways at the sight of the laundry fluttering on the clothesline. Naomi rolled her eyes and slid from the saddle.

"Silly, when are you going to grow up?"

She pulled off the saddle and bridle and turned Hannah into the corral. The smoke from the stove hung low over the house in the dampness, and the clouds looked like they held snow. Hopefully Mrs. Fields wouldn't choose tonight to have her baby and call Naomi's father out in the weather.

She'd stopped by the Pheeney place on her way home to offer her condolences, but she couldn't shake the feeling that Gordon's death was just a nightmare from which she'd wake at any moment. Those few minutes with Ben last night seemed dreamlike, too. She should have insisted he leave her room immediately, screamed if she had to – but she hadn't screamed. Why?

Because deep down, Naomi didn't really believe Ben would hurt her. And while she'd sat there with him, it felt like her loneliness joined with his, like they were floating together in a sea of isolation.

A strong gust of wind made the sheets on the line snap. Chilled from her windy ride home, Naomi hung Hannah's tack in the stable and ran to the house. While she stood by the stove getting warm, her father came in from the sitting room.

"You're back. How's Ethan?"

"Changing his bandages wasn't fun for him or me, but we got through it. No infection so far. Where are Laura and Ben?"

"Ben's up in his room resting, and Laura walked into town to run some errands."

Her father took his usual seat at the table. Behind him, a few snowflakes drifted past the window. Naomi poured herself a cup of coffee, not so much to drink as to feel its comforting warmth in her hands.

"I stopped by to see Gordon's parents on my way home."

Her father patted her chair. "I'll go this evening. How are they?"

Instead of sitting, Naomi leaned against the counter. "They're in shock. They can't believe Gordon won't be coming home. His mother said she keeps thinking a telegram will come tomorrow, saying it's all a mistake. I can't believe it either." Grief settled on her shoulders like a cold hand. "Dad, I think I'll start looking for work after Christmas. It's time I moved on. Mackenzie isn't the same now. It never will be."

Her father's gaze held hers, full of love. When the time came, would she really be able to leave him? "No, it won't ever be the same. Too many of your friends are gone. Have you decided what you want to do?"

"You know I've been thinking about that since I got home. I've seen enough pain. I want to spend my life around happier things."

"I know. I can't blame you for that." Her father glanced down at the wedding ring he'd never taken off. "I also know there's nothing that makes a person happier than being in a good marriage."

Naomi thought about Corinne again, remembered the way she'd looked the other day, alight with joy. "Corinne says the same thing. I don't think she's ever wanted anything else. I look at her and Barry, and I wonder if I even have it in me to feel like that... If I ever had it in me."

The glow of his memories left her father's eyes, making Naomi wish she hadn't spoken. "You do, dear. I know that." Then he squared his shoulders and smiled. "Ben and I had quite a talk this morning after you left. I think he's attracted to you."

"Ben will be on the train out of here as soon as he can manage it."

She'd spoken a little too quickly. Her father lifted a brow and held Naomi's gaze again. "Which has no bearing on what I just said."

Oh, but it did. When the mention of Ben's name was all it took to warm her blood, it mattered. Naomi couldn't afford to forget that he'd soon be gone. She took a sip of her coffee while she chose her words.

"Maybe Ben *is* attracted to me, in a way. The same way he'd be attracted to any reasonably good-looking young woman who looked after him when he was ill. He's lonely, and he's a long way from home. It's only natural."

"You might be right. I'm not pushing him at you, just stating a fact... Though, when it comes down to it, you do have two years of shared experience in common." Her father rose, poured himself a cup of coffee and leaned against the counter beside her, his gaze on Naomi while he stirred in cream. "When Ben leaves, I'm going to ask him to write to us. If I were in his shoes, I'd want friends, whether or not I could say so."

"Of course. I'd like to hear from him, too." As eager as she was to see Ben on his way, Naomi didn't like to think of him alone in a strange place after all he'd been through. She hadn't forgotten how he cut her off when she'd been about to ask him just how awful his time as a prisoner of war had been. Of course, she had no right to his confidence when she'd refused to give him hers, but it would be good for him to get some of that off his chest before he left, to lighten the burden he carried.

Ben might not want to confide in her, but he might talk to Barry if they got to know each other. She'd introduce them, even if Ben didn't think it worthwhile. "Dad, I think I'll talk to Laura when she gets home and invite Corinne and Barry over for supper. They want to meet Ben, and I want him to meet them."

"I think that's a good idea. Now I have to read over my files for this afternoon. I've been lazy long enough. Tell Laura this might be a good time for one of those chickens she's been fattening, to meet its maker. And with two hungry young men to feed, a pie mightn't be a bad idea either, if there's enough sugar in the house."

He shut himself in his office, and Naomi ran upstairs to change out of her riding clothes. She replaced her divided skirt with the black one she'd had on earlier, exchanged her sweater for an ivory flannel blouse, and stood in front of the full-length mirror on the back of the door to see the result. The cut of the skirt flattered her, and her blouse, plain and practical as it was, fit well and highlighted a touch of blue in her eyes. Naomi turned sideways and gathered up her hair in her hand. Almost long enough to pin up, but not quite. Perhaps she should let it grow.

You aren't unattractive, Naomi. You've just gotten out of the habit of thinking about it. Was the girl she'd been in school, the girl who was called a flirt by her enemies, still inside her, or did that Naomi only belong in the past?

She caught herself listening for sounds from the spare room. Was Ben asleep? Should she go and tell him there would be company for dinner? Naomi gave herself a firm mental shake.

He's more a guest than a patient now. You have no more business in his room than he had in yours last night.

Ben might write when he got to the coast, once or twice – or maybe more than that, until he got busy with work, made friends, found a girl. Naomi turned back to her mirror. What kind of girl would appeal to him beyond surface attraction? The old-fashioned type that would be content to keep his house and raise his children?

Maybe, but that girl would also need to be strong enough to stand up to him. Ben seemed the kind of man who would walk over anyone weak enough to let him. A 'new woman,' one who wanted a career and the vote and independence? Perhaps, but she probably wouldn't bring out the gentle side that Ben had shown Naomi last night.

She turned to the window and saw Laura coming up the drive, arms laden with grocery bags. Naomi went downstairs to help, brought up her plan for dinner and got Laura's approval. Corinne accepted the invitation without bothering to consult Barry.

"He's as curious to meet your Mr. MacNeil as I am. We'll be there at six."

My Mr. MacNeil? Naomi would have to clarify that right away.

'Another day, perhaps two, and perhaps you will have learned some respect.'

The young German officer's voice reached Carl through a haze of hunger, thirst and pain. He stood bound to a post in the middle of the prison compound, arms stretched behind him, muscles and tendons at the point of agony. The corporal – nicknamed Quasimodo by the prisoners because of his slightly crooked shoulders – smiled. 'There are idiots in every army, as well as men without honour.'

Idiot. The word echoed in Carl's mind as he woke from the nightmare, muscles frozen, mouth powder-dry. When his blood began flowing again, rage flowed with it. Still on the liminal edge of sleep, he reached under his bed for the bottle of whiskey that should have been there. It wasn't.

Son of a bitch.

Of course the whiskey wasn't there. This wasn't home. Part of Carl's mind recognized the Franklins' spare bedroom, but another part still saw the young corporal's sneering face. Carl sat up and slammed both fists into his mattress, punching hard and fast, longing to feel his knuckles dig into that man's flesh.

He kept punching until he couldn't breathe and his head swam with the pain in his ribs, then he fell back on the bed again, gasping. A man without honour. After all this time, the spiteful words still stung. That made Carl angrier than anything else.

You escaped. You beat him. But what comfort was that when the bastard had lodged himself in Carl's mind and followed him home?

He crossed the hall to the bathroom, splashed water on his face, ran his fingers through his rumpled hair and headed downstairs. He needed some fresh air. Passing the sitting room, Carl got a glimpse of Naomi on the sofa, reading the newspaper. She dropped the paper and called out to him.

"Ben, there's something I want to tell you."

He didn't feel like talking to her or anyone else, but her voice stopped him. Carl paused in the doorway. When she got a good look at him, Naomi's eyes widened and her face paled.

"You're upset. What's the matter?"

She looked scared to death. What was wrong with her? And why hadn't he just kept going?

"It's nothing you can help with."

She stood, took an uncertain step toward him. "Was it a dream?"

Of course she'd figure that out. She must have seen nightmares often enough with her patients. Maybe she had them herself. Carl snapped without meaning to.

"I said it's nothing you can help with."

Naomi took another tentative step. The fear in her eyes softened to sympathy. "What do you have to lose by letting me try?"

Carl's heart started racing. He couldn't talk about the four months of hell he'd endured in the reprisal camp – all because of his own stupidity. He'd been treated fairly while his shoulder wound healed, and when he was sent to a relatively comfortable camp for captured officers, he'd given his word that he wouldn't try to escape. And broken it. And been caught. And paid the price. Period. Was there less honour in that than in playing the game and riding out the war in safety? He'd given up trying to answer that one.

But Naomi stood there, offering… What? Pity?

Perhaps, but she also offered solace.

Carl edged past her and sat on the sofa. Naomi hesitated, then sat beside him. She gave Carl space, but her warmth still penetrated the chill that had settled on him.

"You know, Ben, there's probably nothing you could tell me that I haven't already heard."

"Then there's no need for you to hear it again." Inner strength was written on Naomi's face, in its purity of line and her dignified reserve. She'd come home from overseas with her soul shaken, but intact. Carl would die before he'd chip away at that. "I know you've got a few stories of your own, Naomi, but you're a woman. It was different for you."

She laid a tentative, reassuring hand on his knee. He pulled his leg away, jolted by the way her touch sang along his nerves. A flash of hurt, and then Naomi let it pass. "How do you think it's different?"

Carl let out a long breath and leaned back, avoiding her gaze. "I get angry. So angry I don't know where I am or what I'm doing. Do you ever feel like that?"

"No, but I'd say you have more reason to be angry than I do. What I feel is more a sadness."

He met Naomi's gaze again and saw a wealth of compassion there, more than he could resist. If anyone did, she had a claim to whatever compassion he could muster. They were headed in different directions, but did that have to mean they couldn't give each other something now?

He reached out and traced the curve of her cheek with a finger. Naomi stiffened, and the truth knocked him breathless. Her skittishness around him, what her father had said today. The gun in her nightstand. It all fell into place.

I'm not surprised she's wary around you.

She was wary around him because someone, some man, had hurt her.

Who? Someone overseas? Ninety-nine out of a hundred soldiers would die before they'd harm a nurse, but there was always the hundredth. The one without honour. A world gone mad brought out the madness in people.

How could he not have seen it before this? Carl took a moment to rein in his anger. That wasn't going to get him anywhere. Then he looked Naomi in the eye.

"Naomi, don't lie to me. Someone's hurt you. I can see it."

She edged further away, temper and shock on her face. "Did Dad say something to you?"

He didn't want to frighten her further, but it took every shred of Carl's determination to keep his tone gentle. Naomi had given so much. It was just so damned unfair. "Your father told me nothing. It's obvious. You flinch when I touch you, even accidentally. What happened?"

She shook her head. "Ben, it could have been so much worse. When I think of the terrible things that have happened to women overseas, I—"

"I'm not talking about them, I'm talking about you."

Her fingers curled into the sofa cushions. With obvious effort, she kept her voice steady.

"If you want me to tell you, you'll have to tell me how you got the scars on your wrists."

Their gazes locked in a trial of wills. Carl gave up. If he wanted to keep his own secrets, he'd have to let Naomi keep hers. "All right, have it your way. We both have parts of our lives that we aren't willing to share."

"Thank you."

He lifted his hand to Naomi's cheek again. When she tensed, he simply waited. After a second or two, her eyelids dropped down and her lips parted.

She was too sweet, and it had been too long. Desire took over and Carl slid his hand around to cup the back of Naomi's neck. She pulled back.

"Don't."

Carl lowered his hand. It curled into a fist at his side. Whatever had happened must have been bad, if she couldn't stand a simple touch. "I'd like ten minutes alone with the man who did this to you. Naomi, I've done plenty of things that I'm not proud of, but I've never, ever forced a woman to do anything she didn't want to do. Do you believe me?"

She swallowed, nodded. "Yes."

"Good. Because looking at you now, I think maybe you're feeling some of the same things for me that I'm feeling for you. If I'm wrong, go ahead and tell me so."

Naomi's answer came out small and fearful and she wouldn't look him in the eye, but her words rang with honesty. "I...I wish we could pretend we weren't both so alone."

"Maybe we can." And Carl knew how he wanted to go about it – if he managed not to scare her off first.

He touched her cheek again, just a brush of his fingertips. This time, she didn't flinch. "Naomi, have you been kissed before?

Chapter 7

Colour burned into her cheeks. "Of course I have, but that was before..." Her voice trailed off. Carl tucked a finger under Naomi's chin and very gently lifted it.

"Are you going to let some man take that pleasure from you forever?"

Naomi tensed, but she didn't pull away. She met Carl's gaze squarely, in spite of her obvious fear. "I... No."

"Then maybe you should consider trying kissing again."

Inch by slow inch, he lowered his head. The smell of her hair, the sound of her breath catching. The warmth against his lips when she exhaled. To Carl, a kiss had never been more than a prelude to sex, but none of the few women he'd been with had trembled when he touched them. None had made him tremble in return. He couldn't have rushed if he'd wanted to.

He slid his fingers into the silk of Naomi's hair, tucked a softly curling lock behind her ear and lingered to stroke her there. They were only pretending they weren't alone, like she'd said, but why not pretend while they could?

"Easy… If you want me to stop, just say so." *Hell, she shouldn't have to say so, O'Neill. You don't need her to tell you this is stupid.*

But Naomi said nothing. Their lips met, and Carl's conscience headed south. So what? His conscience had never been much good at keeping him out of trouble, anyway.

He didn't kiss her full on at first. Instead, he teased the corners of her mouth, first one, then the other. Her lips relaxed, but she still held her body tense, ready to run. He ran his fingers up her arms to her shoulders, trying to soothe her, but she flinched. He dropped his hands and gave her a little space. Hell, his own nerves were bowstring tight. He'd never made this kind of effort to be gentle with a woman before. Did he even know how?

"This will be better if you relax."

Naomi turned her face away. "I'm not sure I can."

Carl took her hands and twined his fingers with hers. To anchor her – or himself?

"Don't think. Just feel."

Feel? He didn't have names for the feelings rushing through him right now. He brushed Naomi's lips with his again. Her fingers curled, her shoulders stiffened. Then, between one breath and the next, she relaxed. Her mouth opened, soft and quiet, inviting him to taste her. That was all it was at first, acceptance, but the sweetness of it made him ache.

Then she started kissing him back.

Oh, yeah.

Maybe this was how nice girls kissed. As if Carl would know. Maybe she'd learned from some beau, or maybe she was a natural, but her soft lips and igniting passion took his senses by storm without her even trying.

She pulled her hands away and looked up at him, lips wet, eyes wide. "Ben…I shouldn't have let that happen. It makes no sense."

Still tasting her on his tongue, still smelling her, Carl searched for words to cut this down to size. For both of them. "Does it have to make sense? We're headed in different directions, Naomi. What difference does a kiss make?"

Naomi sat a little taller. "You're right, of course. As long as you see it that way, then there's no harm done."

"None at all." Another lie, and by the way she jumped to her feet, it hurt her. Of course, he should have known he would hurt her. That was how it always worked. Naomi stepped back, obviously eager to put some distance between them.

"By the way, Ben, Barry and Corinne are coming over for supper."

"Barry and Corinne?"

"The friends I told you about. Remember?"

Carl struggled to clear the haze of desire from his brain. "Yeah. Oh, yeah, I remember."

"I should go give Laura a hand."

Naomi hurried out. Carl leaned back and rolled his shoulders, trying to ease the knot of frustration there. *You're an idiot, O'Neill.* All he'd done was upset Naomi and make sure she'd be uncomfortable around him for whatever time they had left together. Why couldn't he have kept his hands to himself?

But the memory of her sweet mouth stifled his regrets. Naomi was an adult who'd had a strong taste of the worst the world could offer, and she had worries of her own. She wouldn't waste time or emotion on Carl once he left, so what did it matter?

Only the ache in his chest and the racing of his pulse said it might matter.

The doorbell rang and the doctor came out of his office to answer it. Thank God Doctor Franklin hadn't heard the goings-on in the sitting room. As badly as Naomi's father wanted to see her settled, a penniless drifter would be his last choice, even though he'd once been a drifter himself.

Carl picked up the newspaper and gave it a shake. What had Naomi and the doctor done to him? He'd always resented people like the Franklins, steady, grounded types. And now, here he was just plain liking them.

What was it Alice had said to him that day in the hospital back in Halifax? "Growing up, none of us liked your friends, but you always stuck by them, even when you suffered for it. Your problem is you've never been able to tell who was worth sticking by and who wasn't." Only Alice could turn that kind of loyalty into a virtue. Of course, she'd never been the smartest girl on the block.

No? If you think about it, Naomi's quite a bit like Alice.

Doctor Franklin and his patient returned to the office. In the kitchen, Laura and Naomi talked as they worked. Carl listened, his whole body tuned to her voice, even though he couldn't make out the words. He rattled the newspaper again in disgust.

You'll never hurt Alice or Mother again because you'll never see them again. So, you know what to do here, too. But the thought of doing what he knew he should only made the ache in his chest worse.

Naomi set the table with her ears tuned to sounds from upstairs. A couple of hours ago, she'd heard Ben go up to his room. She hadn't seen him since she'd left the sitting room after he kissed her.

No. After *they* kissed, and all the tingling, feathery sensations she'd thought were over for her returned.

She darted a glance over her shoulder at Laura stirring flour into her gravy. Time to stop woolgathering. Corinne and Barry would be here any minute. No doubt at dinner, Ben would behave as if nothing unusual had happened today.

So will you, Naomi. For your own sake.

Just after six, the Foleys' truck pulled into the yard. Barry had splurged on the new Ford just after harvest time. Though it meant that Naomi got to see him and Corinne more often than when they'd only had their wagon, she wasn't sure she liked the change. One of too many changes over the last few years.

Barry came in first. Naomi's mood lifted as she greeted him with a hug. Barry had been her first date, her first beau, and though they'd never been serious, he had a corner of his own in her heart.

Barry looked like the farmer he was, blond and heavy-set, with an easygoing expression in his hazel eyes that could turn to steel if he was crossed. By the poorly concealed elation on his face, Corinne had told him her news. Naomi hadn't seen him grin like that since before he shipped out.

"Hang up your coat and sit down. It's been too long." She turned to hug Corinne. "I hope you're hungry."

"I am. Famished, in fact. I couldn't eat breakfast or lunch today."

Laura set a bowl of mashed potatoes on the table, along with the gravy in Naomi's mother's Blue Willow gravy boat. "You're likely carrying a boy, then."

Naomi's father walked in from his office just in time to hear her. His face lit up with a smile. "Corinne, are my ears playing tricks on me?"

"No, Doctor Franklin."

He hugged her as he would have hugged Naomi, had it been her with good news. "Then you and I need to have a visit, young lady."

Corinne nodded. "Book me in whenever you have time and get Naomi to call me."

"It'll be all over town if I make a call. Let's just say next Monday at ten." He turned to Naomi, who was fussing with the dishes. "Where's Ben? We've got a room full of hungry people here. Didn't you tell him we were having company?"

"Of course I did." Surely Ben didn't intend to hide in his room. Maybe it was too soon to expect him to deal with strangers.

He must have heard them talking because there was movement on the floor above them. When Naomi heard his footsteps on the stairs, the relief that washed through her took her by surprise.

Her pulse jumped when Ben entered the room. Their gazes met and held just a little too long. So the kiss had affected him, too. Naomi looked away before anyone could notice.

He *was* handsome, the more so now that he was feeling better and had enjoyed a few days of Laura's cooking, but a different picture of him intruded in Naomi's mind. Ben as a prisoner with his hands bound. That image made her heart lurch.

Barry extended a hand. "Sorry you had such a rough introduction to Mackenzie." Naomi saw Ben sizing her friend up as they shook hands. What would he think if he knew she and Barry had once been a couple?

Ben acknowledged Corinne with a polite but reserved 'pleased to meet you.' Was he actually shy with women? The way he immediately turned back to Barry made Naomi think so. "Don't be sorry. If they'd put me off the train anywhere else, I might not have made it. Mackenzie's lucky to have Doctor Franklin and Naomi."

Barry moved to the counter and inhaled the scent of the chicken waiting to be carved. He and Corinne had both had the freedom of Laura's kitchen since they were children. "We certainly are. Laura, it's been too long since Corinne and I have had one of your meals. I hope you aren't planning on having any leftovers."

"I've fed you often enough to know better, Barry. You and Garnett and Gordon."

Barry's smile faded. "We stopped by to see Gordon's parents on our way here. One of the hardest things I've ever done."

He took his seat next to Corinne. She reached for his hand. "Mr. Pheeney said they aren't going to think about a memorial service right away. They want to take some time to accept that Gordon isn't coming home. Naomi, have you seen Rena yet?"

"No, not yet." Rena Milton had been going with Gordon before he enlisted, and he'd told Naomi things were getting serious. Still, he'd held back on proposing. Now Naomi wished he hadn't. It would have given Rena more of a right to grieve for him publicly.

Naomi's father sat and lifted his water glass. "To good friends. May we not take them for granted." They clinked their glasses. Naomi said a silent prayer that Barry's brother Garnett *would* come home. She wasn't sure she could stand to lose any more friends. Not with Ben leaving, too.

During the meal, Ben surprised Naomi by putting himself out to make conversation. Barry and Corinne warmed to him right away. "I had my first look at the countryside this morning," Ben said as he drizzled gravy over a second helping of chicken and mashed potatoes. "It's like nothing I've ever seen before. I'm impressed."

Barry lifted an eyebrow. "You might change your mind if you spend the winter here. Naomi told us you were on your way to the coast. Warmer, but a lot of rain and fog. Not the best place to get over lung trouble."

Ben shrugged. "I need work, and Vancouver sounds like the best place to find something to do."

With a loaded fork in his hand, Barry paused and looked Ben over. "Dad and I could use help, when it comes to that. He isn't a young man anymore, my brother's still in Europe and the place is meant to be a three-man operation. Might not make as much, but your money would go a lot further here than in Vancouver."

Ben's gaze strayed to Naomi before he answered. "I wouldn't be worth room and board, Barry. I don't know anything about farming."

"You look like you've got a strong back, and that's what we need more than anything. Of course you aren't fit for hard work right now, but you could ease into it as you get well."

Naomi's heart gave a queer little bound. What if Ben didn't disappear from her life in the next couple of weeks? Would it change anything for either of them?

Corinne took notice. She'd thrown Naomi a couple of significant looks since they sat down. Was the offer of work some kind of well-meant conspiracy to keep Ben nearby? It would be weeks before he could be of much use on the farm, and knowing his aversion to taking charity, Naomi didn't doubt he'd say 'no.' At least he did Barry the courtesy of seeming to consider it.

"You're right about the money angle, and I'd like work that would keep me outside."

Naomi's father nodded approval. "You aren't ready to leave here yet, Ben, but when you are, I think the farm would suit you for the winter."

Naomi's pulse tripped again when Ben put down his fork and met Barry's gaze. "Barry, I'm tempted. Tell you what. Let me think about it until Doctor Franklin says I'm well enough to leave. If I come to your place, I'll pay you board until I'm able to be of some real use."

"That won't be necessary, Ben."

"Yes, it will. No offense meant, but I got into this mess because a friend of mine owed money to the wrong people. I'd prefer to pay for my keep until I can earn it."

Barry nodded. "I understand. Think about it, Ben. We'd be glad to have you."

Ben didn't answer. He looked distinctly uncomfortable. It seemed he wasn't used to being welcomed so openly by strangers – first Naomi and her father, and now the Foleys. He was quiet for the rest of the meal. Afterward, he didn't linger at the table.

"I'm sorry, everyone, but it's been a long day and I'm done. Barry, Corinne, pleased to meet you. Naomi, Laura, Doctor Franklin, good night."

Barry and Corinne stayed to talk over coffee, but they'd had a busy day as well and Corinne looked tired. Barry noticed. "Corinne's had a long day, too. Time to head home. Laura, thanks for a great meal. Good night, Doctor Franklin."

Naomi walked them to their truck. Before getting in, Corinne leaned close to Naomi's ear.

"I hope Ben stays. We like him, and he likes you."

Corinne climbed into the truck before she could reply.

Naomi waited in the dark, frosty yard until the glow of the truck's headlights faded into the distance, then she ran inside, chilled and confused. She couldn't doubt any longer that Ben liked her, in one way at least, but even if he stayed in Mackenzie for the winter, there was no real future for him here. Or for her.

The truth could be relentless.

Chapter 8

Tom looked up from his crossword puzzle with a start when Naomi appeared at his office window. "Morning, Naomi. I have a telegram for you."

The early westbound train had left fifteen minutes ago at eight-thirty, leaving the station empty except for the stationmaster. Naomi had chosen her time to arrive for just that reason. Tom fished the telegram from a drawer and handed it over. "Looks like you won't have your patient much longer."

Naomi scanned the slip of paper. *Letter with cash in mail. Take care. Dennis.* So Ben's friend had come through. Under Tom's curious gaze, she tucked the telegram in her purse.

"Guess not. He'll be glad to see this. Thanks." She walked out. If people wanted information about Ben, they'd have to get it from him, and she'd like to see them try.

A tangle of emotions welled up inside her when she thought about the telegram and what it meant. Very soon, Ben would be alone again, among strangers in a new place, and he wasn't ready. His nightmare yesterday had proven that.

Be honest, Naomi. It's not only that he isn't ready to leave. Are you ready to see him go?

She'd been so eager to get out of the station she'd forgotten to pick up the *Regina Leader*. Naomi ducked into the restaurant for a copy. The five tables in the place were empty, with fresh white cloths in place. The morning regulars hadn't come in for their coffee yet.

Sarah MacPherson, a retired farmer's wife, came out from the kitchen at the jingle of the bell over the door. By the look of her wiry figure, no one would guess she'd built a solid little business on the strength of her cooking, but people came from as far as Donwell to enjoy it. Her infectious smile and knack for remembering people, as well as her good food, kept her customers coming back.

"Well now, Naomi, it's been ages, but I guess you've been busy."

"Yes, Sarah. Are those donuts I smell?" The fragrance of frying sweet dough wafting from the kitchen made Naomi's mouth water. She hadn't had breakfast yet.

"Yes, m'dear. Did the doctor send you down for some? Haven't seen him for weeks either, and he's always been partial to my donuts. Of course, I've heard you've had a patient staying with you."

"Yes. Dad's been busy. If you have any donuts ready, I'd like a half-dozen. Cinnamon-sugar, please. And the paper."

"Just took a batch out. Be right with you." Sarah disappeared into the kitchen and returned with two neatly tied white cardboard boxes. "Here you are. Since you have a guest, I thought you might like a full dozen. Up to you, of course."

The aroma coming from the boxes was all the urging Naomi needed. "Ben – Mr. MacNeil – is feeling better now, and I'm sure he'll appreciate these as much as Dad. I'll take them." She tucked the two boxes under her arm with the paper and headed home.

She found Ben sitting on the back step, his grey jacket unbuttoned over his blue shirt, his face turned up to the sun. It gave his hair the gloss of a crow's wing. He was still a bit pale, but the bruises on his face were scarcely noticeable now. The ones on his torso would take a lot longer to fade.

When he heard her, Ben got stiffly to his feet. His eyes held shadows this morning. Had he slept poorly? When he came toward Naomi, a spark kindled inside her.

"Morning."

"Hey. You've been to town already. You must have gotten up early."

"I did, and the early bird got the proverbial worm." Naomi nodded toward the boxes under her arm. "Mrs. MacPherson, at the restaurant, was making donuts when I stopped in for the paper."

"Are they as good as they smell?"

"Yes."

Ben took a step closer. Naomi's breath caught. Was he going to kiss her again? Did she *want* him to kiss her again? To stop him, she held out the donuts and newspaper. "Will you take these? I also stopped by the train station. A wire came in from your friend Dennis."

The glow in Ben's eyes died, leaving the shadows. "Good."

Naomi fished in her bag for the telegram. Ben set the donuts on the step and took it. Caught up in her own ambivalence, she waited for him to say something. Did the thought of his leaving frighten him the way it did her? She hadn't forgotten the look in his eyes yesterday when he came into the sitting room. The anger and horror. It would be so easy for him to give in to it once he was alone again.

Ben scanned the slip of paper, folded it and stuck it in his jeans pocket. "I suppose his letter will be here in a week or so."

"Yes." Too soon. If only Ben would put his pride aside and stay with Barry and Corinne for a while, give himself time to heal.

"You seemed to enjoy meeting Barry and Corinne last night. I'm glad. I was a little afraid you wouldn't be feeling up to dealing with strangers."

Naomi prayed that she didn't sound as manipulative as she felt. Ben's gaze met hers, guarded. Unreadable.

"Barry and Corinne seem nice enough. I wish..." His voice trailed off. Naomi looked away, remembering the last time he'd said those words, when he'd been so ill. This time she wasn't sure she wanted to know, but she couldn't help asking.

"What do you wish, Ben?"

Without answering, he walked past her to the paddock. His hands tightened on the top rail of the fence when Naomi joined him. "I wish I was fit to go to work at something. Anything. Doing nothing isn't good for me."

Naomi followed his gaze out to where sky and grassland met. "Are you seriously considering Barry's offer?"

"I don't know if I'd say 'seriously.'" Ben swung around, a humourless smile on his face. "I wonder what my father would think if he could see me swinging a pitchfork in a barn. Probably that it was all I was fit for."

"Maybe, if he were alive to see you, he'd be proud of you for being willing to work." When he didn't answer, Naomi rounded on him in frustration. "Ben, I don't know why you're so hard on yourself."

He turned away with a shrug. "As far as I can see, I've never been hard enough on myself."

Ben started back toward the house with Naomi at his heels, still riding her annoyance. He had the scars to show what he'd been through. She hated hearing him judge himself more harshly than anyone else would judge him for not having a job yet. "Don't let Barry or Corinne hear you talking like this. Neither of them thinks there's anything wrong with swinging a pitchfork. Both their families have done it for generations."

"I never said there was anything wrong with it, but it would only be a stopgap. Let's go in and have breakfast before those donuts get cold."

Ben's tone told her the subject was closed. His silence during breakfast made Naomi wonder if she'd really offended him. Afterward, her father drove off in the car to make his rounds. Ben cleared the table for Laura before she sent him packing.

"You go back out and sit in the sun. It'll do you good. We might not get another day like this until spring."

His gaze met Naomi's. She turned away and grabbed a dishtowel. "Let's get the dishes done, Laura." Ben's expression said clearly that he'd like Naomi to join him outside, but the atmosphere between them was too charged. She needed distance.

Laura cast a glance out the back door as they started work. "What's going on between you and Ben, Naomi? Has he done something to make you uncomfortable?"

"He's getting restless, that's all. He's edgy, and that makes me edgy. I picked up a telegram for him while I was in town. His friend is sending money."

"So he'll be on his way soon, unless he decides to stay with the Foleys." With another half-guilty glance toward the back porch, Laura lowered her voice. "You know, I've never been one who couldn't admit they were wrong, but I think maybe I was wrong about Ben. I guess he's decent enough."

Coming from Laura, that was high praise. Naomi hid a smile. "I agree, but I don't expect him to stay, Laura. Mackenzie is too small for him." She looked around for a distraction. "I think we should stain this floor before winter sets in. What do you think?"

They talked practicalities until the dishes were dried and put away, then Naomi took the newspaper to the sitting room and kindled a fire. She skimmed the headlines on the front page, saw nothing major in the war news and skipped to the local news. She almost missed the picture at the top of a small column halfway down the page, but something familiar about it caught her eye. When she looked more closely, her stomach turned over.

Familiar, hate-filled eyes looked back at her.

> *Randall Clark, of no fixed address, was arrested by police on October 15 in connection with an indecent assault on a young woman in downtown Regina last week. The accused is expected to appear in court...*

Naomi choked on bile and threw the paper down on the sofa. Again she felt Clark coming up behind her as she walked home from the Granger place that August afternoon. Remembered her first glimpse of his face when she turned to say 'hello.' The desperate urge to run and the shock when he stunned her with a blow that knocked her down. The whole nightmare came back to her, played itself over in her mind in vivid detail. And now he'd attacked someone else, someone who might have been spared had Naomi reported him.

She was still sitting there, caught in the grip of the memory, when Ben walked by the sitting room door. He must have seen her face, because he turned on his heel and covered the distance between them in two quick strides.

"Naomi, you look like you've seen a ghost."

She fought to pull herself together. "I'm...I'm not feeling very well."

"You looked fine at breakfast." Ben sat beside her, not too close. Of course, he already knew more than he should. Naomi avoided his gaze, but she couldn't block out his scent that made her want to lean toward him, be comforted by him again.

The paper rustled as he picked it up. A few seconds later, he went very still.

"This is what's upset you, isn't it?"

Naomi forced herself to face him. Of course the paper had fallen with Clark's picture facing up. Her mind raced. Ben didn't have to know the whole truth.

"Anything like that brings up unpleasant memories."

She braced herself, but Ben kept his voice gentle. "Naomi, I know we agreed to keep our secrets to ourselves, but this is driving me crazy. Was what happened to you as bad as this?"

Unless she lied, he'd assume the worst anyway. Naomi nodded. Ben dropped the paper. "Son of a bitch. Who...?"

"Ben, please. I'm not going to talk about it. I won't relive that day for anyone."

He blew out a breath. "Fine. I won't ask you to, but...Jesus, the thought of anyone hurting you drives me up a wall. Does your father know?"

"Yes. He and Laura know, but nobody else does, not even Barry and Corrine."

Ben looked directly into her eyes. "I've done enough mean things in my life, but nothing as mean as gossiping about this would be. If anyone finds out, it won't be from me."

"Thank you."

He knew, without her saying a word. He knew, and he wasn't judging, blaming or questioning. Her relief took Naomi by surprise. Ben must have seen it, because he slipped his arm behind her.

Naomi jumped. His other hand reached for hers. "Easy. Come here." At first her muscles locked, but slowly, very slowly, her body relaxed. Ben drew her closer, until she leaned against him.

A minute. Only for a minute, while she gathered her strength. After all, if she had to be weak, better with Ben than with her father.

As the seconds ticked by, her breathing slowed to the rhythm of Ben's. Their closeness acted like a potent calming drug, but it seemed to have the opposite effect on him. His body began to tighten. Lost in her own sensations, Naomi laid her hand on his chest. His heart galloped like a runaway horse. She looked up.

"Ben—"

He said nothing, but the heat in his gaze spoke for him. Tension coiled in the pit of Naomi's stomach, but when Ben's lips covered hers, the fear and shame she expected didn't come. There was only pleasure.

She ran her hands over his chest and shoulders and felt a heady sense of power when he shivered. She sensed him fighting for restraint, for gentleness, and that touched a part of her heart she'd thought was dead. She couldn't pretend this time that it didn't matter.

With that thought, the fear came. She caught her breath and turned away. "Ben, we can't do this to each other."

Ben released her hand and shifted to the end of the sofa. "I know. I know this is going nowhere." His eyes mirrored her confusion. "Naomi, at dinner last night, when Barry started talking about me going to work for him, it threw me. I didn't expect it from someone I'd just met, but even if it's an opportunity, it would be stupid for me to accept. I don't belong in Mackenzie."

"I know."

Ben took her hand again. "Trust me. If I stayed here to work with Barry, by the time spring came he'd regret it, and so would I. So would you. As soon as Dennis' letter arrives, I'll be moving on."

Maybe he was right. Maybe a quiet place like this would leave him with too much time to think, too much space for his demons. Naomi put away her pointless, selfish desires.

"Ben, I have a favour to ask. When you get settled, will you write? Don't think of it as an obligation, but Dad and I would both like to hear how you're doing."

Ben let her hand go and got to his feet. By his expression, Naomi wasn't the only one with regrets. "I'm not much for letter writing, Naomi. Or for promises."

"I'm not asking for a promise."

On his way out of the room, Ben paused with his hand on the door jamb. "You make me wish I was the kind of man who could give one."

Chapter 9

The fresh night air was heaven after the heat and smells of the hospital tent. Sweat trickled from under Naomi's head covering and into her eyes to blur her vision. She'd removed her soiled apron, but blood had soaked through it to stain her dress. The metallic scent of it made her empty stomach churn, but at least her shift was over.

Casualties had poured in all day, rife with tetanus and gas gangrene. After ten hours in the operating room, Naomi's mind buzzed with exhaustion, unable to think further ahead than a bath, some food and bed. She stepped out into the blessed freshness, then stopped at a sound from the cot nearest the opening.

This boy must have been brought in with the last wave. He'd been put to bed still dressed. The glow from the overhead light barely penetrated the dimness, but it showed Naomi the blood soaking the blanket that covered him. How could he still be alive?

There were no other nurses nearby. The others on her shift had already left, and the new shift was at the far end of the tent being briefed by the head Sister. Naomi turned to walk away. There was nothing she could do for the patient, and she'd seen enough death for one day. Then the young soldier murmured again. It sounded like 'Maman.'

Naomi looked down at her hands to be sure she'd scrubbed them clean, then moved to the side of the cot. The patient looked to be seventeen or eighteen, dark-haired and olive-skinned. His face hadn't yet lost its young curves. He wore a French uniform. When she knelt beside him he opened his eyes. They were dark brown, their light fading quickly. She leaned closer.

"Comment t'appelle tu?"

The young soldier didn't answer. Not sure he knew she was there, Naomi touched his shoulder. He turned his head toward her and held out both hands. "Maman."

His mother. He's hanging on for his mother. Naomi took his hands. Cool and clammy, they trembled in hers. The boy's eyes lit up with recognition. He thought he knew her.

Naomi did what his mother would have done. She leaned down and kissed his forehead. If she'd been seen, she would have been severely reprimanded, but that didn't occur to her. As she straightened up, the boy's eyes closed and his breathing stopped. She'd given him what he was waiting for.

She woke with her hands ice-cold, the remembered smell of blood in her nostrils. Naomi sat up and took slow, deep breaths until her head cleared and her hands were steady enough to light her lamp. She still liked its soft glow better than the electric ceiling light.

The house was silent. She hadn't awoken anyone. She opened her window and leaned out. The stars stood out clear and bright in the moonless sky, beckoning her. It wouldn't be the first time she'd gone for a late night walk after waking from a dream.

No. Too cold, and her father or Laura might wake and find her gone. It made a lot more sense to go down to the kitchen where the stove would still be warm, and make a cup of cocoa.

She put on her robe, tiptoed downstairs and switched on the kitchen light. The door of Laura's off-the-kitchen bedroom was open a crack to let in more heat. Naomi shut it softly and made a mental note to open it again before she went back upstairs. She fetched milk from the icebox, filled a small saucepan, set it on the stove and sat at the table to wait while it warmed.

The familiar night sounds of the house came and went, as if it breathed softly in its sleep. Silly – or was it? Maybe houses did take on something of the personalities of the people who built them and lived and loved in them. She'd missed this place so much while she was away. How would it be when she left permanently?

Her fancy fell apart when quiet footfalls sounded on the stairs. Ben appeared in the kitchen doorway in his robe, sleepy-eyed, hair standing on end. They spoke at the same time.

"What are you doing up?"

Ben's mouth quirked in a grin. "I was thirsty. I forgot to take a glass of water to my room when I went up. You?"

Naomi nodded toward Laura's door and lowered her voice. Neither her father nor Laura would be pleased to find Naomi and Ben together in the middle of the night like this. "I was thirsty, too. I'm making cocoa. Want some?"

Ben followed her lead and kept his voice down. "Sure."

He joined Naomi at the table and ran a hand through his hair. "We really should stop meeting like this."

When Naomi smiled and rolled her eyes, Carl's heart lifted. He hadn't seen her smile often, and it was worth seeing. She added more milk, cocoa and sugar to the pot on the stove, returned to the table and leaned on her elbows, her pointed chin resting in her hands.

"I noticed the other day that you signed your wire 'Rabbit.' Why?"

Carl gave her the short version. "Someone – I don't remember who – nicknamed me that when I was a kid. It stuck."

Her eyes took on a teasing twinkle. "And you let it stick? That seems out of character for you somehow, but then again, I can see you daring another kid to give you a hard time about it."

She read him well. That was exactly why he'd let the nickname stick, as a way of showing that he didn't give a damn. "Yeah."

Naomi tilted her head, her gaze soft and steady but full of questions. "Ben, I'm curious about your parents."

"You're curious about everything."

"I remember how difficult losing my mother was for me. Losing both parents must have been even harder for you."

Damn. Lying to her got more difficult every time he did it. Her pity was hard enough to take when the reasons were real, but when they weren't, it really stuck in his craw. His answer came out cold and hard. "I was an adult."

His tone didn't seem to faze her. Those clear grey eyes kept looking into his. "Still— "

Carl couldn't take the lie any further. "I was never close to my parents, Naomi. My father drank pretty heavily when I was growing up, and we never saw eye to eye."

Telling just that much of the truth took a weight off his chest. Naomi didn't look too surprised. Maybe he'd said more in his delirium than he'd thought.

"What about your mother?"

"She was the wrong woman for Dad. Too gentle. She couldn't stand up to him."

"Not even for you?"

"Dad didn't beat me, Naomi. We just never got along, and it wasn't all his fault. I caused him enough headaches."

The cocoa began to bubble over. Naomi jumped up and whisked the pot off the stove onto a trivet. "Just in time." She stirred something into the pot before filling two mugs. Carl caught a whiff of spice when she brought them to the table.

"Cinnamon?"

"Yes. Mother always put a bit of cinnamon in her cocoa. When Laura came here, I got her to do the same. It needs less sugar that way." She glanced around the kitchen. "As kids, whenever there was a skating party or hockey game or anything outdoors in the winter, my friends and I used to come back here for cocoa afterward. Gordon and Barry and Corinne and a few others. That seems like a long time ago." She paused, took a moment for her memories. "Leaving here for good is going to be difficult."

Oh, yeah, it was beginning to seem that way for him, too. More than Naomi could imagine. Carl stood and picked up his mug. "I'm going to take this to my room before Laura hears us and we both get into trouble. Good night, Naomi." He paused in the kitchen doorway. "When I get settled, I'll write. That's what friends do."

Naomi woke to bright sunlight and the sound of her father and Laura talking in the kitchen. Her late-night visit with Ben in the kitchen had caught up with her, and she'd overslept.

When she opened her door, the sound of water flowing in the sink told her Ben was in the bathroom. She closed the door and listened for his steps in the hall. Once he was back in his room, she hurried to wash and dress.

The navy blue wool dress with its middy collar was one she'd bought in Winnipeg just before coming home from her stay with Barb. Naomi looked herself over critically and decided she looked neat and practical enough for her visits to a couple of her father's patients this morning, but still feminine. At that last thought, she turned from the mirror in shame. Looking feminine mattered to her again – thanks to Ben. But was that a good thing? When would appearance matter again to that poor girl in Regina, the one she might have spared if she'd been braver?

It's no use thinking that way, Naomi. How hard do you think the police would have searched if you'd reported him? A crime committed in the middle of nowhere with no witnesses. He's been caught now and justice will be done.

She brushed her hair smooth and ran downstairs. Ben followed a minute or so later and took his seat at the table.

His hair was wet, his face freshly shaved. He looked very different from the day he'd arrived here, but the toughness remained. Only now Naomi knew something of what lay beneath it.

If Ben knew the whole truth about that article in the paper, would he think her a coward? He didn't show much tolerance for weakness, in himself or others. As they ate he talked to Naomi's father, casual conversation about the countryside around Mackenzie and the weather, but he had little to say to Naomi. Perhaps he regretted what he'd told her.

When she'd finished eating, Naomi hitched Hannah to the buggy and set out, eager to put some distance between them. She covered the six miles to the Kuchin farm at a comfortable jog. Mrs. Kuchin was recovering from a difficult birth, and Naomi's father wanted to keep an eye on the mother and her newborn daughter. The family's oldest daughter opened the door. At thirteen, Nadia was staying home from school these days to take her mother's place as housekeeper.

Still in its gangly stage, Nadia's body looked its age, but with the face of an adult. It was just past nine o'clock, but she would have already been up for hours, working her way through the chores that filled her days. Her three younger siblings did what they could, but the responsibility of running the house sat on Nadia's thin shoulders for now. Her cornflower-blue eyes lit up with a tired smile as she stepped back to let Naomi in.

"Hello, Miss Franklin. Mum's awake and waiting for you."

Naomi put an arm around Nadia's shoulders and gave her a quick squeeze. "Call me Naomi, Nadia." She breathed in the yeasty aroma that filled the kitchen. "You've been baking."

The young girl's voice held a note of pride. "I put the bread in just after the kids left for school."

"So now you have a little time to relax. Don't work too hard, Nadia. Your mother needs you to stay well."

The Kuchins' one-story farmhouse was smaller than the Johnson home where Naomi had tended little Ethan's scalded arm, but the Kuchin house was in better shape and a whole lot cleaner. Mrs. Kuchin lay in bed in her bedroom off the sitting room, her baby beside her. Newborn Kalyna, named after the rose bush Mrs. Kuchin had brought with her from the old country and which still flourished in the yard, had her mother's bright blue eyes and her father's high Slavic cheekbones, like her older sister. Mr. Kuchin and his bride had come to Saskatchewan from Ukraine fifteen years earlier, built a soddy and then slaved on their land to provide for their growing family, but now they had a comfortable home, and their ten-year-old son would soon be able to do a man's work to help out. Their hardest times were over, though Naomi couldn't help hoping that this baby would be their last. At thirty-nine, the wear and tear on Mrs. Kuchin's body was beginning to tell, though she looked at her newborn daughter with a mother's love.

"She is feeding well, and sleeping a little more. My milk is coming in better, too."

"Good." When Naomi picked up Kalyna, the little one let out a respectable howl of protest. Naomi gave the squirming baby a quick examination and handed her back to her mother. "She looks and sounds perfectly fine and strong to me." She took Mrs. Kuchin's pulse, made sure she hadn't been bleeding excessively, then picked up her canvas satchel. Visiting a healthy mother and child was a pleasant way to start the day.

"You're both doing fine, Mrs. Kuchin, and you have a great helper in Nadia. The more rest you get now, the sooner you'll be on your feet again. You take care of yourself and let Danilo and the children spoil you. Dad or I will come by again in three or four days. If there's any problem before then, send one of the children to town and we'll come out."

"Thank you." Mrs. Kuchin settled the baby beside her and looked up with a thoughtful smile. "You're good with children, *divchyna*. You'll be a good mother, but don't wait too long. It's easiest when you're young."

Naomi knew *divchyna* meant 'girl.' It might have sounded condescending coming from some people, but not the way Mrs. Kuchin said it. Naomi ran a finger through the baby's wispy blond hair and slung her satchel over her shoulder.

"Coming from you, that's a compliment. I'll see you soon."

She said a quick goodbye to Nadia, who was now scrubbing laundry instead of relaxing as Naomi had suggested. She doubted if Mrs. Kuchin would take her advice for long, either. Hard work was the only way this family knew how to live.

Naomi drove to the Clark farm a few miles further out of town, to check on Mr. Clark's cut leg. He'd had a nasty accident with an axe a couple of weeks before. She found him chopping wood again, far too soon, while his fifteen-year-old son half-heartedly pushed a broom in the aisle of the barn. She lectured the father first, then took the son aside and gave him a piece of her mind.

"You're more than old enough to know that your father needs you – never more than now. If I were your mother I'd feel like crying for shame. If you don't want to farm, go to school, graduate and get yourself out of here. Your parents have younger children to feed."

Tears came to the boy's eyes. Naomi knew they were real and wished desperately that she hadn't been so hard on him, but she'd simply lost her temper. He wiped his face with a threadbare coat sleeve and met her gaze. His eyes burned with anger and longing. She knew that feeling.

"They can't afford to send me to school. Dad's been breaking his back on this place for twenty years, and he can't afford to send his kids to school long enough to learn more than reading and writing. You're right, Miss Franklin. I'm going to get out of here, and soon. I'll die before I'll live like this my whole life."

Naomi fought to speak around the lump in her throat. "Ned, I'm sorry. I had no right to speak to you like that. I lost my temper. And I don't blame you for wanting to go your own way. When I was your age, I couldn't wait to do the same, but for the next little while you need to spare your father, or he could get blood poisoning."

"I know that, but I never do anything well enough to suit him anyway."

Naomi shook her head. "You look just like your father when you scowl like that. Do either of you have any idea how much alike you are? He already knows your heart isn't in this place. When he's better, tell him how you feel. And keep in mind that a lot of people have done a lot of things with less education than you have. What do you think you'd like to do?"

Ned cast a glance out the barn door toward his father, then turned back, his jaw set with defiance. "I read the newspapers. The men who go to the front right along with the soldiers and report what's happening... That takes nerve. I'd like to be a reporter. Of course the war will be over before I could ever be one. Hell, it'll probably be over before I'm old enough to enlist."

Naomi rolled her eyes. "Listen to yourself, Ned! Would you like the war to go on for another four years? I've been there, and I certainly wouldn't. As for being a reporter, you keep reading. Start writing, and when you get a chance, talk to Miss Napier at the school. Have you forgotten how good a teacher she is? I expect she'd be willing to lend you some books and help you with your writing. If she says she doesn't have time, I'll help you as much as I can. But for now, you need to help your father."

Ned still looked discontented enough, but the despair was gone from his face. He squared his shoulders and held Naomi's gaze like a grown man.

"I know, and I will. I promise."

As she turned Hannah down the long lane to the main road, Naomi looked back and saw Ned and his father standing by the woodpile. The boy held out his hand for the axe, and his father gave it to him. Perhaps her fit of temper had done more good than harm after all.

She arrived home feeling rather pleased with herself, unhitched Hannah and turned her into the paddock. Naomi's father had taken the car to do his round of visits, and Laura would be sweeping and dusting upstairs, as she always did on Tuesday mornings. How would Ben have put in the hours since breakfast?

As Naomi settled Hannah's harness on its hooks in the stable, she heard a car pulling into the yard. Her father must be home early. She turned to the door and saw an unfamiliar, shiny new Model T coming to a stop. Two men got out, dressed in Mountie uniforms. Dry-mouthed, she went to meet them. Randall Clark's trial was coming up soon. Was this about the rape, or could they be looking for Ben?

The men stopped a couple of paces away and looked Naomi over, a frank and not particularly respectful appraisal. So this was about her. She held her head high and waited. A second or two passed, then the policemen seemed to make up their minds about her. One of them, a lanky blond, touched his cap and nodded.

"Good morning, miss. Are you Naomi Franklin?"

Her heart started slamming against her ribcage. "Yes, Officer."

His face flushed a little with what looked like embarrassment. "I'm Constable Wells from the Yorkton Northwest Mounted Police detachment, and this is Constable Bradley. We got a telegram from the Regina detachment this morning. We need to speak with you regarding a case they're working on."

Naomi treated Constable Wells to a cool stare of her own. This was why she hadn't reported her rape in the first place. She hadn't wanted to be tarred with the same brush as her attacker. "I see. As it happens, you've arrived at a good time. I've just got back from visiting a couple of my father's patients. Come inside."

Chapter 10

She took the men through to the sitting room. The hall floor upstairs creaked under Laura's feet, but where was Ben? Over the last couple of days he'd been spending more time outdoors. Had he gone for a walk? Praying that he'd stay out until this was over, Naomi offered the men coffee. Constable Wells gave her a grateful smile.

"Thank you, miss. We'd appreciate it. We were on the road early."

So far Bradley had said nothing, but it couldn't be clearer that he found the case distasteful. He'd be fifteen or twenty years older than Wells, and the thin mouth under his close-clipped salt-and-pepper moustache was pursed as if he'd just bitten into a lemon. Naomi felt his disapproving gaze on her back as she left the room. She hoped he didn't have daughters.

She put a fresh pot of coffee on the stove to brew and scanned the outside area from the kitchen window. No sign of Ben. Back in the sitting room she sat upright in the armchair, conscious of looking the lady. If her upbringing had set her a bit apart from her peers, she would use it to advantage now.

"The coffee will be ready in a few minutes. Now, officers, you have some questions for me?"

Though Bradley was older, Wells seemed inclined to do the talking. Naomi listened with an ear tuned to Laura's movements. She must have heard the car drive in, but she'd have heard Naomi's voice, too. She'd probably assume the caller was a patient and keep working. Naomi might be able to answer the men's questions and send them on their way without having to say anything to Laura at all.

"Yes. The Regina detachment is holding a man under a charge of indecent assault. They haven't been inclined to take the case too seriously – the young woman involved hasn't the best reputation, I'm sorry to say – but just yesterday the suspect confessed. At the same time, he confessed to assaulting you. He's mentally unstable and can't be taken at his word. We need you to tell us if he's telling the truth."

Naomi breathed a little easier. They weren't asking her to prove the man's guilt, only to confirm what he'd already said. She didn't have to feel as if she were signing his death warrant. "What did he tell you?"

Constable Wells pulled a note pad from his jacket pocket and referred to it. "That on August twelfth of this year, he stole some money from his employer to buy a train ticket and head to the States." The constable looked up. "We spoke to the employer this morning and confirmed that much. The suspect says he came across you alone, several miles from here. He'd been drinking, and he assaulted you."

So the Grangers knew. They'd been angry at being robbed, but they'd feel sick now to hear that their hired man had done much worse than steal from them. They'd known Naomi all her life.

"Yes, I was assaulted on August twelfth, on the way home from the Granger place."

Constable Bradley fitted the tips of his fingers together on his lap and looked down his nose at her. "Why didn't you inform the authorities?"

Naomi caught herself before she rolled her eyes. "Because I knew the case would be impossible to prove. I wasn't beaten bloody and left unconscious. I didn't have much in the way of injuries to prove that I'd been unwilling."

"You didn't fight him?"

"I didn't get the chance. I knew him by sight and had no reason to distrust him, so I didn't think anything of it when I noticed him coming along the track behind me. I thought he was just on his way to town." Naomi's hands moved to hold her stomach as it started to roil. Would it ever really be over? "He caught up to me so gradually that I didn't think he meant any harm. When he came up beside me, I turned to say 'hello,' and I knew then that something wasn't right. I'd never seen hate like that on a person's face." For a moment, Naomi couldn't go on. Her heart hammered and her breath came in gasps as if the attack had just happened. "I would have run then, but before I could, he hit me on the back of the head, hard enough to daze me for a moment. The next thing I knew, I was flat on my back with a knife at my throat."

"Did he make verbal threats?"

"Yes. I'd only seen him once or twice before, just in passing, but he said he'd been thinking about me for weeks, that he'd seen me leave the farm and decided to follow me. He said he'd kill me if I didn't cooperate. I believed him. Excuse me for a moment. I'll get that coffee."

Naomi retreated to the kitchen and managed to fill three mugs in spite of her shaking hands. She'd done it. She'd told her story. When she returned, Wells, who'd been writing busily, closed his notebook, sighed and pinched the bridge of his nose as if he had a headache.

"Miss Franklin, if you'd reported this at the time, Clark might have been caught before he could harm anyone else."

Trust him to stab her conscience where it hurt the most. Naomi sat a little straighter and looked Wells in the eye. "Possibly, but I saw little chance of him being caught. At the time, I just wanted to put it behind me."

Bradley cut in. "Surely a respectable young woman like you doesn't make a habit of wandering the countryside alone."

Naomi almost laughed at him. "Constable, on your way here, did you notice you were driving through open farmland? Everyone here, male or female, from eight to eighty, wanders the countryside alone. There's no choice. As for me, my father is the only doctor in a large area. He uses our car to make his rounds in fine weather, and I don't take our horse unnecessarily in case our housekeeper needs it. I'm a trained nurse, and I help my father regularly in his practice. If I told you I'd been visiting a critically ill patient the day I was assaulted, would that look better to you?"

Footsteps sounded on the stairs. In her temper, she'd forgotten to keep her voice down. A moment later, Laura poked her head into the room.

"Naomi, why are you shouting? Who—"

"It's all right, Laura. These men are from the Yorkton Mountie detachment. They're here to ask some questions about what happened last summer."

"It's about time! What good is—"

"Please, Laura."

At Naomi's pleading look, Laura turned on her heel and walked away. Trust her not to make things worse. "That's our housekeeper. Officers, I'm sorry I raised my voice, but I don't believe my habits are the issue here."

Bradley looked as disapproving as ever, but Wells unbent a little. "I understand your feelings, miss, but we're talking about a capital offense. We have to be very certain of our ground. So it appears that the suspect told the truth. I assume you could identify him?"

She saw Clark's eyes in her mind and shivered. "Yes. I'll never forget his face."

Wells nodded. "Excellent. Your testimony along with that of the other victim should be enough to convict him."

Testimony? Naomi's blood froze at the thought of seeing Clark again, but she wasn't the only victim here. "I'm willing to provide you with a written statement, but I'll want my name kept out of the papers for my father's sake."

Bradley shook his head. "The case will be in the papers, Miss Franklin. You can be certain of that. They may not be able to publish your name, but they will publish the date of the assault and your location. We've talked to the Grangers, and we were seen driving in here. People will put two and two together."

"Yes, they will." Ben's voice. He stood in the doorway, his blue eyes icy. Where had he come from? He'd obviously been in the hall long enough to hear too much, but neither Naomi nor the policemen had heard him. Constable Wells looked from her to Ben, comparing their faces.

"Your brother, Miss Franklin?"

"No. This is Ben MacNeil, a patient who's been staying here for treatment." Now if Ben would only just walk away, but it was already too late. His whole expression as well as his words showed that he wasn't uninvolved.

Constable Bradley looked him over. Naomi saw the policeman react to the traces of bruising on Ben's face. "Do you have any knowledge of the matter we're discussing?"

Ben took a step into the room. His gazed connected with Naomi's, warm and reassuring. "Not really. I've only been here for a few days, and for most of that time I've been too ill to get out of bed. Yesterday I saw Miss Franklin upset over an article in the paper about a rape, and I heard what you just said to her. The thought of anyone harming her bothers me – no, it more than bothers me. She and her father saved my life."

"Do you know Miss Franklin well?"

"No. I was put off the train here six days ago, very ill with pneumonia, and the Franklins took me in. That's the only knowledge I have of them."

Bradley turned to Naomi again. "Does your father often take strangers into his home, Miss Franklin?"

Ben took another step, jaw clenched. Hoping to keep him from losing his temper, Naomi hid her annoyance with a dry smile. "No. Strangers are rare in Mackenzie, but we've had many patients stay here. If they need continuous care or monitoring, it's the only option."

"Yes. Well, Miss Franklin, we'll get a written statement from you while we're here. Mr. MacNeil, will you be staying in Mackenzie for a while?"

"I'm not planning on it. As soon as I'm well enough, I'll be moving on to the coast to find work."

"I see. I'll ask you to provide Miss Franklin with a forwarding address when you leave. We may have questions for you at some point. Now if we can get your statement, miss, we won't trouble you any further today."

Naomi wrote out her statement and walked the policemen to their car. Ben and Laura were waiting in the kitchen when she returned. Laura held out her arms, and Naomi walked into them for a hug.

"Hold your head high, child. You aren't the one who's committed a crime here."

Naomi clung to Laura for a long moment, then stepped back…to be enfolded in Ben's arms.
He took her so completely by surprise that she had no time to shy away. She couldn't believe he'd hug her in front of Laura. He held Naomi stiffly because of his ribs, but the contact warmed her whole body. It also nudged a door in her heart a little further open. She had only one secret left to keep from Ben now.

Only a second or two, and he let her go. "Laura's right, Naomi. The people who matter will know the truth. Ignore the rest."

Easier said than done, especially where the practice was concerned. Neither she nor her father could hide. Naomi hated the thought of how hard this would be on him.

Ben grabbed his jacket in the porch and walked out. Laura stood looking after him. "Naomi, that young man is starting to care for you."

"I'm afraid so." From the window, Naomi watched Ben disappear around the stable. Hurting him was the last thing she wanted to do, but it looked like she'd have no choice. Whatever their feelings for each other, they had to go their separate ways. Laura spoke beside her.

"A few days ago I couldn't have imagined saying this – but you could do worse."

"That's far from the point, Laura. Ben can't stay here, and neither can I. We both need to find work. The timing is all wrong."

Laura put a hand on Naomi's shoulder, turned her and looked into her eyes. "You're starting to care for him, too, aren't you?"

Naomi shrugged. "If I am, that doesn't change anything."

Laura folded her in another hug. "Child, feelings change everything."

On the same rise where he and Naomi had stopped on their first walk together, Carl settled on a patch of sun-warmed grass and stretched his legs out in front of him. The emptiness and silence had no charm for him this time. All he could see was the face of the man in that newspaper article, the man who'd raped Naomi.

He tore up a handful of grass and tossed it aside. Why on earth hadn't she reported the rape when it happened? If she had, the bastard responsible might have met his richly deserved, sorry end before now.

Hold on. First thing, she's a woman, meaning you don't have a clue what she's feeling. Second thing, she's thinking about her father and Laura. How nasty is this going to get in a small town like this?

Face it, O'Neill. The thought of another man touching her, let alone raping her, drives you up the wall. You're hooked, and you have been since you woke up and looked into her eyes. So are you going to be a gentleman, keep your feelings to yourself and do the right thing – stay away from her 'til your cash comes in, then get on the train without looking back? That's the ticket, isn't it? An officer and a gentleman.

The brisk wind found its way through Carl's open jacket. He pulled it closed and crossed his arms, but the wind carried remembered voices, too, voices that wouldn't be blocked out.

"It will be cold tonight. What do you think, Otto? Should we give him something to eat?"

The young guard peered at Carl, pale blue eyes distorted by the thick lenses of his glasses. "If we don't, he might be dead by morning."

He spoke with a heavy Northern accent, but Carl had learned German well enough to understand in spite of it. He lifted his head and glared at Otto. Then I'll see you in Hell, little weasel.

After two days standing bound and immobile in the cold spring wind with no coat, no food and very little water, Carl figured Otto might be right. Quasimodo stood beside him, a cigarette between his lips. He removed it and waved the tip close to Carl's eyes, smiling.

"Oh, I don't think so. He's as thick-skinned as he is thick-headed, this one."

Carl braced himself. The bastard wouldn't blind him, but he'd burn him without blinking an eye. Otto put a restraining hand on Quasimodo's shoulder. "That's why the commandant wants him alive. If he isn't ready to fight again by next week, our asses will be on the line."

Quasimodo brushed the tip of the cigarette across Carl's cheek, more to frighten than to really burn him, then turned away. Smart man. Major Bueller wouldn't be pleased if a member of his 'boxing club' got badly damaged.

Otto laughed. "You're right, his skin is thick. That's why the Major values him. Better give him something..."

Carl caught himself before he could fall further into the past. He jumped to his feet, cold to the marrow of his bones. Strange how his body seemed to remember as well as his mind.

The hell of it was, when he got to Vancouver things would be just like they'd been in Halifax. The terrors, the nights when only whiskey would allow him to sleep. And this time he'd be completely alone. No job, and no money coming in until he found work. No family.

Yeah, right.

Way too late to be thinking of his family. Pointless to admit that he was tired of being alone. And alone was alone, no matter which coast you were on.

No Naomi. The thought left him as empty as the landscape around him.

Grow up, O'Neill. You've known her a week. Besides, you have nothing to offer her, not even your real name.

Maybe...maybe the smart thing to do was not to make any big moves right now. After all, for the short term he had an out. He could accept Barry Foley's offer of board and work, give himself time until his ribs healed. Meanwhile, Carl could keep an eye on Naomi from a safe distance, while she rode out the inevitable gossip when her rape was made public. Once they weren't in constant contact every day, the connection between them would surely fade like it had with the few other women he'd known. Then maybe it would be easier to move on.

Maybe.

Chapter 11

"You're sure?"

In spite of herself, Naomi's doubts came through in her voice. Ben noticed and replied with a bit of an edge.

"Why not? There's nothing waiting for me in Vancouver. The shape I'm in right now, no one is going to hire me right away, and Barry is right. My money will go further here. Since he made the offer, I might as well accept. I'll pay him board until I can earn my keep. The other day you were acting like you thought I should accept Barry's offer. What's different now?"

They'd walked a bit further this time, past the rise where they'd stopped before, to a little dip in the prairie that offered some shelter from the wind. Still, it ruffled Ben's black hair and brought the blood to his skin. Looking like this, it wasn't hard to picture him wearing clan colours and carrying a claymore. Naomi had never thought to ask, but likely his ancestors were highland Scots like her own.

She hadn't meant to sound that way, but too much had happened too quickly. Their kisses, the visit from the Mounties. That was only yesterday. She and Ben had been dodging each other since then, while things unsaid built up between them. Meanwhile, Naomi had started looking at employment listings in her father's medical journals.

Running away? Perhaps. Things wouldn't be pleasant for her here this winter, but Naomi couldn't pretend town gossip was her only reason for taking steps toward moving on. And now Ben had decided to stay. The kaleidoscope kept on shifting, leaving her no certain ground, no patterns to depend on.

Naomi knew Ben had done his share of drinking, but he'd had no liquor since he'd come off the train. Yet he never mentioned it, showed no outward signs of craving it. He seemed restless around her, but now he'd chosen to stay nearby. The contradictions threw her. Ben's kisses did magical things to her body and took her heart out into deep water, way over her head, but Naomi hadn't let herself imagine that he was getting in over his head, too. Now she wondered, and that was a problem. She tried to think out the kindest possible words, then gave up. She'd have to just blunder through.

"Ben, I don't know how to say this well, so I'm just going to say it. This...attraction between us... I won't pretend I don't feel it, but to base important decisions on it would be a mistake. For both of us."

"Is that what you think I'm doing?"

Of course he wasn't going to make this easy. "I don't know what you're thinking. I only know that I don't want to hurt you."

Ben stopped and turned to face her. "I don't want to hurt you, either."

"I know you don't." In spite of the wind, Naomi's face started burning. He had a way of looking at her that called all her motives into question. "Ben, the truth is I've only gone out with men three or four times since high school."

His grin did nothing to soothe her. "Why? I can't believe you haven't had your chances."

Why? Now that was a question. Naomi had never come up with an answer that made sense. Growing up as the only child of a busy, widowed country doctor, she'd become self-sufficient while very young, just as Ben had, but that didn't mean she hadn't been lonely. Still, something had always held her back from offering her heart.

"Not that many, really. Nursing school was busy, the field hospital was even busier, and there were strict rules. And now, after what happened last summer, I—" Oh, Lord, this was difficult. Ben's kisses had been so gentle, so patient. Could she make him understand? "I'm feeling very confused. A few kisses are one thing, Ben, but when I think of anything more, I know I'm not ready. I don't know if I ever will be."

Ben lifted his hand to her cheek. Of their own volition, her lips parted slightly. Around him, her body seemed to have a will of its own, and that scared her more than anything. He shook his head.

"You will be, Naomi. Trust me on that." The pad of his thumb, warm and slightly rough, brushed her lips and her stomach quivered. Then he dropped his hand. "Don't worry, I'm not reading anything more into what's happened between us than you are. And since we're being honest, I haven't been involved with many women, either."

In spite of his attractiveness, Naomi believed him. She doubted there had ever been much softness in Ben's life, and since he enlisted, there'd probably been none. That was one of the things that drew her to him. A longing to comfort, to take him in her arms and hold him close. She wouldn't deceive herself about that.

"Why? I can't believe you haven't had *your* chances."

Hearing his words tossed back at him brought an ironic smile to his face. "None of them quite suited me."

The trace of wistfulness behind the irony caught at Naomi's heartstrings. From what he'd told her about his childhood, she guessed Ben had learned early on to guard his feelings. Now he needed someone who could open his heart, not a woman just as guarded in her own way.

"When you get to Vancouver and get settled, I know it won't be long before someone wonderful comes along and sweeps you off your feet."

Ben's blue eyes turned serious. "And when you leave here, I'm sure it won't take long 'til that happens to you. Just don't be too quick to give up your work. Not many men will realize how much it means to you. Hold out for one who does."

Naomi smiled to hide how much his concern and understanding touched her. "I'll likely be an old maid, then."

Their gazes met. The glow in Ben's eyes unsettled Naomi further. "There's no old maid in you, Naomi."

Naomi broke eye contact and walked on. This conversation was hitting too many touchy points. Time to change the subject. "Are you getting tired?"

"No, I'm fine."

"Then come on. There's a place I'd like to show you."

Naomi led the way to a deeper hollow that held a small pond, skimmed over with ice and fringed with dry, frosted cattails. The glassy surface mirrored back the few cotton-wool clouds that floated above it, together with her and Ben's faces – his curious, hers a little sad.

She couldn't put a finger on why she'd brought him here, other than that the place had always grounded her, given her calm. She'd sat here the night before she'd left Mackenzie to ship out for Europe, and the night after she got back.

With the toe of her boot, Naomi broke the ice at the pond's edge. "I've been coming here for as long as I remember. My friends and I played here all year round. Did you have a favourite place at home?"

Ben spared the pond a brief glance before locking his gaze on Naomi's again. "I guess my favourite spot as a kid was the rail yard near our house. I used to imagine climbing into a boxcar and heading west, to parts unknown." Emotions Naomi couldn't read crossed his face before he smiled. "Now here I am."

She didn't mean to blurt it out, but after a few seconds of awkward silence the words said themselves. "Ben, I've started looking for a job. I worked on a couple of applications this morning."

He went very still. "Where?"

"Calgary and Halifax."

She saw Ben's stomach draw in as if from a blow. Oh, she was in over her head all right, and it looked like he might be, too. Hurting him twisted a knife in her heart.

He hid it quickly. "I'd say that's smart. Things are going to be difficult for you here this winter, I think." He touched her cheek. "I wish you luck, Naomi." Then he turned on his heel and started striding back toward home, leaving her behind.

Carl set his teeth against the jarring to his ribs as the truck left Mackenzie's main street for the rutted road leading into farm country. Barry looked over at him in concern and slowed the truck.

"Sorry. I've had broken ribs before. Fun it's not."

Carl turned to the window and looked out on the landscape Naomi loved. And now planned to leave. "They're starting to heal."

Barry's concern turned to curiosity. "I'd have bet that you weren't going to take me up on my offer. What changed?" When Carl was slow to answer, Barry's gaze sharpened. "Naomi?"

Yeah. Seven ways to Sunday. What would Barry think if Carl told him? Not much, probably.

"Naomi's started looking for a job. She's sent away a couple of applications." Wouldn't it be poetic justice if she ended up in Halifax, the city Carl had run from?

"So you're not staying because of her?"

Carl shifted to ease his ribs and held back a sigh. Barry wasn't stupid, and he wouldn't appreciate being lied to.

"Naomi and I have gotten to be good friends. If things were different, if we weren't both moving on, maybe we could be more. But we are both moving on."

Barry took his eyes off Carl long enough to swerve around a pothole. "Well, as long as you both know that, I haven't got a problem."

Barry's tone raised Carl's hackles. Or was the problem really that Barry's tone made Carl jealous? *Put a lid on that, O'Neill. You've known her two weeks, and he's known her for years. Long enough that he can be of a lot more help to her than you can.*

"Glad to hear it."

The frost in Barry's gaze thawed a little. "Did Naomi tell you that she and I kept company for a little while just after we got out of school?"

Jealousy stabbed Carl a little deeper. She'd only gone out with a few men. Was Naomi still carrying a torch for Barry? If so, she had more generosity than the other girls he'd known. Carl couldn't picture any of those girls staying friends with a former beau who'd gone on to marry their best friend.

"No, she didn't tell me."

"Yeah. I thought about asking her to marry me."

"Why didn't you?"

"We were both too young, and I knew Naomi wasn't keen on the farming life. Before she went away to university, we agreed we were meant to be friends like we always had been."

For a moment, Carl considered telling Barry about what had happened to Naomi, that she was going to need her friends more than ever when word got around town, but he thought better of it. Barry and Corinne would find out soon enough without him saying anything.

"Naomi's lucky to have you and Corrine for friends. Barry, believe me, with what I owe her, hurting her is the last thing I want to do."

They fell silent. The cold, bare countryside slipped past, but Carl barely saw it, his mind back in town, standing in the yard saying goodbye to Doctor Franklin and Naomi.

Of course, he'd only be five miles away and he'd be seeing her again. That was the whole point of his staying with the Foleys, but it was hard to remember that when she looked up at him with those beautiful grey eyes.

"We'll see you soon, Ben. I'll call when Dennis' letter arrives."

"Yeah. Naomi, Doctor Franklin...thanks again for everything." Knowing he'd take her in his arms if he stood there any longer, he'd walked away. Now here he sat, feeling more adrift than he had since he'd gotten off the ship in Halifax.

What's the matter with you, O'Neill? If it's going to be like this, you'd be better off just getting on the train. That would certainly be easier for him, and maybe for Naomi, too, but damned if he was going to leave until... *Until she leaves, too? That could be a month or a year from now.* Carl swore quietly. Barry looked over at him. "Hang in there. Not much further."

Ten minutes later the truck pulled into the farmyard. As Carl got stiffly out, a big, lolloping mongrel of a dog galloped from the barn. He looked to be only an over-grown puppy, with a thick shaggy coat and a ragtag face. Barry clapped him on the head.

"Go on, Tank."

Carl snorted with laughter. "Tank?"

Barry rolled his eyes. "He's as strong as a tank, and just about as smart. We took him in from a neighbour whose bitch had a litter of nine. When he saw how big they were going to be and how much they could eat, he decided only to keep one and shoot the others if no one would take them. Corrine had to save one. Don't know if Tank'll ever have the sense to be of any use on the farm, but he makes Corrine laugh, and that's enough for me. There she is at the kitchen window. Come on."

The crunch of their boots on the frozen earth of the yard echoed in the stillness. The wind was barely a breath here, sheltered as they were by the weathered grey barn and the faded white farmhouse. All around them was open prairie. Near the horizon a few cattle grazed, behind a wire fence turned to gossamer by distance. Carl paused to look around. Peaceful and somehow soothing, like the landscape in back of Naomi's place.

"How much land do you have?"

"Four sections, between me and Garnett and Dad. Dad's house is half a mile further down the road. There's a rise in between or you could see it from here. There's another house on the place, too, across from Dad's. It was my grandfather's, and it'll be Garnett's when he marries."

"The one who's still overseas?"

"Yeah."

The stove's heat welcomed them at the kitchen door. The Foleys' kitchen had the same air of comfort as the Franklins', with blue gingham on the table and at the windows. The well-scrubbed pine floor looked fairly new, as did the furniture and the stove. No doubt Barry and Corinne had done some work on the place when they moved in. Of course, none of the houses out here were old compared to many back in Halifax. Thirty years ago most people here had been living in soddies, and many still did.

Corrine greeted them with a kiss for Barry and one of her bright smiles for Carl. "You're here. Welcome. We're going to give you the room off the kitchen. It isn't as big as the spare room upstairs, but it's warmer. Bring your bag."

She led him to a small bedroom, the kind of room where they might put a hired hand to sleep. It contained nothing but a bed and a dresser, but it was clean and warm.

"Thanks." Carl dumped his duffle bag on the bed and stood, wondering how on earth he was going to put in his time here. He'd drive Barry crazy tagging along after him when he couldn't do anything useful on the farm, but he'd drive himself crazy sitting around the house, getting in Corrine's way. And the whole district seemed as dry as dust with prohibition. If he didn't get back to work soon, he'd be a raving lunatic by Christmas. Meanwhile, Corinne was watching him.

"I may not be able to be of much use to Barry right now, but if there are any small jobs to do around the house I'll be happy to oblige. I'm not used to doing nothing."

"I don't suppose you are. I'll see what I can find. In the meantime, Barry will be glad to have your company on the farm whenever you feel up to it. It'll do you both good. He misses Garnett. Now lunch is ready. Come and sit in."

Carl put away a healthy serving of Corinne's ham, scalloped potatoes and biscuits with homemade butter. Rationing didn't have much meaning here, except for sugar. One advantage, at least, to landing in farm country. After the meal, he followed Barry out to the barn and watched him fork some hay down from the loft into a wagon. "I'll be taking this out to the cattle. Come along if you want. The track's pretty rough, but it's not a long ride."

Next, Barry had to change the dressing on the hoof of a cow with foot foul. The big Hereford was closely tethered to a ring in the barn wall, and Barry got a rope on one of her hind feet and tied it to the wall as well, but she still managed to kick and plunge as he wrestled with her infected front hoof. Carl didn't doubt that doing something like this was how Barry had gotten the broken ribs he'd mentioned. He stayed well back, out of range of flying hooves and cow shit, until the job was over.

Barry wiped himself as clean as he could with a burlap sack and went on to a pigsty at the other end of the barn. A big sow lay in there on her side, nursing a litter of… Carl counted eight wriggling, voracious pink piglets. The sow cast a wary look at him and opened her mouth, revealing a formidable set of yellow tusks. Instinctively he took a step back.

In North End Halifax, where he'd grown up, some of the neighbours had kept a milk cow and raised chickens, even a pig or two, but not his family. A manager at one of the city's largest factories didn't have the time or the need to raise his own food. A few times Carl's sisters had brought home stray dogs or cats, but the animals never stayed for more than a week or so before his father found them another home, or said he did. One time, Carl had told his father about a cat Alice was hiding in the cellar. He'd been annoyed with her for some reason. The cat disappeared. Shame goaded him at the memory.

Feeling very much the inadequate city boy, Carl watched while Barry picked up and inspected each piglet in turn. Then it was time to take the hay out to the pasture. After a very few minutes of being jostled on the wagon seat, Carl decided it would be easier on his ribs to walk. He climbed down and kept pace with Barry's plodding team of Belgians until they reached their destination. By the time Barry had finished unloading the wagon, the cold wind had found its way through the thick jacket Carl had borrowed. Corinne gave him a concerned look when they got back to the warmth of the kitchen.

"Naomi will sharpen her tongue on me if you get sick again. Stand by the stove and thaw out."

Barry rolled his eyes at Carl and mouthed, *women.* Carl glanced out the window, where the sky was darkening to dusk. The hours had flown by instead of crawling.

After supper, Carl pleaded fatigue and retreated to his room. He wasn't lying, but he also had no desire to intrude on Barry and Corinne's evening. This was when he'd expected the third-wheel feeling to set in, and it did.

Sleep was going to be hard to come by. He resigned himself to that when he put down the book Naomi had lent him, blew out his lamp – the Foleys didn't have electricity – and closed his eyes. With no distractions, the nagging craving that had been creeping up on him for the last few days made itself felt again.

He'd done his share of drinking before he enlisted, and more since coming home, but his craving for alcohol had never become physical like his father's. Liquor eased his restlessness and helped him to sleep on those nights when the four walls of a room – any room – felt too confining. He sure as hell could use a drink tonight. Barry and Corinne would be up at daylight, and Carl didn't like the thought of facing them and trying to be civil after a sleepless night.

At home, he'd made a habit of staying outside most of the night – before he'd been beaten up. The first few nights he'd spent in the veterans' hospital after the fight, confined to bed, dizzy from blows to his head and so sore he could barely move, had been the worst nights of his life.

It wasn't until quite a while after Barry and Corinne went upstairs that Carl managed to fall asleep. The next thing he knew he was sitting up in bed, drenched in a cold sweat, with Barry standing there in the glow of the oil lamp.

"Must have been a bad one."

"Yeah." Carl swallowed, took a few deep breaths and tried to muster some dignity. He must have yelled. He glanced at the clock on the dresser. Three a.m. "Sorry I woke you."

He'd never felt more foolish, but Barry just shrugged. "Don't be. I can fall asleep at the drop of a hat. You still having nightmares?"

"I wouldn't call them nightmares, at least not all the time. I mean, I don't often remember them." But, with the suddenness of a switch being flipped, he remembered this one.

The remains of a French village with a name he couldn't recall. The broken brick walls of a shop of some sort, the front window empty and black behind a streaming curtain of rain. The bodies of six of his men lying in the square around the village well, victims of the machine gun hidden by the darkness of that empty window. Carl was the only one still standing.

At least two of the gunners were wounded or dead. Whether they were still mobile, or whether there was anyone else in there, Carl didn't know, but he was sure they knew he was there and still on his feet. He crouched behind the well, knowing that the moment he showed himself might well be his last.

Peering through the rain, he judged the distance between the well and the rubble of the church, the nearest cover. Finally he ducked low and made a run for it. Nothing happened.

Perhaps there was no one left alive in the shop. He waited, heard nothing, and emerged from his cover. On his belly, out of sight from the front of the shop, he crawled until he reached the side wall. The back of the building had been blown away. He got to his feet and crept along the wall until he could peer around it.

One of the German gunners lay slumped over the machine gun. Another sprawled on the ground nearby. A third sat with his back against what was left of the back wall, his rifle beside him. With his own rifle at the ready, Carl stepped over a pile of smashed bricks. The sitting man opened his eyes. His hand moved toward his rifle. Carl jumped forward and kicked it out of reach.

The soldier looked to be about Carl's age, blond, with eyes a lighter blue than Carl's. Blood from a shoulder wound soaked his uniform jacket and one of his legs was bleeding, too, but it looked like he had at least a chance at survival. His eyes widened in appeal as Carl approached.

"Help. No?"

Carl stood there with his rifle aimed at the man's forehead, his finger on the trigger. His men lying outside – he'd led them into this. Ben MacNeil had a wife and young son. Cam Johnson also left a widow and family. Carl looked into those hope-filled eyes and shook his head.

"No."

He pulled the trigger.

Carl dragged himself out of the memory to find Barry sitting on the end of his bed. "You remember this one, don't you?"

"Yeah." And that seemed to be happening more often since he'd landed in Mackenzie, almost as if some door in his mind refused to stay shut any longer. Maybe Carl owed the German gunner that much.

"Barry, while you were overseas, did you ever kill anyone you didn't have to kill? Anyone who wasn't shooting at you?"

Barry frowned, shook his head. "No. You?"

"Yes."

Barry didn't ask why, but seeing the acceptance on his face, Carl told him anyway. "He and his mates had killed six of my men."

Barry's answer was immediate, firm and clear. "I'd have done the same thing."

Carl had ever thought he had much of a conscience, but now, as the burden lifted, he started to wonder.

Barry rose. "I'll go put on a pot of coffee and—"

"Don't bother. I'll be able to go back to sleep now."

"All right. Ben...just remember I've been there, too."

Barry left the room. Carl blew out the lamp again. Stillness settled on the house. Eventually he drifted off to sleep again, and this time, he dreamed of Naomi. She stood with him on the rise behind her house, with the wind ruffling her hair and the look in her eyes he'd seen the day he walked out there with her. The look of accepting that you're home.

Chapter 12

Carl dropped his book at the sound of the kitchen door closing. Tank set up a frantic racket in the yard. Probably Corinne, back from town. A chair scraped back from the table as Barry got up to greet her.

"You're cold." Paper rustled. Carl pictured Barry taking grocery bags from Corinne's arms, then hugging her in the silence that followed. "Looks like winter's here."

Winter. Could it be November already? A week and a half since Carl had come out to the Foley place. A week and a half since he'd seen Naomi.

It seemed like a lot longer. The routine of the farm, the easy friendship Barry and Corinne offered, still felt new and strange. As for Naomi, Carl might have been able to kid himself that her grip on his heart was loosening, if not for the way it jumped whenever her name was mentioned.

They'd spoken twice on the phone – brief, frustrating conversations. Even when Barry and Corinne were considerate and left Carl alone to talk to her, the words he wanted eluded him. After all, she'd made herself clear when he told her he was staying. She wasn't.

Metal scraped on metal as Corinne pulled the kettle to the front of the stove. "Yes, it does feel like winter. Where's Ben?"

"In his room, I think. He disappeared when we came in from the barn. Anything new in town?"

"Yes." Corinne hesitated. "I think I should tell you later."

Carl sat up on his bed. He might be jumping to conclusions, but he knew of one piece of news Corinne wouldn't want him to overhear.

"Ben's probably asleep. I don't think he slept well last night," Barry said. "You've got me wondering. You may as well tell me now."

A knot formed in Carl's chest in the moment before Corinne spoke. "All right. You remember that article in the paper, about the Grangers' hired man being arrested for rape? In the store today, I overheard Ann Draper and Jeannie Holdman talking, saying that the Mounties were in town last Monday calling on the Grangers and the Franklins. Ann and Jeannie made a couple of nasty insinuations about Naomi before they realized I was there."

So the word was out. Carl swore and got off the bed. Barry's voice sharpened. "That would be Ann and Jeannie. They've been jealous of Naomi since school, and they're cats to begin with. Did you tell her?"

"No. I suppose I should, but I just didn't know what to make of it."

Carl stepped out into the kitchen. "I know what to make of it."

A guilty blush spread over Corrine's face. He shook his head. "I already knew, Corinne. I walked in on her just after she'd seen that article in the paper, and I was there when the Mounties came. The bastard assaulted her before he left town. I promised her I wouldn't say anything."

Barry's fist hit the table. "Why the hell didn't she report him?"

Corinne rounded on him. "Think, Barry. Where would that have gotten her?"

"Probably nowhere." Barry pulled out a chair and dropped into it so hard it almost tipped over. "I'd like to be there to see him get what he deserves."

Carl joined him. "So would I. Anyone I hear say a word about Naomi is going to be sorry."

Corinne fixed both of them with a glare. "Listen, you two. I know how you feel. I feel the same way, but you aren't going to make this harder for Naomi. The less said, the quicker the gossip will die down. I wonder if Laura and Doctor Franklin know."

"They do. They've known since it happened." If they hadn't, staying away from Naomi might have been impossible. At least she had her father behind her.

"Good." Corinne turned to Barry again. "I wish she'd told us, too, but that's Naomi. She's always kept her troubles to herself, ever since she was little. I'll pay her a visit tomorrow. If I were in her shoes, I'd be relieved not to have to keep it secret anymore."

Yeah. There'd been relief on Naomi's face the day Carl found out. She didn't have to keep her secret from him any longer. Would he ever be able to feel that way about his own secrets?

Corinne moved to stand behind Barry and rested her hands on his shoulders. "I heard something else in town, too. I ran into Mr. Pheeney. He told me the memorial service for Gordon is going to be Thursday night."

Barry reached up to lay a hand over Corinne's. "It's time. Ben, will you go with us?"

"Of course. He was your good friend, and Naomi's." And Carl wanted to be there if those spiteful cats, or any other spiteful cats, took the opportunity to insult her.

Naomi turned Hannah into the corral and stalked to the house, scattering squawking hens as she went. Laura met her at the kitchen door.

"You're home. And you're in a temper. I haven't seen you look like that since before you went overseas."

"I haven't felt like this since then. I stopped at the Johnson place to change Ethan's dressing, and they were positively cool to me. When I was finished, Mr. Johnson said they'd heard some things that made them think they'd rather Dad tended to Ethan from now on. When I asked him what he'd heard, he wouldn't say – but he didn't have to."

"And if Ned Johnson has paid the doctor a dollar for everything he's done for that family, I'd be surprised. The ingrate." Laura let Naomi in and slammed the door. "Your father will put him in his place, you can be sure of that, but I wonder who's been gossiping? I haven't seen anything more in the paper, but I didn't look at yesterday's. Your father didn't get home with it until late."

"I don't think he read it either. He had his supper and went right to bed, and I went up too, right after I finished my Toronto application. The paper's still in the sitting room. I'll get it."

Naomi returned with the newspaper and laid it on the table. There it was, on the second page, the news she'd looked for with a sinking stomach every day since the police visit.

> *The suspect, who was employed on the farm of Michael Granger near Mackenzie over the past summer, has also confessed to assaulting a young woman from the area in August. The Mounted Police have the victim's statement corroborating the confession. "We are deeply sorry," Mr. Granger told police when he was interviewed. "We know this young woman well and are saddened that this outrage happened to her."*

Naomi dropped the paper, a painful lump forming in her throat. In the next instant Laura was there, with a comforting hand on Naomi's shoulder.

"It had to happen, Naomi. You know that."

"I know. Laura, I should have reported him. If I had, he might have been caught before he hurt anyone else. Instead I was selfish, and what did I gain? The whole town will know now anyway."

The hand on her shoulder squeezed gently. "You did what you thought was best at the time. That's all anyone can do. And you were thinking as much of your father as you were of yourself."

The simple truth, but it didn't go very far toward easing Naomi's guilt. "I hate the thought of how this is going to hurt Dad. Oh, I know people won't say anything about me to his face. They won't dare, but they'll talk behind his back, saying the assault was my fault, and that will hurt worse."

"It'll be old news soon enough." Laura turned to the window. "That's Corrine driving in. I'll fill the tea pot."

Naomi took Corinne's coat and wrapped her in a hug. "Good morning. I was going to call you today. You look well."

129

Corinne looked rosy and healthy enough, but she wasn't wearing her usual smile. That was enough to tell Naomi that Corinne had heard the news, too. "Yes, the morning sickness is easing up."

"Good. How's Ben?"

"Feeling better every day. He's started helping Barry a bit around the place."

"That will ease Ben's mind a little. We miss him."

Corinne helped herself to a molasses cookie from the crock on the counter while Laura poured hot water into mugs to warm them. "He misses you, too. Naomi, you made quite an impression on Ben."

Naomi held back a sigh. If Corinne read Ben as easily as she'd always read Naomi, there was no point in denying it. "I suppose so. He was pretty sick when he landed here, remember?"

Corinne pointed with her cookie and looked Naomi in the eye. "I think he made quite an impression on you, too. If he hadn't, you'd be calling every day to check on him." Corinne sighed when Naomi didn't react. "Well, I'm not going to pry."

That came out as if she were writing lines on a school blackboard. Naomi had to smile. Her friend shrugged. Corinne would be the first to admit that delicacy wasn't her strong point.

"Have you heard that the memorial service for Gordon is going to be next Thursday?"

"No. I haven't been in town for a couple of days. Dad has some patients right now that just need monitoring, so I've been busy." Truth was Naomi hadn't spared Gordon much thought since Ben left for the farm. Her old friend deserved better.

She braced herself when Corinne took a deep breath. Here it was. "I heard something else in town yesterday, too. Some nasty gossip. Naomi, all fall I've had the feeling something was bothering you. I figured you'd tell me when you were ready, so I didn't press you, but now I know."

"Ben told you."

"No. He only confirmed it after I'd already put two and two together. He also told me that Laura and your father know, or I wouldn't be saying anything now."

A little bit of hurt came through in Corinne's voice. Another stab of guilt in Naomi's heart. She *had* been selfish, even though she'd been trying to spare others pain. "I couldn't talk about it, Corinne. Not even to you."

Corrine finished her cookie and came forward with another hug. "I understand. Now the man has been caught. He'll get what he deserves, and people will find something else to talk about. You can put it behind you."

"I had put it behind me, until the police showed up here."

"Or was it until Ben showed up here?"

Maybe talking about Ben was a little less difficult than talking about the rape, but only a little. "Corinne—"

"Don't worry, I'm not going to badger you, but Ben admitted to Barry that he really likes you. Of course, Barry had to worm it out of him. They're becoming friends pretty quickly."

Laura poured tea for the three of them. "I'm glad." It still surprised Naomi how Laura's attitude about Ben had changed in such a short time. Corinne accepted her tea and helped herself to another cookie.

"So am I. Naomi, I think you were right about Ben having a bad go of it overseas. Barry's gotten up in the night with him a couple of times."

Naomi remembered Ben in her room, offering comfort the night they'd heard about Gordon. How she ached to do the same for him, but Barry could help him more, because Ben would tell Barry things he'd never tell her.

Ben. Oh, how she missed him.

"I know I'm right. A friend like Barry is just what he needs."

Over the rim of her mug, Corinne held Naomi's gaze. "We'll look after your wanderer, Naomi. But don't be surprised when he moves on, because he will, unless you give him a reason to stay. He told Barry you were applying for jobs away…"

Naomi changed the subject, and Corinne didn't bring up Ben's name again, but her words niggled at Naomi for the rest of the day. Of course, well-meaning as she was, Corinne couldn't understand. Only a woman who'd been raped could know how the experience filtered into every cell, how you became a stranger in your own body, and certainly no man could understand, not even Naomi's father, as much as he'd hurt for her. As for Ben, Corinne had left Naomi even more certain that she'd done the right thing in backing away. He'd forget her soon enough once he started his new life.

At supper, Naomi told her father what had happened at the Johnson place. "Dad, I hate that you have to deal with this." His face flushed and his eyes kindled.

"They've got a hell of a nerve treating you like that. This was none of your doing, Naomi."

"But if we start losing patients—"

"Don't look so dismal, sweetheart. It isn't as if the Johnsons can go out and find another doctor who'll treat them and wait for his money. Their place will be first on my list tomorrow morning. I'm going to give them a piece of my mind. Don't give it another thought." Just what Naomi expected, but that didn't ease the humiliation of not being welcome in a patient's home.

You take things too much to heart, Naomi. You've been told that before.

Like her feelings for Ben.

Naomi went to bed with a dozen conflicting emotions pulling at her. She closed them off and thought over the letter she'd finished last night, for the hospital in Toronto. The most interesting job of the ones she'd applied for so far, involving mostly surgical work. If she got it, she'd be there by Christmas.

She shivered under the cold quilts. If only it could be summer, like summer used to be with leisurely months that seemed to stretch on and on. Now everything moved too fast.

Naomi closed her eyes and pictured the pond in midsummer, concentrated until she smelled the warm grass and the earth-flavoured water, felt its coolness on her feet and the sun's heat on the back of her neck. She was ten, and Barry and Corinne and Gordon were there with her, splashing, giddy with freedom.

Then the picture shifted. The pond still shimmered under the bright summer sun but a different boy stood with her in the water, a black-haired boy with dark blue eyes and a smile on his pugnacious face.

"Come on, Naomi." He reached for her hand and they stepped out onto the grass together. Only now the hand that held hers was a man's, and its pressure made her feel anything but childish. She looked up and saw Ben's face as she'd never seen it before, open and smiling, with no shadows.

He gave her hand a gentle tug. Without a word, she followed him. The dream faded, but Naomi woke at dawn with all its colours and sensations and feelings clear and vivid, the smell of the grass and Ben's scent mingling in her mind.

As if he'd somehow reached inside her, found her soul and claimed a part of it.

Foolish. You've been thinking of him, and now you've dreamed of him. Naomi pulled on her robe and went down to breakfast. Her father had already eaten and left. Laura set a steaming bowl of oatmeal on the table.

"Eat it while it's hot, Naomi. I'd like to be a mouse in the corner at the Johnson place this morning when your father gets there."

"So would I." In the stable, Hannah whinnied for her breakfast. Naomi hurried through her porridge, dressed in riding clothes and her warm jacket, and headed outside. Maybe a brisk ride would ease her restless mood.

She set out in the general direction of the Foley place. The saddle was stiff and the mare edgy with cold, so for the first few minutes Naomi had to concentrate on keeping her seat, but once she got warm she let Hannah set her own pace. The familiar landscape, frozen now under a dull November sky, tugged at Naomi's heart. How many more times would she ride through it like this?

Placid as the horse usually was, Hannah could get her blood up when she chose, and today she chose. They'd covered half the distance to the Foley's when another horse and rider appeared on the horizon. Naomi recognized the horse as Bess, the Foleys' mare, but that wasn't Barry or Corrine in the saddle. They were both as comfortable on horseback as Naomi, and this person didn't look like they knew how to sit a horse at all. She caught a glimpse of dark hair under the rider's cloth cap.

Ben, you infernal idiot.

Naomi sent Hannah along at a gallop and came up on Ben so fast his horse almost shied. Embarrassed as she was angry, Naomi reined her own sidestepping mount to a halt.

"Have you lost your mind? Do Barry and Corinne know where you are?"

Ben threw her a cocky grin. "No. Corinne thinks I'm with Barry, and Barry thinks I'm in the house. Neither of them will miss me until lunch time."

Naomi sat there, blood racing with fury and the impact of Ben's closeness. He held himself a bit less stiffly now, his colour was good and the bruising on his face had disappeared. He'd gained some weight, and altogether he looked impossibly attractive, even in one of Barry's old jackets. "Remember when you said I could puncture your lung with a punch? Right now I'm very tempted to do just that. Have you ever ridden before?"

Ben rolled his eyes. "Of course I've ridden before. Come on, Naomi, this horse is as gentle as a kitten. I'm sure you know that."

Naomi nudged Hannah closer. Yes, Bess was gentle. She thanked heaven Ben had the sense not to take Kaiser, Barry's mean, jug-headed brute of a gelding, but she doubted Ben had been on horseback since before he enlisted. "The quietest horse can bolt if they're frightened."

One thick black brow lifted. "Yes. You almost proved that a minute ago."

Naomi sighed and backed Hannah off. Where was the smart comeback she needed? She'd been attracted to men before, but never to the point where she lost her self-possession.

"What are you doing out here anyway?"

"Coming to town to see you." Ben slid awkwardly to the ground. Good. Breathing a little easier, Naomi dismounted.

"You could have phoned."

The horses wandered a few feet off to greet each other. Ben came toward Naomi until they stood with only a hand's breadth between them. Longing, frustration, doubt – those blue eyes reflected all the feelings tangling in her chest, drying up her throat.

"Naomi, I saw that new article in the paper, and so did Barry and Corinne. I wanted to be sure you were all right."

Ben was only a bit taller than average, just over six feet, and not as heavily built as some men his height, but everything about him was so completely male that Naomi felt dwarfed by him, even though she only had to tilt her head slightly to meet his gaze.

"I am." Naomi paused to moisten her mouth. "Corrine said you were feeling better. I wasn't sure I believed her – you haven't had much to say on the phone – but I believe her now. You're looking well."

"I can't say what I want to say to you on the phone." Ben's hands settled on her shoulders. Naomi's heart started hammering against her breastbone. By the light in his eyes, she guessed his was racing, too. "It's no good, is it, Naomi? As soon as we're together, there it is again. Maybe staying with Barry and Corinne was a bad idea."

In spite of the cold, Naomi's face burned. The heat from Ben's hands seeped through her coat and soaked into her body, turning it molten. She struggled to find her voice. "I don't have the answers, Ben. I only know that I've missed you. More than I expected to."

Ben's hands slid from her shoulders to her back as he enclosed her in his embrace. "I've missed you, too."

He bent his head and nipped lightly at her jaw. Fire rocketed down Naomi's neck, and her lips tingled. If this was what a few days away from Ben did to her, what chance did she have? Her stomach swarmed with nerves, but her spine relaxed and her head fell back to give him better access to her throat.

Flames where Ben's lips touched her, ice when the cold wind blew over the moisture he left behind. When his lips finally claimed hers, all Naomi could do was wrap her arms around him and hold on. The kiss was fierce, almost desperate, nothing like the kisses they'd shared before.

It left them both breathless. Ben released her and shook his head.

"I shouldn't have done that. It isn't going to make things any easier for either of us."

Oh, it certainly wasn't. Every time Ben kissed her he captured another piece of her heart. At this rate, he'd leave her with nothing, but right now her body was doing the talking. Naomi took Ben's hand and interlaced her fingers with his.

"Are you sorry?"

He shook his head. "The truth? No."

"Neither am I."

And no amount of logic, no tally of all the pain Naomi was inviting for herself and Ben, could change that. They couldn't give each other anything but memories, so she chose to make them good ones. Naomi released Ben's hand and met his gaze again. "One of my teachers at nursing school had a saying. 'If you don't know what to do, do what you'll wish you'd done when you're eighty.' We don't have a lot of time, but if we don't take what we have, when I'm eighty, I think I'll regret it."

He lifted her hand to his cheek. "I know I will. I just wish—"

But neither of them could afford the kind of wishes Naomi saw in Ben's eyes. She turned away. "If wishes were horses, beggars would ride. Come on, I'm taking you home for lunch."

Carl climbed out of the truck in the darkness of the Franklin yard. The night was starlit and perfectly still, so quiet his heartbeat sounded painfully loud in his ears. Would Naomi hear it on the walk into town for the memorial service?

Light poured from the kitchen doorway. Laura came out, followed by Naomi and her father.

Had Naomi said anything to the doctor about the change in their relationship? Too bad Carl hadn't asked. It would have made this a lot less awkward.

Since the day they'd met out on the prairie, Carl had seen Naomi once at her place and once at the Foleys'. The doctor hadn't been home and Laura had found a reason to go to town and leave them alone – so he knew Laura, at least, didn't disapprove. Corrine approved too strongly for Carl's taste. Barry was reserving judgment.

"Naomi's a grown woman and she's no fool, but she's vulnerable, Ben. Be honest with her, or you'll have me to answer to."

Honest. What would Barry think if he knew Carl had been lying since he arrived here, to him and Corinne, to Naomi and to the doctor?

'If wishes were horses, beggars would ride...' He couldn't change what was done, but he could do his best to keep his lies from spoiling whatever time he had with Naomi.

Barry and Corinne started off, with Laura and the doctor behind them. Carl and Naomi fell in behind. No one talked much on the way to town. The Franklins and the Foleys had a lost friend to remember. Carl shrugged off the frankly curious looks as they joined the crowd filing into the Presbyterian church, but the few less than friendly glances directed at Naomi were a lot harder to ignore.

They found seats in a pew near the back. Naomi ended up beside him. Not smart, perhaps, but it felt good to be near her, to think she wanted to be near him at a time like this.

In minutes, it was standing room only in the small, low-roofed wooden church. Not much like stately old St. Joseph's at home, with its facade of mellow red brick, dark polished pews and brass memorial plaques on the walls – some dim with age, some new and gleaming. Here the pews were of plain, blond varnished softwood, and no stained glass embellished the whitewashed walls. But there were gleaming new memorial plaques here, too, bearing the names of young men Naomi had grown up with. Now there would be another.

Carl reached for Naomi's hand. She didn't look at him, but the way her hand trembled a little, then settled in his, said as much as a glance. She wanted the contact, wanted his support tonight. Had anyone else ever turned to him at a difficult time?

Not that he could remember.

As the service went on, the tables turned. Carl needed Naomi's support as much as she needed his. He'd attended enough funerals for men buried in the field, but never a ceremony like this with grieving friends and loved ones. Ben MacNeil and the others who'd died in that French village, the German soldier who'd asked Carl for help... Who had grieved for them?

He held fast to Naomi's hand, closed his eyes and filled his mind with the memory of her kisses, until the service ended. Then they were out again in the cold, quiet night, walking behind Barry and Corinne. As they turned the corner onto the street where the Franklins lived, Naomi tucked her arm through Carl's. He almost jumped. The doctor and Laura were right behind them. They couldn't help but see.

If this was Naomi's way of telling her father she and Carl were more than friends, it was as good as any. After all, what words could explain their relationship? None that would satisfy a parent.

Then again, Doctor Franklin was a perceptive man. Perhaps he already understood.

Chapter 13

Carl did up the last button on the grey pin-striped shirt Corinne had made for him, and stuffed the shirt tails into his stiff new jeans. It irked him that she'd spent the money and the time, but she refused to listen to reason.

"You can pay us back when your money arrives, and I like sewing. You want to impress Naomi, don't you?"

Corinne had him there. He'd convinced Naomi to go to this dance against her better judgment, so he wanted to make it worthwhile. And since Corinne had been the one to bring it up, perhaps it was only fair that she provided the clothes.

Naomi had dropped by, found Corinne sewing and asked what she was making. "A dress for the Thanksgiving Dance. What are you wearing?"

Carl might have thought the two of them had planned it, if not for the obvious discomfort on Naomi's face. "I'm not planning on going." When Corinne just waited, Naomi's cheeks coloured. "It's been four years since I've been to the Thanksgiving Dance, Corinne. It won't be the same."

Corinne let it pass, but that night at supper she'd brought the subject up again and dragged Carl into it. "You know, Ben, I'd bet five dollars that Naomi would go to this dance if you asked her."

He'd had no intention of asking her. She didn't want to go, and neither did Carl. The last time he'd gone to a dance back in Halifax, at the parish hall in his old neighbourhood, it hadn't turned out well. He arrived drunk and ended up in a fight with his sister Georgie's escort. Going to this affair with Naomi and meeting a crowd of strangers who would be at best, curious, and at worst, hostile... How had he convinced himself that was a good idea?

Instead, why not spend the evening with Naomi at her place? It was time he had a talk with the doctor. Doctor Franklin must have misgivings about Carl's friendship with Naomi already, knowing that Carl would soon be moving on. Naomi's father might think Carl didn't want to be seen in public with her, especially now with gossip going around about the rape case. Maybe Naomi would think so, too.

So, in the end, he'd ridden into town and asked her. As he expected, she said 'no.' As he hadn't expected, he wouldn't take her 'no' for an answer.

"If you don't go, everyone in town will think you're ashamed. Maybe you are – ashamed to be seen with me, that is."

That roused her temper. "You're talking nonsense. I just think it would be foolish to make things more difficult for both of us, just for the sake of attending a dance neither of us would enjoy anyway."

Carl shook his head. "The last dance I went to was a fund-raising affair in the church hall at home. I showed up drunk and got into a fight. I've never liked crowds, and since I got home from overseas I can barely tolerate them, but I want to prove to myself that I can get through something like this without alcohol. And I want you with me."

"Ben—"

"Of course, if you'd rather, I could just come over here and spend the evening with you. We'd both enjoy that more."

He brushed his thumb over Naomi's lips and watched them part. She reached for his hand and lowered it, clasped warmly in hers.

"We both know that would not be a good idea."

"Then come to the dance with me."

So Naomi had agreed to go. Now, Carl scowled at the reflection in his mirror.

You're in it up to your eyeballs, aren't you, O'Neill? It's a good thing you can't get your hands on a bottle of whiskey, or you'd be three sheets to the wind by now. So are you going to be a good boy tonight and not make her wish she'd never set eyes on you?

He turned his back on his reflection and walked into the kitchen. Barry looked Carl over and grinned. "Not bad."

Corinne stepped up and straightened the tie Carl had borrowed from Barry. "Not bad at all."

Carl frowned. "I'm glad you approve, since it's your money and your work I'm wearing."

She rolled her eyes. "I'll charge you interest if it'll make you feel better. As far as I'm concerned, it'll be worth every penny to see Naomi's face when she's dancing with you."

Carl had to admit he looked quite different from the man who'd landed in Mackenzie three weeks ago. For one thing, he was sleeping better. His ribs no longer kept him awake at night, and when dreams woke him he'd lay there listening to the silence around him, and thinking of Naomi.

A vision of her, tall and slender in a soft, flowing dress, floated in Carl's mind. He shook it off. Tonight was going to be about self-control, not self-indulgence.

Corinne looked very pretty herself tonight, dressed in a rich brown that made her hair glow. Barry pulled her close for a quick kiss. "Naomi won't be the only one turning heads at the dance. Corinne, there's one bottle left of that dandelion wine you made last year, isn't there? What do you say we open it so Ben and I can have a Thanksgiving toast before we go?"

"All right, why not?"

Corinne brought the bottle and two glasses from the pantry. "Ben, have you ever had dandelion wine?"

"No, I haven't."

"Would you like to try some?"

Carl looked at the bottle, imagined the wine's flavour, the alcohol easing his nerves. One glass...

No. Tonight, he knew he wouldn't be able to stop at one glass.

"No thanks, Barry. I don't handle it well."

Barry and Corinne exchanged a half-guilty glance. Carl didn't like making them feel awkward, but he wasn't about to let Naomi down before the evening even got started. Barry rose.

"All right, we'll save the wine for another time. Let's go then."

By the time they reached the outskirts of town, Carl regretted refusing the wine. It would have made it easier to face the crowd, but this might be his only chance to spend an evening out with Naomi. He'd be damned if he was going to ruin it.

Naomi smoothed her hands down the front of her dress and gave the skirt a tug. The lamplight gave the pale green, finely woven wool a faint lustre that brought back memories of the damp London evening when she'd found the dress in a small out-of-the-way shop. That had been on her last leave, and she'd never worn it before.

It looked as well on her as she remembered, but it seemed to belong to another place and time. She stood straighter and tried to quell the butterflies swarming in her stomach by thinking of Ben's eyes when he saw her.

It doesn't matter who else looks at you and whispers. You're doing this for him.

There'd been whispering enough, she knew. A couple of her old schoolmates, girls she'd liked, and who she had thought liked her, had pointedly snubbed her the other day in town. Naomi wished people would gossip openly so she could counter them, but of course they didn't dare because of her father.

After experimenting with a few ways of doing her hair, Naomi just left it loose to fall softly around her shoulders. Simple, the way she liked it best. She thought Ben did, too, though he'd never said so. A little shiver ran through her at the memory of his fingers running through it.

She ran down to the sitting room, where her father was reading by the fire. He looked up with a smile.

"If your mother could see you tonight, she'd be very proud."

Naomi sat next to him. "You talk about Mother more now than you've ever done before. Why?"

Her father put down his book and leaned back into the corner of the sofa. "I suppose it's because you're just about the same age she was when we met. You look very much like her, Naomi."

Naomi had heard that all her life, but she'd always wondered if it were true. Time had blurred her memories of her mother, and when she looked at the few pictures of her in the family album, she only saw a superficial resemblance.

"Do I? It's hard to tell from her pictures. She looks so...stiff."

Her father laughed. "Suzanne didn't like having her picture taken, but she was anything but stiff. She loved to laugh and tease. She thought you were very serious as a child."

Serious? Naomi had never thought so, at least not before she went overseas. Maybe her mother hadn't known her as well as Naomi had always thought – or wished? Somehow, her mother seemed further away than ever these days.

"Was I?"

"Maybe a little." Her father rested a hand on her knee. "You've had reason enough to be serious lately, Naomi. You've seen too much for a girl your age, but I've noticed a change in you over the last couple of weeks." He looked into her eyes. "Is it Ben?"

Naomi laid her hand over his. She hadn't said much to her father about Ben, other than that they'd become 'a bit more than just friends.' What else was there to tell him? And he hadn't pressed her. That had never been his way. "You're a grown-up now, Naomi, and I trust you," he'd said. "Life is short. If you see a chance to be happy, even for a little while, take it. Just remember to use your head as well as your heart."

Naomi let out a sigh. That would be a lot easier if her head and heart weren't pulling her in opposite directions. "Life is strange, isn't it? He lands on our doorstep out of nowhere, and now...it scares me to think of him leaving in the spring."

Her father shook his head. "Spring is a long way off, Naomi. For now, I'm just glad to see you and Ben enjoying each other's company. You both deserve it. There he is now."

Laura answered the kitchen door. Naomi heard her laugh at something Ben said. No one would think now that Laura had been ready to believe Ben was a German spy. He really had no idea how much the doctor and Laura and Barry and Corinne liked him. Intuition told Naomi he'd never been good at seeing things like that.

She ran out to meet him. A spark flared in his eyes at the sight of her. Dressed in new jeans and his grey jacket, his freshly shaved face flushed with cold, he looked better than she had ever seen him. The butterflies in Naomi's stomach fluttered at the thought.

Carl stood there dry-mouthed and speechless. He'd never seen Naomi dressed up before. He took a step forward and swallowed the lump in his throat.

"Hey. You look great. Bet you didn't get that dress in Mackenzie."

A flirtatious smile flashed across Naomi's face. "You can't get any kind of a dress in Mackenzie unless you make it yourself. I got this in London."

Doctor Franklin joined them. "Hello, Ben. You've been making yourself scarce. It's good to see you."

A needle of guilt pricked Carl, as it always did around Naomi's father. If the doctor only knew that Carl would hurt as much as Naomi when the time came to leave. Maybe more, because she no longer had lies to regret.

"Evening, Doctor Franklin. You can blame Barry. Ever since the first time he saw me on a horse, I've had a hard time convincing him to lend me one."

That made the doctor chuckle. "Barry was more or less born on horseback."

Carl laughed with him. "I wasn't."

The Foleys had dropped Carl off at the Franklins' and continued on to town. The doctor kissed Naomi's cheek. "You two should be going. Barry and Corinne will be waiting for you at the hall."

Carl picked up Naomi's coat, which was warming over a chair by the stove, and held it for her. As she slipped her arms in, he fought a wicked temptation to kiss the nape of her neck. Then they were out in the frosty night. As they walked down the frozen lane, he took her hand.

"I don't know if I'm ready for this."

Naomi giggled. "It's just a dance, Ben. You've survived a lot worse." Her hand tightened around his as she looked up at him. "I'm nervous, too. I went to one social not long after I got home from Europe, and I didn't enjoy it. People acted as if I were a stranger instead of someone who grew up here. So, I didn't go to another."

Carl tried to put himself in Naomi's shoes. She'd feel out of place going to social functions alone, or as a constant third wheel with Corinne and Barry, though they wouldn't have minded. And the men who might have asked her probably weren't men she'd consider for more than an occasional evening out. In a small place like this, a couple of dances or dinners could easily lead to expectations of more. As much as Naomi loved Mackenzie, she'd been raised to leave it. Not that Carl blamed the doctor for that.

Carl looked up at the dark, crystal-clear sky. He still wasn't used to the sky out here, day or night. It dwarfed everything, held people the way the ocean held some people at home. Naomi would leave Mackenzie, but he didn't doubt she'd stay out here somewhere. He could picture her as a maternity nurse, bringing babies into the world in some small town, seeing life begin instead of end – then, at the end of the day, going home to a family of her own.

But what if she marries some selfish clod who makes her give up nursing? Someone who won't look further than the end of his own nose and see how much her work means to her? That's her choice and none of your business, O'Neill. You've got nothing to offer her but lies.

They walked in silence until they reached Railway Street. As they stepped onto the lighted roadway, the stars vanished and Naomi gently pulled her hand from Carl's.

"The hall's just a block away."

In other words, time to be careful. Carl increased the distance between them slightly. Barry's truck was parked with others along the street, and the voices of couples and groups going into the hall carried clearly on the still air. A few people paused to look as Carl followed Naomi inside.

Folding tables had been set up on the scarred hardwood floor, and four middle-aged men were placing stools and unpacking their instruments on the low stage at the end of the room. The knot in Carl's stomach tightened as a flood of memories hit him. Sneaking out of a dance with a girl to steal his first kisses. The last social he'd attended, with rum simmering in his blood and rage riding him.

Naomi's gaze met his, soft with concern. Carl pulled himself back to the moment. The woman at the door took their admission money, then they hung their coats on the rack inside and joined Barry and Corinne at their table in a back corner. Carl thanked them mentally for choosing an inconspicuous spot. No doubt Naomi appreciated their consideration, too.

As they crossed the room, several heads turned. Two young women paused in their conversation to look Naomi's way, then turned to each other again, tongues clacking. Naomi ignored them, but Carl sent them a scathing look. Were they the ones Corinne had heard talking? A man was no man if he struck any woman, but witches like those two made the thought more than tempting.

Carl and Naomi chatted with Barry and Corinne while the hall filled. As the minutes went by, Carl realized that he'd never done this before, never gone out for an evening with people he not only liked but trusted, and who liked and trusted him. When the band began playing a waltz, Barry took Corinne's hand and led her out onto the floor. They danced discreetly enough, but the way their gazes locked made it clear that there was no one else in the room for either of them. Carl glanced at Naomi out of the corner of his eye and saw a far-away look on her face.

"Penny for your thoughts?"

She shrugged. "Just feeling a little nostalgic, I guess. I used to look forward to the dances here for weeks."

"You sound like an old woman."

"I suppose I do. I'm sorry." A smile chased the shadows from her eyes.

Carl reached for Naomi's hand under the table. "Got your copper-toed boots on?"

Her smile became a grin. She nodded, and Carl led her to the edge of the dance floor. As the band slid into another waltz, he took her in his arms.

As a kid, he'd bribed Georgie to teach him to dance because he'd figured out that it impressed girls, but he'd never really enjoyed it. There were many more interesting things to do with a girl in his arms, but maybe there was something to this dancing thing after all. The musicians weren't flashy but they were smooth, and the music worked its way into Carl's mind as they circled the floor. He drew Naomi closer and she lowered her head, bringing her lips close to his neck. The other dancers seemed to disappear. Carl slid his hand up her back and threaded his fingers into her hair. She looked up, and all thoughts of discretion vanished from Carl's mind. He would have kissed her right there if the music hadn't stopped, bringing them back to earth.

Corinne and Barry followed them back to the table. Corinne looked at Naomi and grinned.

"Enjoying yourself?"

"Yes."

That couldn't be more clear. Carl couldn't believe the change in her. With bright colour in her cheeks and a sparkle in her eyes, she looked no more than eighteen. This must be what she used to look like. What she was meant to look like.

Barry picked up on Naomi's mood and shot Carl an amused glance. As much as he liked Naomi's friends, this would be a hell of a lot easier if they were alone, and if he didn't have to go home with the Foleys afterward.

That's pretty rich after all they've done for you. Carl tried to remember a time when he'd felt real gratitude, and decided he hadn't – until now. His mother, his sisters, even his father – had he ever said a sincere 'thank you' for anything they'd done for him? Had the thought even crossed his mind? It was too late for that, but it wasn't too late for the people with him now. He swallowed a lump in his throat.

"Barry...all of you...thanks."

His feelings must have shown on his face. Nobody spoke for a long moment, then Barry lifted his glass of punch.

"You're more than welcome, Ben."

They all drank and the awkward moment passed, but the evening was changed. Carl knew it, felt it, tried to shelve it for later, but every dance with Naomi took him further down a road he'd never taken.

They were taking a break between dances when he noticed a man standing just inside the door, someone he hadn't seen in the hall yet tonight. One of the local farmers by the look of him – perhaps thirty, with a round, tanned face. He joined a group Carl had noticed before and made a mental note to avoid, for Naomi's sake. Two of the women were the ones who had given Naomi the evil eye when she and Carl walked in, and the men looked just the type to make Carl forget his promise to himself to stay out of trouble.

Loud laughter came from the group as the newcomer settled in. Carl turned away, longing for a shot of whiskey to settle his jangled nerves. A minute later Naomi froze in her seat, then shifted abruptly to turn her back on the newcomer's group. She said nothing, but all the enjoyment drained from her face. Carl looked toward the man who'd just come in. He was staring at Naomi and wore a satisfied smirk.

Anger just as intoxicating as liquor ran through Carl's veins. He should have known better than to come here tonight, but right now he just didn't give a damn. He touched Naomi's hand to get her attention.

"Do you know that man?"

She jumped, and Carl's anger rose a notch. "By sight, like I know everyone in Mackenzie."

"Why are you afraid of him?"

"I'm not afraid of him. I've never had anything to do with him. I just don't like him, and neither does anyone else around here."

"What's his name?"

"Mark Jakeman."

"Does he live in town?"

"No, his family has a farm a couple of miles out."

"Well, if he looks at you again the way he just did a minute ago, he won't be getting home tonight under his own steam."

Naomi's eyes opened a little wider. "Ignore him, Ben. He's an ass, and everyone in Mackenzie knows it. Don't let him bother you."

"You let him bother you."

She let out an impatient sigh. "Look, I don't handle any kind of attention from men very well these days. You know why. I'm not going to let him ruin our evening. Let's dance."

Carl took a calming breath and got a grip on his temper. After all, he'd come to this dance for Naomi's sake. He led her back onto the dance floor, took her in his arms and did his best to help her forget Mark Jakeman. As she relaxed into the music, Carl forgot Jakeman, too, until he appeared at Carl's elbow.

"Naomi, who's your friend? The one who got dumped off the train?"

The woman Jakeman was dancing with threw a malicious smile Naomi's way, then looked up at her partner. "Mark, behave yourself."

Her tone made it clear that she really didn't care if he behaved or not. Naomi gave Carl's hand a warning squeeze, but he was in no mood to pay attention. "Naomi, will you do the introductions please?"

She glared at him, then rolled her eyes. "Ben MacNeil, this is Mark Jakeman and Lucy Hampton. Now let's—"

Carl cut her off. "Thanks. Been back from overseas for long, Mark?" He deliberately made his use of Jakeman's first name as insulting as possible. He might be wrong, but he'd have bet the man hadn't been overseas. When Jakeman didn't answer, Carl put on an insolent grin.

"Oops. I guess that was a little rude."

Lucy spoke up. "Rude and uncalled-for. Mark's needed on the farm. His mother's a widow."

Jakeman's face flushed. Carl's blood started to run fast and light. He'd made an honest effort not to embarrass Naomi, but Jakeman had come asking for trouble and he wasn't going to take no for an answer.

"Oh, so he's doing his bit for the Empire – growing wheat?"

Mark had gotten his composure back. He raked his gaze over Naomi again, slowly, suggestively. "Yes. I take it you've been over there. Is that where you and Naomi met? It's obvious that you've known each other for some time."

Carl smiled, savouring his anticipation. It had been a while since the fight back in Halifax, long enough for his fists to need a target. "Sorry, but you're mistaken. We got to know each other while I was her father's patient."

Jakeman took a step closer and locked gazes with Carl. "I'm sure that wasn't difficult."

"Meaning?"

"Meaning Naomi isn't exactly a difficult woman to get to know."

Oh, this was going to feel good. "Maybe. Then again, she only knows you well enough to call you an ass. I don't know you at all, but I agree with her."

Naomi said something, but Carl didn't get the words. All his attention was focused on Jakeman. This feeling wasn't like the blind rage that had overcome Carl when he sailed into Georgie's friend at the dance at home. This felt more like the fire of whiskey in the blood, heady and intoxicating. He let go of Naomi and jerked his head toward the door. "You called the tune, Mark – so let's dance. Come on."

Helpless, Naomi watched Mark and Ben walk out. She should have known better than to come here. To bring him here.

Eyes bright with malice, Lucy put a hand on her arm.

"Don't worry, Naomi, Mark won't kill him, but you might not find your soldier boy so pretty when he's through with him."

Naomi shook her off and threw her a killing look. "Mark had better look out for himself." She had no doubt that if he were healthy, Ben would be lethal in a fight. He had the strength and he had the temper, but right now, with his ribs only half healed, he'd be risking his life.

She'd learned enough about men overseas to know that nothing she could say would change Ben's mind now. Barry and Corinne had been too wrapped up in each other to catch the byplay on the dance floor, but Barry saw Ben and Mark leave and met Naomi at the door.

"What's going on?"

"They had words, and Ben couldn't let it go."

"All right. I'll see what I can do."

Barry sidled past Naomi and jogged outside. Corinne joined Naomi and they followed, to find Ben and Mark circling each other while a small group of interested bystanders watched. Barry stepped in between them.

"Ben, you don't need to do this."

"Yes, I do. He insulted Naomi."

"Fine. Leave him to me."

"Sorry, Barry. I appreciate it, but this is my party."

Mark took a step forward. "Get out of the way, Foley."

Barry stared him down. "You put him down, and I'm next." He stepped aside. "I've got your back, Ben."

Naomi stood there seething with frustration. Surely Barry could have done more to stop this, but a look at his face told her he was itching to fight Mark himself, that he was using all his self-control not to. She tried to take comfort from the thought that he'd step in if Ben got into trouble, but that might be too late.

Right now, Ben looked to be enjoying himself. With a grin on his face, he circled Mark one more time, then stepped in and threw a quick, compact punch that landed hard in Mark's belly. Standing beside her, Barry put a hand on her shoulder. "Well now. The man knows how to box. I think I'm going to enjoy this."

He might enjoy it, but Naomi's breath left her when Mark countered with a right to Ben's midsection. Ben knocked Mark's fist aside and threw another short punch with timing that told her Barry must be right. She'd spoken the simple truth when she'd called Ben a fighter.

Mark clearly saw it, too. He circled Ben again, buying time while Ben waited, fists up, still wearing that cocky grin. Naomi remembered that Mark had done his share of fighting in school. This wasn't over yet.

In the next moment, Mark threw himself at Ben's legs. Ben jumped aside just in time and Mark rolled past him. Mark scrambled to his feet and charged in, punching furiously. Ben couldn't parry every blow. Mark's right caught him in the belly, winding him. Before Ben could catch his breath another blow landed on his jaw. Naomi winced, expecting him to fall, but he stayed on his feet. Off balance, Mark walked into a hard left. Then Constable Walters broke through the ring of bystanders, rifle in hand, and fired a shot in the air.

"Gentlemen, this is over."

The shot got Ben's and Mark's attention. Barry stepped between them. Constable Walters lowered his Winchester.

"Okay, Barry, tell me what happened."

Mark spoke first, wiping blood from his cut lip. "He threw the first punch."

Barry glared at him. "You provoked him, asshole." He turned to the constable. "He insulted Naomi, Jack."

"What did he say?"

"I didn't hear it, but—"

He stopped when Constable Walters raised his rifle again. "We'll sort that out at the jail. You two, march. Now."

They marched. Naomi knew this wasn't Mark's first encounter with Jack Walters, and she guessed Ben wasn't a stranger to the law, either. Both apparently knew better than to give the constable grief.

Once they disappeared down Railway, headed toward the lockup, the group in the yard broke up. Naomi discovered she was freezing. She didn't have her coat, and neither did Ben. He'd be chilled to the bone by the time he reached the jail.

He can't be badly hurt. If that punch had landed on his ribs he'd have fallen. Corinne appeared with Naomi's coat and laid it over her shoulders.

"He'll be all right. It'll all get sorted out in the morning. We'll come in to pick him up. It's time to go."

Naomi shrugged into her coat, buttoned it and followed Corinne to the truck. "I knew I shouldn't have come."

"I'm sorry it ended this way," Corinne said as she climbed in next to Barry. "But before that, you and Ben were both enjoying yourselves. I was watching you." A rueful grin spread across her face. "If Ben were completely well, I would have liked watching him trounce Mark. He deserves it. You know that."

Yes, but the last thing Ben needed right now was attention from the law. This might just be enough to send him running again. "Which is exactly why Ben should have ignored him."

Barry glanced over at her. "It doesn't work that way, Naomi. If Ben had ignored him, Mark would have just kept pushing. That's what he's like. Remember?"

Naomi sighed. "I know. I wonder where Ben learned to box? He certainly knows how."

"In the Army, probably. It's a good thing he learned, or he might be seriously hurt right now. Mark's no slouch in a fight either. Never has been."

Naomi leaned against the frosty truck window and closed her eyes. They should stop by the jail and make sure Ben was all right.

No. Ben wouldn't want to see her tonight. After what he said when he asked her to the dance, about proving to himself that he could handle it – he'd wanted to do that for her, and it hadn't worked. She knew him well enough by now to be sure that his failure to control his temper would hurt more than the blows he'd taken. That was why she ached for him, that and the look in his eyes when he held her on the dance floor, the look that had made the rest of the world disappear.

No, she shouldn't have gone to the dance. It had only made everything worse.

Chapter 14

Carl glared at Jakeman through the bars between their cells. Thanks to that idiot, he'd broken his promises to Naomi – and to himself.

Well done, O'Neill. Bloody well done.

This wasn't the first night Carl had spent in jail. He'd been picked up and taken to the drunk tank a couple of times in Halifax, but that was before he enlisted. Now, being locked up had an entirely different meaning.

Damned if he'd let Jakeman see him sweat. Carl threw the man another glare and settled on his cot. The jail smelled like the others he'd been in, of stale alcohol, urine and vomit, with a strong overlay of some lye-based cleaner. The whitewashed walls showed a dent or two where they'd been kicked or punched. On the other side of the bars, a heavy maple-stained desk and a scratched black metal filing cabinet were the only furnishings.

Constable Walters sat at the desk, filling out a form. When he'd finished, he scraped back his chair and turned an icy look on Jakeman, then Carl.

"I'm going to make a phone call. If I hear a sound from in here, you'll both be my guests for a week." He rose, stalked into the small outer office they'd walked through on the way in, and closed the door. Carl lay back on his bunk, fists clenched.

What would any cop, even in a hole in the wall like Mackenzie, do with a stranger in his custody? Ask questions. Walters didn't strike Carl as a fool. He wouldn't forget to contact the Army. How long would it take him to find out that Ben MacNeil from Newcastle, New Brunswick, was dead – and for the Franklins and the Foleys to find out Carl had repaid their kindness with lies? A few days, probably. Then the dream world Carl had been living in would collapse. He could only hope that the constable would release Carl before he got answers and that he'd have time to get out of town if he had to. Of course, for that to happen, he needed his money from Dennis.

Bile rose in his throat. If the Army caught up with him, it would mean prison or being sent back to the trenches. He was AWOL all right, but with his medical leave taken into account and the need for men at the front, any confinement would probably be short. More than likely, to be rid of him, they'd just strip him of officer status and put him on the next troop ship. What was it Liam Cochrane, Georgie's beau, had said to him?

'I think you'd rather die than go back, and that's what you're trying to do.'

Maybe Liam was right. The thought of being in the trenches again, the stink of death all around him – Carl couldn't survive that a second time. And maybe when he first came home, some desperate part of him had been trying to die – but not now. Not any longer. Never before had life meant what it meant to him now. Something good. Something promising…

That was because of Naomi, and if he ran, he'd be running from her.

Not that it mattered. All would be ruined with or without his help. When Naomi and her father found out he'd lied to her, she'd be lost to him anyway, and he'd be back where he started. Alone, which was probably how he was meant to be.

Then why did that thought hurt so badly?

He heard the constable on the phone, but couldn't make out the words. In the next cell, Mark sat on his bunk, glowering at the ceiling. Carl decided the entertainment of baiting him wouldn't be worth the effort and closed his eyes.

His house of cards was falling all around him, and he hadn't even had the satisfaction of demolishing Jakeman. Carl had learned to box, after a fashion, as a teenager, from a friend who trained at a local gym. When he'd quarrelled with his parents and enlisted, a more than usually perceptive drill instructor had picked up on his anger and steered Carl to an informal boxing club that had sprung up among the recruits. He'd gotten into some trouble for loose interpretation of sporting rules, but he won his matches and thrived on it. Then, in the reprisal camp, when they found out he could fight... He shut the door on that memory. Of course his ability and training wouldn't have impressed Naomi, if she'd even noticed his skill.

Naomi. She was a lady to the core, and if Carl read her right, a little bit of a small-town princess. Her father had raised her to expect a lot from a man. Why would she waste time or emotion on one who couldn't keep his temper or his fists down?

Carl swore under his breath. Soon enough he'd have to learn not to think of Naomi, but that time wasn't now. He let his mind take him back to the dance, to when he held her in his arms. With that memory he fell asleep.

Laura put a mug of coffee in front of Naomi as soon as she sat at the table. "You don't look like you got much sleep. There's no point being upset over what happened last night, Naomi. You knew Ben was a fighter. That's how he ended up here, remember?"

Naomi's father grinned. "And a competent one, from what you told me. Laura's right. As for Mark, it's not the first time he's pushed someone too far, and I doubt if it will be the last."

Naomi reached for a piece of toast. Had Ben had anything to eat yet? Had he gotten any sleep? "I'm upset for Ben, that's all. I know he was trying to prove something to himself by going to the dance, and it didn't work." She hadn't told her father and Laura what Ben had said about the last social he attended. Nor could she tell them that her biggest worry was that this would make Ben change his mind about staying in Mackenzie.

The phone rang. Laura answered it. "Naomi, it's Corinne."

Corinne sounded as bright and cheerful as always. These days, nothing could dim her spirits for long.

"Morning, Naomi. Barry just finished in the barn and he's on his way into town to get Ben. Do you want him to pick you up?"

"Of course I do. Ben got into this because of me." Naomi couldn't wait to see him, to reassure herself that he wasn't badly hurt. Whenever and however Ben left Mackenzie, he'd leave knowing that she didn't judge him on anything but by the way he'd treated her.

Half an hour later, Barry parked the truck in front of the jail. A chill ran through Naomi when they walked into the outer office. Spending the night behind bars couldn't have been easy for Ben after being a prisoner of war.

Constable Walters met them with a frown. "I guess you're here to pick up your hand, Barry. He can go, but don't be surprised if he skips out on you."

Naomi looked over Constable Walters' shoulder at the closed door behind him. Ben must be back there. How long was this going to take? Barry sighed as if he were thinking the same thing.

"Why do you say that?"

The look Constable Walters gave Barry made it clear he didn't appreciate the challenge. "I've got a feeling that he isn't who he says he is. I put out a few inquiries last night and this morning, but of course I haven't got any answers yet. Anyway, I can't hold him on a hunch."

Naomi's temper rose. After all, Ben wasn't the only one to blame here. "Where's Mark? He started the whole affair."

Constable Walters raised an eyebrow. Naomi's face heated. Was he wondering about her and Ben, as well as about Ben's past? "I let him out half an hour ago. I'm sure he did start it, but MacNeil wouldn't tell me what Mark said, so there was nothing else I could do." Constable Walters' shrewd dark eyes looked her up and down. "I can make a pretty good guess, though."

Naomi's face burned hotter. "I heard what he said, and it was insulting."

"If I'd heard it, I'd have done exactly what Ben did," Barry added.

"Looking at Mark's face this morning, I'd say he's paid plenty for it. Wait here."

Constable Walters disappeared into the other room and returned with Ben. His cheek was bruised where Mark's fist had connected, and he held himself as if his ribs were sore. Naomi struggled with an urge to wrap her arms around him. When Ben saw her, his mouth set in an angry line.

"You shouldn't be here."

But she also saw relief in his eyes. It made her urge to hold him even stronger. "Considering this happened because of me, I disagree. How are you feeling?"

"It didn't happen because of you. It happened because of Jakeman. I'm fine. As you know, this isn't the first fight I've been in. Barry, I've wasted enough of your time. Let's get out of here."

Out on the street, Naomi took a deep breath of clean, cold air. Ben did the same. Barry went on ahead. Naomi and Ben fell into step a few paces behind him.

Ben walked along in silence, not returning Naomi's gaze. Was he going to shut her out? Her heart sank. Perhaps he'd already decided to leave.

"Where did you learn to box? It's clear you know how."

Ben answered without looking at her. "In the Army. As you must have figured out by now, I have a temper, and I ran into a drill instructor smart enough to give me something to do with it."

"Good for him." Naomi stopped and laid a hand on Ben's arm to make him face her. Come what may, she wanted him to know she didn't blame him. "Ben, I was furious with you last night for taking such a risk on my account, but I know Mark wouldn't have given you a choice. Would have kept pushing. Now I'm just glad you're all right."

"Thanks." Ben moved toward her and for an instant Naomi thought he'd kiss her right there in the street, but he stopped. His sigh voiced Naomi's frustration. Then he grinned. "I can't remember when I enjoyed myself so much at a dance."

He touched her cheek. Skin tingled at his touch, and Naomi held his gaze. "You enjoyed the fight, too, didn't you?"

"Yes, I did." Ben's hand slid around to cup the back of her neck. "Come to think of it, I've never played the knight in shining armour before. I enjoyed that, too."

Barry had reached the truck. Carl and Naomi hurried to catch up. Before he and Barry drove off, Ben leaned out the window.

"Goodbye, Naomi."

With a chill in the pit of her stomach, Naomi watched the truck out of sight. *Goodbye?* Ben had never said that to her before. It sounded so final.

Before going home, Naomi stopped to pick up the mail. Heat from the stove touched her face when she stepped in, reminding her of Ben's warm hand against her cheek. How long would it be before the part of her heart that he'd claimed was her own again?

"Any news from Charlie, Mrs. Anderson?"

The Andersons had run the store for as long as Naomi could remember. Their son Charlie had been overseas for three years now. Mrs. Anderson nodded.

"We had a letter last week. He was well when he wrote. There's mail for you." She pulled a few letters from under the counter and glanced at the return address on the top one before handing it over. "Are you thinking of leaving again, Naomi?"

"Just making some inquiries." A response from the military hospital in Calgary. Naomi's heart beat a little faster. Mrs. Anderson leaned on the counter.

"Don't blame you. Mackenzie must seem pretty slow to you now, though I hear there was excitement enough at the dance last night."

Naomi put on a smile and refused to rise to the bait. "I've never found Mackenzie slow, but it's time I was doing something more with my life."

"I suppose so. Here's a couple of letters for your father and one for that patient of yours."

Naomi took the envelopes. The letter for Ben had a Halifax address. That must be his money.

He'd be free to go on his way now.

Naomi thanked Mrs. Anderson and got herself out of the store before her feelings could show on her face. On the street, she tore open her letter from Calgary.

They'd declined her application.

Dread settled like cold iron in Naomi's stomach. There were other experienced nurses out there, nurses who lived a lot closer to the bigger hospitals. Nurses with city connections.

What if she couldn't find a job? To be trapped here in Mackenzie after Ben left…

Trapped? At home? Naomi stuck the letter in her coat pocket. The rejection didn't weigh as heavily on her heart or in her hand as the letter with Ben's name on it.

Naomi arrived home to a kitchen full of the smell of fresh bread. Laura had just taken the loaves from the pans and set them on a rack to cool. She looked over her shoulder as she set the bread pans in the sink.

"So how is Ben?"

He's fine. Mark didn't hurt him badly. I stopped for the mail on the way home. I got a 'no' from Calgary, and Ben's money is here."

Out of nowhere, Naomi's eyes filled with tears. In the next moment, Laura had her arm around her.

"Child, sit down."

Naomi dried her eyes on her coat sleeve and sat at the table. "I don't know why I'm being so silly. It's only one application, and it wasn't my first choice anyway. And I knew Ben's letter would have to come soon."

Laura pulled a chair around to sit beside her. "But you didn't know it was coming today."

Naomi gave herself a little shake. Yesterday, she'd been content to accept whatever time she had with Ben as a gift. What right did she have to complain now if it were taken away? And if she'd let herself forget that he had secrets, that was no one's fault but her own.

"Laura, we've suspected all along that Ben wasn't telling us the whole truth. Jack Walters thinks so, too. I should never have let myself get so involved."

Laura shook her head. "Sometimes it isn't about choice. If you really care about Ben, maybe you need to have a little more trust, rather than less."

Trust. Naomi turned the word over in her mind. "Trust in what?"

"Trust that things will work out the way they're meant to."

Bitterness welled up in Naomi, and strong words rushed out before she could stop them. "But things don't work out, Laura. They didn't for Mother. They didn't for Gordon. They didn't for a lot of my patients overseas. And they aren't going to work out for me and Ben. I've always known that, but I still let myself fall in love with him—" Naomi stopped short. *In love? With a man she'd known a month?* "Oh, I'm being ridiculous."

Laura's tone sharpened in response to Naomi's words. "No, you're being human. Which means you can't predict the future any better than anyone else. The only way you can be sure things won't work out for you and Ben is if you give up on him." She took a breath and went on more gently. "I don't blame you for being afraid, Naomi. You have reasons enough, but I also know you're stronger and braver than you think. Remember that. You'd better call Corinne and tell her the letter's here."

"Get out of the way, dog, or you're going to get hurt." Carl leaned on his pitchfork and waited while Tank ran around the stall. The fool beast thought anything that moved was meant to be chased, and that included tools.

In a minute or two, Tank decided the game was over and ran out to follow Barry's trail to the cattle. Carl went back to work spreading straw until Corinne called him from the porch.

By the look on her face, she had news. Carl's stomach lurched. Had Constable Walters gotten his answers already, or was there more trouble for Naomi?

But Corinne didn't look upset or suspicious. Carl crossed the yard to meet her.

"Ben, Naomi just called. She picked up a letter for you this morning. It's from your friend in Halifax."

Good. He wasn't trapped any longer. Now he'd be able to pay the Franklins and the Foleys what he owed them before he left them behind...left Naomi behind.

Carl had awoken in his cell that morning thinking of her, knowing what he had to do. He could stay here until Constable Walters proved him a fraud, and find himself on the way to an Army stockade or shipped overseas. Or he could go before that happened, and perhaps spare Naomi some pain. Before long, she'd be able to see that she was well rid of him.

"Ben, are you all right?"

He barely heard Corinne's voice. "I'm all right. If it's okay, I'll ride into town and pick up the letter this afternoon." Carl turned on his heel and headed back to the barn, leaving Corinne standing there, puzzled.

He sat on a sawhorse, leaned back against the wall and swore. Now wasn't the time to remember Naomi's comforting touch while he was sick or to remember being in her room in the middle of the night, but those memories came back to him more strongly than her kisses. With his next breath Carl was on his feet with a shovel in his hands. He slammed it against the wall with enough force to bend the metal.

You knew how this was going to end, didn't you? So pay your debts and get out. Only he could never repay Naomi and her father, or Barry and Corinne for what they'd done for him.

Another memory rose up, of his parents standing on the kitchen step at home, the morning he shipped out. His father stiff but with a grudging pride beneath his frown, his mother white to the lips, rigid with the effort to hold back her tears. The girls had said their goodbyes in the kitchen. Georgie with a forced smile, Alice quiet as always but with signs on her face that tears had been shed in the night. Alice had always shed her tears in private.

Carl had walked away without a backward glance. He'd always had a certain respect for Georgie, because she could be as hardnosed as her father and took nothing from anyone, but had he ever offered his mother and Alice anything but contempt? If he could see them now, tell them—

But he couldn't and wouldn't. Ever. His lies ensured that.

Loneliness hit him like a fist to the gut, leaving him breathless. Carl slumped on the sawhorse again and took in great gulps of air. Scalding tears leaked from his tight-shut eyes and trickled down his bruised cheek. Christ, when was the last time he'd cried? How old had he been? Six or seven?

He curled his hands into fists and kept taking slow breaths until his tears stopped, then he walked out into the yard, to where the farm lane met the road. Corinne had gone in. Carl looked across miles of grey-brown prairie and hard blue sky.

Maybe he did belong in the Army. He couldn't say he'd had real friends overseas, but he'd had comrades, men who respected him. Men who'd trusted him with their lives, and whom he'd trusted with his.

And he'd let those men down, just like he'd let down his mother and Alice. Now he would do the same to Naomi and her father and the Foleys. The pattern of his life...only this time the regret came first.

An urge swept over him to start walking, just put one foot in front of the other until he couldn't go any further...

There's an easier way than that, O'Neill. There's a rifle in the porch, and you know how to use it.

He didn't walk. He ran, until his lungs were ready to burst and his head swam with lack of air. He stopped and waited, doubled over, hands on his knees, until he could breathe again. When he straightened up, he saw the spire of Mackenzie's Catholic church in the distance. Only another mile to town.

Instead of running away from Naomi, he'd run toward her.

Chapter 15

Naomi came through from her father's office to the kitchen at the sound of their ring on the phone. Corrine was on the other end, her voice strained.

"Naomi, is Ben at your place?"

"No. Is he on his way?"

"I-I'm not sure. I thought he finished in the barn and had gone out to help Barry, but Barry just came in for lunch alone. The horses are both in the barn. Ben said he was going to head over to your place later to pick up his letter, but..." Corinne's voice trailed off. She wouldn't say more on the phone, but her worry came though to chill Naomi.

"Did he take his things?"

"No, but it isn't like him to disappear like that at meal time."

Careful. You don't know who might be listening. "I'm sure he's just gone for a walk and lost track of the time. Call me when he gets back."

Naomi hung up and returned to the office to finish the notes she'd been making about yesterday's home visits, but she couldn't write anything that made sense. Could Ben have hitched a ride in a passing vehicle? Was he in so much trouble with the law that he'd choose to run without his money or his belongings?

After twenty minutes or so, a knock on the kitchen door made Naomi jump. There stood Ben, looking like he'd been chased all the way from the farm by the devil himself. "Ben, what on earth? Corrine called. She's worried about you. How did you get here?"

He stepped past her and shut the door behind him. "I walked."

"Sit down. I'm going to call Corinne and—"

"No, don't call her yet." Ben moved to the stove, turned his back and held his hands out to warm them. Naomi walked up behind him and put her hand on his shoulder. His whole body stiffened.

"Ben, you're upset. I can see it. Talk to me."

He shook his head. Tension rolled off him in waves. "I don't know what to say."

With a firm hand, Naomi turned him to face her, looked into his eyes. She'd never seen them so haunted. She didn't know what to say either, so she simply wrapped her arms around him and laid her cheek against the wool of his jacket.

And she felt Ben's heart gallop like it had that first day when he was so ill. She ran her hand over his back, helpless to comfort him in any other way, since she didn't know what was wrong. But perhaps that was what he needed, because his arms came up to pull her closer and his cheek brushed her hair. As the seconds ticked by, his heart slowed and his body relaxed. Naomi looked up, tried to read the emotions mingling behind Ben's eyes, and failed.

"Ben, you look like you ran all the way here. What happened?"

He pulled out of her embrace and moved to the window, turning his back on her again. "I don't understand it. I was puttering around in the barn, and Corinne came out to tell me that you'd called, that my letter had arrived. I was thinking 'good, now I can pay my debts and make some decisions,' and then I started thinking about home – how I left – and the next thing I knew I was running here as hard as I could."

Naomi had seen Ben angry, she'd seen him upset, but she'd never seen him so confused. Somehow, his mind had connected leaving Mackenzie with leaving his family, but she knew too little about them to puzzle it out.

"What happened when you left home?"

Ben turned around. He wouldn't meet her gaze, but shame came through in his voice. "I'd been fighting with my parents – they aren't dead, Naomi. That was a lie."

Somehow, she wasn't surprised. The few times Ben had spoken of his parents, the memories had sounded too fresh, too immediate. So he had family, but he'd chosen to cut himself off from them. How...how terribly lonely he must be.

"Why?"

"I didn't want you contacting them. You know my father and I never got along, and my mother…" He swallowed, then went on, his voice thick like the sound of fabric tearing. Or his soul. "I treated her like dirt. I only enlisted because they were ready to throw me out." He shook his head. "I'm her firstborn. Her only son, and I let her think I was dead. I didn't even write to tell her I was coming home from overseas."

Naomi swallowed the painful lump that had risen in her throat. She'd lost her mother, but she had precious memories of her. Of them. How lost must Ben feel, to not even know what he'd missed?

"Her only *son*?"

Ben nodded. "I have two younger sisters."

"Is Alice one of them?"

"Yeah." As if his regrets goaded him, Ben spun on his heel and returned to the stove. "I hurt her, too. I lost my temper with her and hit her. I put bruises on her face. I'd just wakened from a nightmare and didn't know what I was doing, but I hurt her. Even then, she was the one who came to see me in the hospital after I got beaten up."

Oh, Ben. He'd carry that regret for life. No one but his sister could ease his guilt, and she wasn't here. Still, Naomi had to try. She moved closer and took Ben's hands.

"Then she cares for you. I'm sure she understood that you didn't mean to hurt her."

He shrugged. "Maybe. Alice never saw me very clearly. Maybe my father did, and that was our problem."

Naomi looked into Ben's eyes. The pain she saw there could only be a measure of the good in him. Alice must have known that, too. "Or perhaps Alice saw you more clearly than anyone else."

"I don't think so."

And that was the saddest thing of all. Ben judged himself more harshly than Alice probably had, more harshly than his mother could ever have judged him. The way he spoke of them told Naomi that.

"I do. Ben, you fought for me at the dance. You came to my room in the night when I was upset, because you cared. I didn't think I'd ever want a man to touch me again, and you've changed that. Those are the things I'll always remember about you." Naomi paused. She didn't want Ben to think she judged him, but... "If you're sorry about the way things were with your family, why don't you tell them so?"

He pulled his hands from hers and turned away. "I can't expect them to forgive me."

"Ben, my mother has been dead for fifteen years, and never a day goes by that I don't think of her and long for her. If you have regrets now, they'll be worse once your parents are gone."

Ben didn't answer, but at least he didn't look angry. Good. She'd let it lie for now. "I'm going to call Corinne and let her know you're here."

Naomi kept the call brief, just telling Corinne that Ben was there, safe, and she'd call back later. Ben still stood by the stove. Naomi joined him. "Take off your coat. You're staying with us tonight."

"I don't know if that's a good idea."

"I do." Until that haunted look in Ben's eyes faded completely, Naomi wasn't letting him out of her sight.

Naomi hung Ben's coat in the back porch, then took his hand. "Come." She led him to the sitting room. On the sofa, she held out her arms to him. After a long hesitation, he sat down and settled into her embrace.

"Where's Laura? If she comes in—"

"Laura went to town. She won't be home for another hour or so, and Dad won't be home until suppertime." Naomi drew him closer. "We have some time."

For awhile they just sat there, not talking, sharing each other's warmth. How many more times would they be able to do this? Ben spoke first, in a drowsy murmur.

"Do you ever get confused about time, Naomi? So you're not sure if something is happening now, or if it happened in the past, or if it's a dream?"

"Yes, once in a while." Her fingers slid into his hair. "I think that's part of shell shock, Ben. Has anyone ever talked to you about that?"

He nodded. "Before I was sent home from Europe, I saw an Army doctor. He said I didn't have it. The doctor I saw at the veterans' hospital in Halifax disagreed."

Typical. Naomi had worked with both kinds of doctors – the ones who only believed in wounds they could see, and the ones who accepted that war damaged minds as well as bodies. She held Ben a little closer and thanked heaven he'd had at least one doctor with a heart. "I was taught that shell shock happens to soldiers because the brain gets injured from concussion by artillery, but I've never believed that's all there is to it. If so, why would it happen to me? I was never close to an artillery barrage. I think sometimes it happens when your mind just can't take any more."

"Maybe."

"It makes sense, doesn't it?"

Ben lifted his head. "It makes sense, but it's still not an excuse for hurting people."

Naomi looked into his eyes. How had he become so dear to her so quickly? "Ben, if I learned anything over there, it's that life is too short for regrets about things we can't change."

Her fingers brushed through the short, soft hair at the nape of his neck. Ben's eyes took on a glow. "Naomi, this is bound to get really complicated."

"It already has, don't you think?"

Ben sighed and lowered his head. His lips found the corded muscle at the side of Naomi's neck. He nipped her gently, soothed the small sting with his tongue, then nipped her again.

Heat rocketed from Naomi's neck down her arms. Her palms burned and her body went lax. With one hand she pressed Ben closer, while her other hand slid up his back to his shoulder. Her fingers found the spot where the bullet had passed out of his body. She brushed the scar's rough edge in a light caress. If only she could soothe his inner wounds that easily.

But he'd soothed hers. He'd brought joy back into her life with his touch, and touching him felt just as wonderful. The muscles of his back tensed and released under her fingers, so that she itched to delve beneath his shirt and let them play across his taut skin. Even through his clothes, the warm, solid feel of him made her bones melt.

Ben's eyes held no shadows now, only heat. Naomi reached for his mouth and it sealed to hers, hot and demanding, taking her from sensations she never expected to feel again to ones she'd never felt before.

She let herself fall back against the arm of the sofa and took Ben with her. Time wasn't tricking them now. It no longer existed. Naomi had no idea how long they lay there kissing, lost in each other, before Ben suddenly sat up. "Someone's home."

Naomi hadn't heard the door, but now she heard Laura in the kitchen. How embarrassing would it be to be caught here spooning like a pair of randy teenagers? The way her face burned, it must be beet red. She straightened her blouse and skirt, ran her fingers through her hair and stood to check her reflection in the mirror over the fireplace. Her lips were swollen from Ben's kisses, and her eyes – she turned away. No chance that she'd fool anyone.

Laura called out from the kitchen. "Naomi, are you home?"

"Yes, I'm in here. Ben dropped in." After their talk earlier, Naomi doubted that Laura would intrude on them. She returned to the sofa. The passion between her and Ben had cooled for now. He looked troubled again.

Naomi had been there with Corinne the day most of Mackenzie's young men left on the train. She'd watched their families say goodbye, some determinedly cheerful, some keeping a stiff upper lip, some shedding tears. What must it have been like for Ben to leave in anger? She took his hand and linked her fingers with his.

"Your friend, Dennis. Were you and he close overseas?"

Ben folded Naomi's hand in his. "No, Dennis and I aren't particularly close. I got you to contact him because he owed me a debt. I told you I got in a fight helping out a friend. He was the friend."

Naomi shifted to press lightly against him, offering comfort. Ben had fought for Dennis, even though the man hadn't given him real friendship. He'd fought for her, even though he knew he'd be moving on soon. Did he have any idea how much generosity he'd shown?

"What happened?"

Ben rested their joined hands on his knee and turned to face her. "I was in Halifax for a few weeks before I headed west. Dennis has a bootleg operation there. He owed the wrong people money. I went with him to try to help him make a deal, and it turned sour."

Bootlegging. That fit. "Did Dennis get beaten up, too?"

A rueful shake of Ben's head. "No. He ran."

Naomi didn't bother trying to control her temper. What a sorry excuse for a man, let alone a friend! "Then he's a despicable coward." Ben shrugged off her anger.

"Or a smart man. It depends on how you want to see it."

"I know how I see it." Naomi held Ben's gaze. "Have you ever run out on a friend?"

He looked away. "There are a lot of other ways to let people down, Naomi."

His tone tore at Naomi's heart. It sounded so bleak. If only Ben could see even a glimpse of himself as she saw him. A man who'd served his country, stood up for her, stood by his friends even though they didn't deserve it... "Do you even know that you have a keen sense of honour? That you don't let people down when they need you?"

A short, bitter chuckle. "Alice said the same thing to me once. She always was pretty naive."

Naomi didn't care for his dismissive attitude. She put some steel in her voice. "Would you say I'm naive?"

Ben hesitated. "No. You've seen and experienced things Alice couldn't even imagine."

Trust that things will work out the way they're meant to. Could it be that Laura was right? If Naomi hadn't gone overseas, if the rape hadn't happened, Ben wouldn't be able to say that now. Maybe there were reasons for the good and the awful things that happened to people. If Ben had landed on her doorstep three years ago, would he have been drawn to her at all, or would he only have seen a young country girl as naive as his sister? And would Naomi have seen him as anything but an angry, reckless young man?

"Yes, I've seen a lot, and so have you. And we've both survived. You don't have to worry about hurting me, Ben. I'm here for you to lean on and I'll be here when you leave, though I hope you won't just yet."

Ben frowned and pulled his hand from hers, but longing showed on his face. Naomi simply waited. After a minute or so, Ben lay back and rested his head on her lap. She ran her fingers over his temple with light, soothing strokes.

"Close your eyes."

Within seconds, he was asleep. Naomi watched the tense lines ease from his face. When he'd arrived in Mackenzie, she'd thought he could easily pass for thirty, even older, but not now, and not just because he'd had a few weeks of rest and square meals. Whether he realized it or not, Ben had changed since coming here. And it showed.

She ran her fingers through his hair again. Ben had come to her today because, on some level, he knew he needed her – but he had no idea how much she also needed him.

Chapter 16

Her skin burned from head to toe, but she still craved the heat. It washed through her in waves, beginning where Ben's fingers traced a blazing trail down her side and over her hip. Meanwhile his lips moved over hers, making them ache and tingle. His taste filled her mouth, and the spicy male scent of him filled her nose.

But his touch, his flavour, his scent all faded with her next breath. Naomi sat up in bed, shivering, to find the quilts down around her waist.

How long had it been since she'd had a dream like that?

She'd never had a dream quite like that.

This afternoon, Ben had slept with his head on her lap for nearly an hour before her father arrived home early. There'd been no further chance to be alone with Ben. Naomi told her father and Laura that Ben had come to pick up his money and stayed for a visit. He'd walked because he wanted the exercise, and of course, there was no question of him walking back out to the Foley place after dark.

Her father and Laura didn't question her. At supper, Ben apologized for what had happened at the dance, then the rest of the evening had passed in casual conversation — but no one looked casual. Everyone clearly felt something in the air, and every time Naomi looked at Ben, she saw her own churned-up feelings reflected in his eyes.

And later, those feelings had invaded her sleep.

There'd been no further mention of the money. It seemed that her father and Laura didn't want to bring it up any more than Naomi did. It smacked of finality.

A faint glow of light leaked under Naomi's door. Was her father up for some reason? She hadn't heard the phone ring. She crawled out from under the quilts, slipped on her robe and opened the door a crack.

The light came from Ben's room. Naomi's heart started to race as her mind filled with thoughts of going to him, making her dream a reality.

For shame, Naomi. She closed her door, turned around and got back into bed. But that light continued to tease her.

You've had your body stolen. Ben gave it back to you. Would it be so wrong to share it with him now?

Maybe not, but no one else would see it that way.

If she were honest, it wasn't the thought of her father that held her back, or even the thought of another pregnancy. Shame scorched Naomi's face. No, the only thing keeping her in her room was fear.

Fear of what?

She knew Ben wanted her. His kisses left no doubt about that. So what was she afraid of?

Her own words came back to remind her. 'Things don't work out, Laura. They didn't work out for Mother. They didn't work out for Gordon. They aren't going to work out for Ben and me.'

Was that it, then? Other than her youthful flirtation with Barry, she'd never had a relationship with a man. While her nursing school classmates danced and flirted as much as strict rules would allow, she'd spent most of her time studying. The few times she'd been attracted to a man, she'd backed off. Because they weren't right for her, or was it because she couldn't risk losing another person she loved?

But you're going to lose Ben. That's not a risk; it's a fact. Will it be easier if you tell him how you feel, or if you don't?

It all came down to that one choice, and this might be Naomi's only chance to make it. Maybe someday, someone else would come into her life and set her on fire the way Ben did. Maybe they wouldn't. After all, her father had never remarried.

When you're eighty, what will you wish you'd done, Naomi?

Naomi got out of bed, switched on the ceiling light and put on her robe. She stood in front her mirror for a moment, then took the robe off and dropped it on the bed. Her flannel nightgown covered her from her neck to her toes, but at least it was new and pretty. She ran her fingers through her hair to fluff it a bit. It was so fine.

She opened her door and stood, her pulse pounding, while her mind whirled with all the reasons why this was a very bad idea. Maybe Ben wouldn't want to hear what she had to say. Maybe that quixotic sense of honour of his would kick in and he'd send her back to her own room, humiliated.

You're stronger and braver than you think. Holding that thought, Naomi took a step out into the hall. Then another.

No sound came from Ben's room. Perhaps he'd fallen asleep with the light on. She stopped outside his door, gathered her nerve, and knocked softly. No response.

"Ben? Are you all right?"

He didn't answer. Naomi eased the door open. Ben sat up in bed, naked at least to his waist. She hadn't seen him that way since his illness. The bruises on his torso were gone now, leaving smooth skin underlaid with muscle. The fresh bruises on his face stood out against his fair skin.

A fighter. He frightened her – and she'd never wanted to touch anyone so much in her life. With racing heart, Naomi stepped in and closed the door.

Jesus, Mary and Joseph. Why couldn't she have taken the hint when he didn't answer her knock? After several hours of broken sleep and disturbing dreams, Naomi in his room was the last thing Carl needed. But here she stood, as if she'd stepped out of the dream that had wakened him. Of course he hadn't pictured her in a flannel nightgown, but her softly parted lips, the tangle of her fine hair framing her face – that fit his dream, all right.

All the emotions of the day still churned inside him, draining his will. She was everything he'd never dared to want, and just what he couldn't have.

"You shouldn't be here."

Naomi swallowed, took a step closer. Her mouth curved in a tentative smile. "If I remember correctly, I said something like that to you once. You didn't listen either."

She visibly shivered. Nerves? Or maybe she was just cold. The room was chilly, but Carl couldn't feel it for the heat in his blood. Holding his gaze, her beautiful grey eyes wide, Naomi crossed the room and sat on the edge of the bed. "I woke up and saw your light on... Couldn't sleep?"

"No."

"Neither could I." Naomi took a breath as if gathering her courage. "I was thinking about you. About us."

Her scent reached Carl, tinged with musk. Desire. Just like this afternoon. Carl's pulse started pounding in his ears. "So was I."

A long pause. Naomi laid a hand on Carl's shoulder. "We don't have much more time together. I don't want you to go without knowing how I feel about you."

Her fingers trailed down his arm. He swallowed the lump in his throat. "Naomi—" Carl's voice failed him as her touch broke the connection between his body and his brain. Then she lifted his hand to her cheek and kissed his palm.

"Ben, I love you."

Carl's breath left him in a rush. *Love?* He'd never imagined it, never thought about it. He wanted Naomi, needed her, had been driven to her today when he'd tried and failed to face the fact that it was time to leave, but did that mean he loved her, too?

Yeah, he guessed it did.

But Naomi couldn't really love *him*. She didn't even know his name. Maybe Carl had a conscience after all, or maybe it was just her touch wreaking havoc on his ability to think, but he couldn't lie to her any longer.

"My name isn't Ben."

Naomi moved back a little and folded her hands in her lap. She looked serious, but not too surprised. No doubt she'd wondered.

"What is it, then?"

"Carl O'Neill. Ben MacNeil was killed the day before I was captured. And I'm not from Newcastle. I'm from Halifax."

Naomi gathered up a handful of his quilt, as if bracing herself for bad news. "Why did you hide your real name from us?"

"I haven't been discharged, Naomi. After I escaped, I was sent home on leave. When it's up, I'll probably be sent back to active duty. I don't have the guts to go back over there. One way or the other it would kill me. So...I ran. I'm AWOL now, but I'm not a deserter – yet."

The disgust Carl expected didn't come. He would have welcomed it instead of the sadness and regret he saw on Naomi's face.

"It isn't a matter of guts. You've done your share. There shouldn't be any question of your going back, but I know the Army doesn't work that way." Her eyes looked into his, soft with compassion. "If you were sent home, you must have had a worse time as a prisoner than you've told me. Your shoulder wound wouldn't have been enough. I nursed more than one soldier who'd been wounded before, and they were judged fit to go back to the trenches, even one with a metal plate in his head where his skull had been fractured."

"What I told you about being a prisoner was true."

Naomi's finger traced the scar on Carl's right wrist. "It wasn't the whole truth. I already know that."

He pulled his hand back. His family had never noticed those faint, telltale scars. He'd never let them close enough. Even in hospital, Carl's doctor and nurses hadn't noticed them. They'd been too busy and too concerned with his obvious injuries, but he owed Naomi some kind of explanation. She had a right to know the truth about the man she said she loved.

"When I was captured, they patched up my shoulder and sent me to a prison camp for officers. I'd made lieutenant a couple of months before. The camp was deep inside Germany, near Brandenburg, well away from the fighting. They were decent enough to me there. All they asked was that I follow the rules and give my word that I wouldn't try to escape. So, I promised and settled down to ride out the war in safety."

Carl closed his eyes and pictured the room where he'd been debriefed before being sent home, the faces of the officers to whom he'd told his story. He couldn't tell it again any other way.

"I've never been very good at being told what to do, and the longer I sat in that camp, the harder it got. There I was, out of harm's way, just marking time. I got into trouble a couple of times for breaking minor rules, and then I tried to escape. And got caught."

Naomi's hand touched his. "What did they do to you?"

Carl inhaled, filled his nose with her scent before going on. "They sent me to another camp, near the front. One of the ones the Germans built to try to force the French to move their prison camps back out of artillery range."

He heard Naomi's sharp intake of breath. "A reprisal camp."

Carl opened his eyes. "What do you know about reprisal camps?"

"Only what I've heard second hand." Her expression told Carl she'd heard enough. That she understood. "How long were you there?"

"Four months." Of lice in his hair. Rancid food. Cold and hunger and blows. Forced work and mind-numbing exhaustion. Hours standing bound and immobile, until his joints froze and he fainted with pain. Four months of Otto and Petr. Carl saw his memories reflected in Naomi's eyes.

"What happened to you there?"

Carl looked away. "I got off a little easier than a lot of the other men."

"Why was that?"

She doesn't need to know that. Haven't you already hurt her enough? But with Naomi's soft gaze on him, the words seemed to say themselves.

"One of the other prisoners was a real piece of work. They didn't feed us much, and this man stole food from anyone who he thought wouldn't fight back. He tried to steal from me, and I fought back." Carl reached for Naomi's hand and folded it in his to steady him. "They threw me in solitary confinement for a few days, but it turned out that the camp commandant liked to watch a good fight. He chose me and eight or nine other prisoners and set up matches. He called it his boxing club, but boxing had nothing to do with it. There were no rules."

Naomi let out a little gasp and laid her other hand on Carl's knee. Tears shone in her eyes. "I can't imagine that."

"The winner ate that day, and the loser didn't. Lose too often and you were out, and on half rations from then on. But we made a few rules among ourselves. We had to be careful – we didn't dare throw a fight – but we made sure no one got too badly hurt, and no one lost too often. Even so, we weren't much better than animals when it came down to it."

Naomi shook her head, sending a tear trailing down her cheek. "None of you had a choice, so you did what you could to keep each other alive and reasonably strong. That sounds smart to me."

She moved closer and slipped her arm around him. Carl pulled back. Smart? She didn't know the whole story. "Once in a while we were made to fight someone who wasn't really up to it, as punishment for them. We were expected to destroy them."

Naomi wiped her eyes. "Carl—" Her voice caught. Carl rushed to finish the story, to get to the end of the lies and half-truths once and for all.

"It only happened to me twice. I did my best to walk a fine line, to do enough damage to satisfy the commandant without doing too much, but one of those men died."

Now she knew. And the look in her eyes hurt Carl more than anything that had happened to him. She held on to his hand when he tried to pull it away. Then against all caution, Carl gave in. After laying his soul bare for her, he needed that connection more than he'd ever needed anything.

"What would have happened if you'd refused to fight him?"

"I would have been thrown out of the club at the least, executed at the worst, and someone else would have had to fight him."

Naomi reached out to touch Carl's bruised cheek. Her tears flowed freely now. "You tried to save his life."

"Yeah." And hearing Naomi say it eased his burden of guilt, even though he'd failed. "Everything I told you this afternoon was the truth, about my parents and my sisters, about how I got beaten up. Only thing I didn't tell you was that after Corinne told me about Dennis' letter, I thought about taking Barry's rifle and making sure I never hurt anyone again."

"But you didn't. You came here instead. There's something in you that's stronger than what's trying to pull you under."

Naomi laid her hand against his chest. The gentleness of her gesture tore something in Carl wide open, releasing a flood of pent-up longings. Longings he couldn't indulge – not if he wanted to live with himself. He trapped her hand under his.

"Naomi, I can't tell you how much you mean to me, but I don't need any more regrets."

Eyes still misty, she held his gaze. "I have regrets, too, Ben – I mean Carl. I wonder how long it will take me to get used to that?" She gave him a shaky smile. "I haven't told you the whole truth either. The day we met, I wasn't just coming home from a visit to a friend. I'd been to see a doctor because I was pregnant."

For a moment, blind anger surged through him. Carl held still, forced himself to wait until his temper ebbed.

"The rape?"

"Yes. I've destroyed a life, too."

"Does your father know?"

"No. I couldn't tell him. I know he wouldn't have blamed me, but I just couldn't."

How alone she must have felt, making that decision. Carl pressed Naomi's hand more closely over his heart. What right did he have to judge her for holding back, when he'd held back so much himself?

"No, your father wouldn't have blamed you. I don't blame you either."

Naomi smiled. "But I needed to tell you. Carl, I understand that you don't want more regrets. Neither do I. That's why I'm here."

She leaned in and touched her lips to his, only a whisper of a kiss, but it set a match to powder. She could never be his, but just this once, couldn't he be hers?

Carl gripped Naomi's shoulders and eased her down on top of him. Her mouth found his again and they melted together like snow under the spring sun. He undid the top buttons of her nightgown, slid his hand inside and found her breast, warm satin to his touch. Her small gasp of pleasure went from her mouth to his as her body shivered in response.

Christ. Was he going to be able to keep this gentle for her?

Yes, said his heart. At the moment nothing mattered but Naomi. When he did leave, she'd have the memory of what being with a man should be like. It was Carl's job to make the memory so strong she'd never settle for anything less or be haunted by the violence of rape.

He lifted Naomi's nightgown over her head and took a moment to just enjoy the sight of her. Sitting astride his thighs, her fine, wavy hair falling softly around her shoulders, she was beautiful, but it was the play of emotions across her face – desire, tenderness, uncertainty – that took his breath away. He'd never seen tenderness in the eyes of any other woman he'd been with. It touched raw places inside him, made them ache and sting.

"Naomi, this is new to me, too. I've never been anyone's first. Show me what you want."

"I want to remember you. Everything about you." She bent and touched her lips to the hollow at the base of his throat, swirled her tongue against his skin. "The way you taste and smell. Here...and here..." Her fingers trailed down his torso, traced along one rib, crept lower to run along his oblique. "I want to know you so I'll never forget you."

Her hand shifted to the long muscle of his inner thigh. Carl's belly jerked tight as bolts of heat streaked to his groin. Naomi looked up with a sultry little smile.

"Do you like that?"

"Oh, yeah." He slid his hand down the satin skin of her back to the mounds of her buttocks and cupped her there. "Want to know how much?"

He dipped his fingers between her thighs and stroked her. Her body rocked back. "Carl – I..."

She was on the edge already, and so was he. Carl settled his hands at her hips and pulled her forward, ready to join himself to her with one thrust of his aching sex, but he had just enough mind left to overcome that instinct. He lifted Naomi and settled her beside him.

"I don't want to rush this. It's too important."

"Yes, it is." Naomi brushed her thumb over his lips. Then she kissed him, slowly, gently. With a sweetness that made a lump form in his throat. "Come here," was all she said.

Carl shifted to lie over her and buried his face against the side of her throat. His eyes stung with tears. He needed her so damn much, as much or more than she needed this. Naomi welcomed him, cradling his weight with her body. His refuge, his anchor. She soothed the raw emotions running through him. Left him free to be with her, body and soul.

More soft kisses, more light caresses. A murmur, a sigh. Each touch made him burn and his mouth made her arch against him. There was no way Carl would risk getting her pregnant again, so he used his hand to bring her to her peak, and she did the same for him, stroking him until he came to a shuddering climax that had him biting his lips to keep from crying out and waking the house.

He came back to reality with Naomi watching him, poised on one elbow, wearing a smile full of feminine sensuality. A vixen's smile. She pressed a soft kiss to his mouth, then settled into his arms.

"Whatever happens, I'm never going to regret this. I didn't know anything could feel so good."

Carl held her close. "Neither did I. Don't ever forget, Naomi."

Her fingers trailed across his chest. "Don't you forget, either." She looked up with another impish smile. "You know, Ben – Carl – I should have guessed you were Irish, not Scottish. You've got a real Irish temper."

Body replete, mind adrift on a sea of contentment, Carl grinned. "And where do the Franklins come from?"

"Edinburgh."

"Of course." Carl tucked a lock of her soft hair behind Naomi's ear. If the glow in her eyes was any indication, he'd done what he set out to do. She had some idea now of what being with a man should be like. That would count for something when he left her – for both of them. Naomi nestled close to him again. "I think that deep down, I always knew Ben wasn't your real name. When I asked you your name that first day, you seemed to have trouble remembering. Sick as you were, that's something a person doesn't forget. Do you have a middle name?"

"Of course. My mother is a staunch Catholic."

He felt her lips curve. "Let me guess. Joseph?"

"No, Carl. My first name is Francis, after Dad, but no one has ever called me that."

"Francis Carl O'Neill. I like it."

"What about you?"

"My middle name is Suzanne, after Mother."

"Naomi Suzanne Franklin." Carl kissed her hair. "It's beautiful, and so are you."

For a few minutes they lay there, not talking, just holding each other. How perfect would it be to hold her like this every night, to have Naomi always there when he woke in the dark? Crazy ideas started spinning in Carl's mind. He could send for her as soon as he found a job in Vancouver, and she could find work nursing. They could find places not too far apart, give themselves some time, and then—

Yeah, right. Marry, have children, and raise them under a false name? Because you can't marry her as Carl O'Neill.

Carl eased out of Naomi's embrace and out of bed. Naomi's sleepy gaze followed him as he grabbed his robe, opened the door and peered around it. The house was silent. He padded down the hall to the bathroom.

You're going to wash, and then you're going to send her back to her room. But when he returned, Naomi was asleep. Carl took off his robe and stood for a moment, shivering with cold, trying to muster the resolve to wake her.

He couldn't. He crawled into bed beside her and kept his distance, not wanting his chilled body to touch hers, but Naomi shifted and pressed herself to his side, one arm across his chest.

In seconds he was warm again. And he knew then with a clarity he couldn't explain that it didn't matter how much or how little time they had. All the time in the world would never be enough.

Chapter 17

Naomi woke when the sky outside the spare room window had just begun to fade from deep blue to grey. She should get back to her own room before her father and Laura woke, but she couldn't bring herself to leave Carl just yet.

He still slept, his face close to hers, his arm around her waist. Would this be the only time she'd know the pleasure of waking up close to him? Perhaps, but she'd remember him every morning for the rest of her life, for the pleasure they'd shared and because of what he'd told her.

Carl hadn't said exactly how he'd gotten the scars on his wrists, but he'd told her more about what he'd been through than she'd ever expected to know. It touched Naomi to think he trusted her that much. She'd only heard bits and pieces of stories about reprisal camps, but she didn't doubt he had fuel enough for a lifetime of nightmares.

Francis Carl O'Neill. She studied his face and tried to picture his family. Did he resemble either of his parents? She imagined him with silver threads in his dark hair, his eyes a colder blue, his features grown harsher with time. Was that what his father looked like? From what she gathered, the man even intimidated his own wife. And Carl's sisters – did either of them resemble him? Did they have any idea of what he'd suffered?

Did they miss him at all?

The kitchen floor creaked and the poker rattled in the stove. Laura was up and starting the fire. Naomi couldn't stall any longer. She slipped out of bed, ran her fingers over the curve of Carl's shoulder and down his arm, 'til he woke with a sleepy smile on his face.

"Hey."

"Hey. I'm going to get dressed and go down to help Laura."

Carl stretched, sat up and glanced out the window. "I guess you should." His smile faded. "I'll tell her and your father everything this morning."

Naomi sat on the edge of the bed and looked into his eyes. "Dad isn't going to blame you, Carl. Neither will Laura."

"Maybe not. We'll see."

But his expression said it was Naomi's opinion that mattered most. She touched her lips to his. "Didn't I make myself clear last night? I don't blame you either. I'll see you downstairs."

After a quick bath, Naomi dressed and headed down to the kitchen. She sliced bread while Laura mixed milk into her scrambled eggs and sliced ham for the skillet.

"You're up early."

"I heard you up and decided to give you a hand, since we have company."

Laura set her mixing bowl on the counter and held Naomi's gaze. "Naomi, is Ben all right?"

In the process of filling the coffee pot, Naomi slopped hot water from the kettle onto the stove. A hiss of steam covered the rather unladylike word she muttered under her breath. Did Laura know something she shouldn't?

"Yes. Did you think he wasn't?"

"I wondered. I slept poorly, and I heard someone get up in the night. Then I thought I heard your voice."

Before Naomi could answer, footsteps sounded on the stairs. Carl walked into the kitchen with her father behind him.

At the sight of her Carl's heart did a flip, partly from nerves and partly from the memory of what he and Naomi had shared in the night. Her scent, the feel of her skin, the way she'd looked into his eyes as her pleasure peaked... In that moment, she'd held nothing back.

Neither had he. Though he hadn't been inside her, part of his soul had merged with hers. And now the piper had to be paid.

A leaden weight settled in Carl's stomach. Naomi might believe her father wouldn't blame him for running away, but he had his doubts. If only he didn't like Doctor Franklin so much.

Everyone took their seats at the table. Doctor Franklin took his coffee from Laura and looked Carl over with a critical eye. "What's going on with you, Ben? You look as if there's something on your mind."

"There is." Carl took a deep breath and stole a quick glance at Naomi. She sent him a silent message of encouragement. "Doctor Franklin, I've lied to you. I've lied about a lot of things, and I don't feel good about it. I've told Naomi the truth, and now I want to tell you."

The doctor's face went very still, with an expression Carl guessed was the calm before the storm. Doctor Franklin turned to Naomi first, searching for hurt in her eyes. She met his gaze, gave him a small smile. With a resigned sigh, her father shifted in his chair to face Carl. "I'm listening."

Why couldn't the man be angry? If Carl had taken in a sick stranger off the street and that stranger repaid him by lying and playing with his daughter's affections...

But you'd never dream of taking in a stranger, would you?

No, and in the doctor's place, he'd be furious, but Doctor Franklin apparently cared more about Naomi's feelings than his own pride. And that only made Carl's guilt worse.

Carl told the doctor what he'd told Naomi, leaving out his time in the reprisal camp. Then he waited while Doctor Franklin studied him, brow furrowed as if he were thinking about a perplexing case.

"Well, I can't say I'm surprised. A man as badly beaten as you were doesn't travel halfway across a continent unless something's driving him. When is your leave up?"

"The middle of December."

"So do you plan to live under someone else's name for the rest of your life?"

Naomi leaned forward, waiting for Carl to answer her father's question. What did she expect? She deserved a man strong enough to go home, face the Army and his family. Hell, she deserved a man strong enough to die for her if he had to.

There are fools in every army, as well as men without honour. Fools who'd fought for the enemy's amusement to keep their own bellies full. Naomi deserved a man a hell of a lot stronger than that.

"Ben MacNeil was one of my men. A good one. I guess there are worse things I could do than use his name, as long as I don't disgrace it."

Naomi's shoulders slumped. Her father shook his head. "I don't judge people when I haven't walked in their shoes. There shouldn't be any question that you don't belong on active duty, but I know the Army doesn't always make common sense decisions. Still, forever is a long time to live a lie. And what about your family?"

The thought of them brought back the ache of emptiness that had driven Carl here yesterday. "Things with my family have always been complicated. That's as much my fault as anyone else's. It'll be best for everyone if I keep my distance."

The doctor sighed again. "That's your choice, of course. Just be aware that the day will come when it'll be too late."

"Doctor Franklin, I think it's already too late."

Naomi straightened and met her father's gaze, then Carl's. The disappointment he saw on her face cut deep. The price they both had to pay for last night. After all, *she'd* come to *him*. He spoke to the doctor, but his words were for her.

"I'm not cut out to be a family man. I've always known that, but you all make me wish I were different. No one has ever done that before. I'll be in your debt for the rest of my life. And speaking of debts, I'd better open Dennis' letter."

Naomi rose and pulled an envelope from the mail holder on the counter. Carl opened it and pulled out a sheet of writing paper wrapped around ten ten-dollar bills.

This should see you through. Feel better soon.
Dennis

Carl peeled off two of the bills. "Doctor Franklin, this is for you." He readied himself to insist, but Doctor Franklin took the money without argument.

"Thank you, Carl."

Carl looked him in the eye. "Thank you for understanding."

Through all of this, Laura had gone about preparing breakfast, her lips pressed together. Her silence must be costing her dearly. Carl knew she loved Naomi more than her own life.

Laura set the plates on the table and took her seat. No one spoke while they ate. As soon as he'd finished, Carl pushed back his chair.

"I should write to Dennis and tell him his letter arrived."

Upstairs in his room, Carl wrote a quick note to Dennis and then sat at the desk, breathing in the scent of sex that still filled the air. To wake up beside Naomi every morning, to lose himself with her like he had last night... Someday, some other man would have that privilege.

Restlessness prodded Carl to his feet and set him pacing. He should get started on his way back to Barry and Corinne's, tell them the truth as well. Then what? Spend a few more days eating his heart out for Naomi? Until another black moment sent him running here again, or running for Barry's rifle?

Time to go, O'Neill.

The westbound transcontinental, the train he'd arrived on, left Mackenzie at one o'clock. Carl had heard it whistle every day he'd been here, but there was a morning train as well. Naomi had told him that it came from Regina and went as far west as Edmonton. He could make a connection to the coast from there.

He'd left nothing at Barry and Corinne's that he couldn't do without. There was nothing keeping him from being on that train this morning. Nothing more to say to Naomi – but he couldn't leave without a word. Carl pulled another piece of paper from the desk drawer.

Dear Naomi,

We've both known this day was coming. It might as well be today. If I wait any longer, I don't think I'll be able to find the nerve to leave.

You told me last night that you love me. I'll take that with me and keep it forever, and I'll do my best to live up to your regard. I can give you that much at least, even if I can't give you my name.

I'm leaving you ten dollars for Barry and Corinne. Tell them I'll never forget them or their kindness. You father, too.

Goodbye, my beautiful girl.

Carl

Carl tucked the note in an envelope with the money, wrote Naomi's name on it and checked the clock by the bed. About half an hour until train time. He'd heard the doctor's car leave while he was writing, and Laura was doing the dishes. Naomi usually went out to feed Hannah after breakfast. He wouldn't get a better chance.

He stuck his note to Dennis in his pocket, picked up the envelope for Naomi and crossed the hall to her room.

Her scent hung in the air here as well, as palpable as his memories. Naomi ordering him out of her room at gunpoint. Naomi in his arms. And her words, 'I wish we could pretend we weren't both so alone.'

But they had no more time for pretending. Carl left the envelope on Naomi's bed. Downstairs, he took his jacket from the hall closet, struggled with the sticky front door, and slipped out.

He paused and listened. Naomi's voice carried on the still air as she spoke to Hannah in the stable. She'd probably go up to her room to change when she went in, and find his note. Carl waited a moment longer to be sure Laura didn't come outside, then he headed toward town at a jog. He didn't stop until he got to the train station.

Carl hadn't made the effort to get to know anyone in town. He'd never taken the time to walk the streets or step into any of the businesses. At first he hadn't been up to it, and then it hadn't seemed worth the bother. He thought he recognized the man behind the ticket counter from Gordon Pheeney's memorial service, but he couldn't be certain. The man gave him a sharp glance.

"You're the one the Franklins took in, aren't you? The one who got into a tussle with Mark Jakeman the other night?"

"Yeah. Ticket to Edmonton, please. One way."

"Sure. They'll be boarding in about ten minutes."

Carl paid for his ticket and took a seat on one of the station's wooden benches, close to the wood stove. Outside the window, clouds of steam rose from the waiting train. Had Naomi found his note yet?

He pushed the thought of her away. He couldn't afford to dwell on his regrets. His money wouldn't last long in Vancouver. Better think about finding a place to live and getting a job. Now that he was healed, finding work shouldn't be difficult, but in a place where he knew no one, it might not be as easy as he hoped.

The call came to board.

The hollow ache in Carl's chest grew sharper as the train pulled away. It only took a few seconds for Mackenzie to disappear behind him. Now all that mattered was what lay ahead.

You'll make this work. That's one promise you're going to keep. For once in Carl's life, he'd done the right thing. If it hurt like hell, that was no one's fault but his own.

Naomi came in from the stable and ran upstairs to wash and change. The door to Carl's room was open, but he wasn't there and she hadn't seen him downstairs. Maybe he was in the sitting room. She hadn't bothered to ask Laura. He wouldn't have started on his walk back to the farm without saying goodbye.

She wished she hadn't let her disappointment show at breakfast. Had she really expected Carl to say he'd go home? Of course not, but the idea of him perhaps spending a short time behind bars, then being discharged, had taken hold before Naomi could help herself. The thought of Carl free to make amends with his family, free to come back to her, robbed her of common sense.

She had no right to judge him. She wasn't judging him, but Carl was giving up so much along with his name if he didn't face his responsibility head on. He couldn't go home to his family. He couldn't marry and have a family of his own.

But he would be alive. There was that.

The thought of Carl going back to the front hurt as much as the thought of him spending his life alone.

Be honest, Naomi. Do you really think he'll spend his life alone?

No. There would be women in Carl's life, but he deserved what he'd never had. A real home.

Naomi dried her hands and returned to her room. When she saw the envelope on her bed, her stomach plummeted. She'd heard the morning train whistle as it left the station a few minutes ago. Carl couldn't...

But he had.

She dropped Carl's note and the money on the bed and ran down to the kitchen. "Laura, did you hear Carl go out?"

Laura threw down her dishtowel. "I heard the front door close a while ago. I thought he'd gone out to talk to you."

"No. I think he caught the train. He left a note on my bed with some money for Barry and Corinne. As if they'd want his money any more than we did."

Naomi's voice vibrated with anger, hot and satisfying. The hurt would come later. Laura drew her into a hug.

"I'd have thought better of him, Naomi. He can't run from his problems forever."

Naomi stepped back. "I'm not angry with him, I'm angry with myself. Why should I be disappointed? He never lied to me about his feelings. He never made any promises, because he knew he couldn't keep them."

"But you're disappointed anyway. Because you love him."

Oh, yes. So much that Naomi didn't even regret telling him so. So much that it had made her selfish. Her feelings weren't the only issue here. "Laura, Carl told me some things... He's been through so much. He deserves better from himself."

"Yes, he does, but he has to make that choice." Laura gave Naomi another quick hug. "It'll get easier, Naomi. I know you don't feel like that right now, but it will."

"I'll have to trust you on that."

Naomi helped Laura finish the dishes, then got back into her barn clothes and rode out to the Foleys' to give them Carl's money. The landscape she'd ridden through so often looked harsh and unfamiliar, brooding under a grey sky. Only a few hours ago, she'd been warm in Carl's arms. Now he was gone from her life. A door had closed. How long would it take to get used to the emptiness?

She found Barry in the kitchen with Corinne, grabbing a second cup of coffee after finishing the barn chores. When Naomi told them about Carl and gave them his money Barry was hurt, but Corinne was simply furious.

"Naomi, that man was in love with you. His eyes lit up every time your name was mentioned. And he runs off like a coward without even saying goodbye!"

Barry cut in. "He's no coward. I can tell you that."

"No, he's not." But Carl seemed to think he was. Naomi blinked back tears. "He thinks he's doing the right thing."

"The right thing?" Corinne dumped the dregs of her coffee in the sink and set her mug down with a clatter. "He's running from his family and his feelings for you. Neither is going to go away."

Naomi found herself rushing to Carl's defence. Corrine didn't know the whole story. "I'd rather think of him starting a new life as Ben MacNeil than going back overseas."

But Corinne wouldn't let go of her anger that easily. "I just don't like seeing you hurt, Naomi."

Neither did Naomi's father. The look on his face when she told him before supper hurt most of all. Standing by the sitting room fire, he held her close.

"It's at times like this that I really wish your mother were here. But I haven't quite forgotten how it feels to be a young man, and I know this – that young man cares for you."

"Yes, he does, in a way." Enough that he'd mentioned giving her his name. Had Carl really meant that, or were they just words?

Her father looked into her eyes. "He cares, Naomi. Hold on to that."

But at the moment, those two words didn't feel like much to hold onto.

Chapter 18

Before Naomi knew it, Carl had been gone a week. A week she'd filled as completely as possible. The practice helped. Her father's pointed comments to a few patients had at least driven gossip underground, and there were a fair number of cases that could do with Naomi's care instead of his. She threw herself into the work with all the determination she could muster, for her father's sake.

Meanwhile, Naomi wrote some letters inquiring into training as a midwife. Perhaps there could be a place for her here in Mackenzie after all. Being able to stay with her father and Laura would almost make up for what might always be missing in her life, a husband and children. As for her old sense of adventure, it seemed to have deserted her. Life away from here would be too lonely without her father and Laura, Barry and Corinne.

Naomi came home from one of the outlying farms one afternoon to find Jack Walters in the kitchen with Laura, in uniform, looking much too official for comfort. Did he have some information about Carl?

"Hello, Constable Walters. Are you here to see me?"

"Naomi. Yes, I am." Constable Walters pulled two folded pieces of paper from his shirt pocket and opened one. "This is from a friend of my brother's who has connections in Maritime Command in Halifax. I figured that since Ben MacNeil was an Easterner and he'd been overseas, he would have shipped out from there. Well, he did, and he was killed at Guillemont last year. Your patient gave you a false name. I hear he skipped town over a week ago. Do you know where he went?"

At least she didn't have to lie. "No. He left without saying a word to anyone. I think he caught the morning train."

Walters shrugged. "Of course I heard the word around town that he was headed for the coast when he landed here. A deserter, most likely. Well, that's the Army's problem, not mine. He's out of my hair and yours, but I thought you should know."

Naomi dropped her eyelids to hide her relief. Constable Walters wasn't going to pursue the matter any further, and chances were the Army wouldn't, either. Then Walters unfolded his other document.

"That's not the only reason I'm here. This is a subpoena from the crown prosecutor's office in Regina. You're required to testify at Randall Clark's trial on November tenth."

Naomi's stomach heaved. She ran to the sink and leaned over it, gulping air to avoid being sick, while Laura held her shoulders.

"It'll be all right, child. You'll go and tell the truth, and it will be over once and for all. Your father and I will be right there with you."

"They want your testimony in person to add weight to the prosecutor's case," Constable Walters said. "It could be the difference between Clark getting what he deserves and him getting away scot-free, Naomi."

Naomi straightened up. If she could do it, if she could look Randall Clark in the eye, at least she would have done something to help ensure his conviction. She struggled to keep her voice even.

"You're right, Laura. Constable Walters, I'll be there."

The night before the trial, Naomi lay awake in her hotel room. Would she disgrace herself in the courtroom tomorrow, faint, be sick or unable to speak when she saw Randall Clark's face? How hard would it be for her father to watch her do this?

Laura snored softly in the other bed. Tomorrow would be hard on her, too. Then there would be the wait until the jury reached a verdict.

Dear Lord, what if they find him not guilty?

No. That man robbed you of a piece of your soul. You and that other girl. If not for Carl, he'd have robbed you of part of your future, too. You aren't going to let him get away with that or have the chance to do it to another woman.

At first light, Naomi gave up trying to sleep, got up and ran a bath. Later, with her father and Laura, she worried down some breakfast in the hotel dining room. Then it was time to go to court. Thank God she'd been instructed to wait in a small office down the hall from the courtroom until she was called. If she'd had to sit in the same room with Clark all morning, she would have lost her nerve. Her father and Laura waited with her, her father with Naomi's hand in his.

"You have nothing to hide and nothing to be ashamed of, Naomi. Remember that."

"I will. I'll be fine." She smiled for him. "Dad, I've been thinking about Carl this morning. I suppose he's found a job by now."

"Probably. You miss him, don't you?"

"Yes, I do. I expect I will for a while."

"I'm sure he feels the same. It'll get easier, dear."

"I keep telling myself that."

Her father squeezed her hand. "I know you really cared for him."

"Yes, I did."

Her father held her gaze. "Naomi, I know you were with Carl in his room the night before he left."

Naomi glanced over at Laura. She must know, too, or Naomi's father wouldn't have brought it up with her in the room. Naomi spoke to both of them.

"I went to tell him I loved him. I didn't want him to leave without knowing."

Her father nodded. "And did he say he loved you?"

"Not in words. I don't think he knows how. Dad, we didn't do anything stupid. I couldn't do that to you."

"I'm not angry with you, Naomi. I admire your courage." Someone knocked on the door. Her father stood and squared his shoulders. "It's time."

When Naomi stepped into the courtroom, her head whirled. A waft of body odors, perfume and tobacco rose from the full gallery of spectators. She took her seat on the witness stand and there in front of her, sat Randall Clark, at a table with his lawyer. Her stomach heaved.

Carl. Think of Carl. She closed her eyes and took deep breaths while the oath was given. Her 'I do' sounded firm and clear.

I won't let him rob me of anything more. Not now, not ever again. With the memory of her night with Carl clear in her mind, Naomi looked Clark in the eye while her written statement was read. The prosecutor asked her a few questions confirming her statement, then it was Clark's lawyer's turn.

"Miss Franklin, why didn't you report the assault when it happened?"

"Because I saw little chance of it ever being proved."

"The medical report you submitted from Doctor James Brantley in Yorkton indicates carnal knowledge, but no injuries to speak of, only a few minor contusions. Didn't you fight him at all?"

"Didn't you listen to my statement? He had a knife at my throat."

"How do you expect the court to take this case seriously when you didn't take it seriously enough yourself to report it to the police?"

Naomi met the gaze of Clark's other victim, who sat with her parents in the front row of the gallery. She appeared to be seventeen or eighteen, pretty in an overt way, with thick, curly dark hair and a high-coloured complexion. 'None too good a reputation,' the police had said. Naomi wished she'd been allowed to speak to the girl, to apologize for her selfishness.

"I regret that decision now, but that doesn't alter the facts."

Naomi looked at the jury and saw sympathy there. They believed her. Clark's lawyer saw it, too. He played the only card he could.

"It's been proven that carnal knowledge of these two young women by my client did occur. What has not been proven is that either woman resisted him as strongly as they might have. Given this lack of resistance, and the unstable mental condition of Mr. Clark, he might have taken their lassitude for permission, so I argue that he cannot be held fully responsible for his actions."

Not responsible? When he'd told Naomi that he'd been thinking about her for weeks, that she 'belonged' to him? The thought revolted her more than ever now that she knew what belonging to a man meant.

"I could have cheerfully shot that lawyer as well as Clark," her father said when it was over and they were back in the blessed peace of the hotel, "but I couldn't have been prouder of you, Naomi. You didn't let either of them shake you."

"I just kept picturing Carl, imagining him there with me. Whatever happens, I'm through letting Randall Clark have any part of me."

They expected the jury's deliberation to take at least until the next day, but the prosecutor's office called later that evening. Clark had been found guilty and fully responsible. He would hang.

Naomi put down the newspaper and gazed out the sitting room window into the fading dusk. The fine snow that had been drifting down all afternoon had changed to a thick curtain of white. Good thing her father had switched the buggy from wheels to runners yesterday. The clock on the mantel chimed four. Time he was home.

She rose, added wood to the fire and did a restless turn around the room. Since she'd gotten home from the trial, she couldn't seem to settle down to anything. She turned to the window again. Had Carl found work and a decent place to live? He probably wouldn't write, not after the way he'd left.

Was he as unhappy as she? Had he written to his family? Perhaps he'd decided to go home and report, face whatever discipline the Army chose to give him. He might even be on his way back overseas. Naomi saw his face among the hundreds that lived in her memory. Lifeless faces.

Hannah appeared outside the window, a moving dark blur against the curtain of snow. Naomi hurried out to the kitchen, where Laura was starting supper. A few minutes later Naomi's father stepped into the porch, stomping snow from his boots. He hung his coat on its hook and started to step over the threshold into the kitchen, then pitched forward onto his knees.

Naomi's first thought was that he'd caught his foot on the ledge between the porch and the kitchen, but then she saw him clutching his chest. She and Laura got to him at the same time, rolled him onto his side and helped him sit up, but he fell back against Naomi's shoulder, his face grey with pain. He couldn't catch his breath.

"Laura, call Doctor Brantley. Hurry." Naomi spoke on instinct, but she knew Laura might as well save her breath. Doctor Brantley was an hour away by car, and the snow would make it two. Even if he were five minutes away, there'd be little he could do. Naomi had never seen a heart attack patient, but she'd learned enough in school to know the reality.

She held her father close, supporting him against her shoulder while she laid a hand over his heart. She didn't know how to read its fast, erratic rhythm. "Dad, are you taking any medication?"

"No. There's none that can help." He looked up, struggled to speak through his shortness of breath. "Sorry, Naomi... I should have told you."

"You knew you were ill?" Of course he knew. The signs were there, but Naomi and Laura had simply refused to see them – Laura out of love, and Naomi because she'd been too wrapped up in her own problems.

210

Her father nodded. "Saw Brantley just before you got back from overseas. My heart – decided to get old without asking me."

"Dad, if I'd known I wouldn't have gone overseas. I wouldn't have given up that time with you."

He took her hand, squeezed it as he looked into her eyes. "Don't you dare feel guilty. Nothing you could do." He struggled for another breath. "If I could have seen you settled and happy... But that would be having everything, and no one has everything. You came home to me safely. That's enough."

Laura's hurried conversation with Doctor Brantley filled in the pause while Naomi fought to master her voice. "No it isn't. It isn't enough."

Her father gripped her hand tighter as another spasm of pain hit him. When it passed, he looked into her eyes again. "Naomi...look after Laura. She doesn't have anyone else."

"I will. I promise."

"You're the daughter she never had." He released Naomi's hand and touched her cheek. "My beautiful girl. Your mother and I are so proud of you. Always will be."

"Dad, I—" Before she could say 'I love you,' his eyes closed. His heart stilled under Naomi's hand.

How could hers keep beating? She'd never let herself imagine life without her father. Then Laura was kneeling beside her, tears running down her face.

"I'll call Corinne and Barry."

Naomi walked through the next few days as if she were walking through a moonscape. Nothing seemed real. They buried her father on a bright, diamond-hard morning. Barry and Corinne had stood by her through it all, but after the funeral and the reception, Naomi gently asked them to go home. "I need to be alone for a little while and catch my breath. Please understand."

Corinne hugged her. "Of course we understand. If you need anything, we're only a phone call away." Then she and Barry drove away, leaving Naomi and Laura to go home to the empty house.

Naomi retreated to her father's office, sat at the desk and tried to gather her thoughts. She'd gone through the practice finances yesterday. Her father had never talked much about money, but he'd left everything in order. Thankfully, the house was paid for and there were no debts, but the money in the bank would only keep her and Laura for three or four months. Unless Naomi found work very soon, they'd have to take out a mortgage to live.

Chances were that when a new doctor came to Mackenzie, he'd buy the place, but that might not be 'til spring – if it happened then. The practice wasn't exactly a gold mine that would attract an ambitious young man, even if any were to be found with the war on. She still had hopes for the job in Halifax, but she couldn't afford to sit here nursing her grief and waiting to hear from them. She'd better start writing more application letters.

Naomi pulled a sheet from the note pad on the desk and jotted down the names of a few hospitals where some of her classmates were working, then she wrote her name and address at the top of a sheet of writing paper, but she couldn't muster the will to start a letter.

If she did go to Halifax... What if Carl were there? Would she run into him one day on the street? Naomi shook off the thought. She couldn't afford to think of Carl any more than she could afford to think about the loss of her father.

Laura came in and set a cup of tea on the desk. "What are you doing in here, child?"

"I've got to start thinking about work." Naomi looked up at her. "What's the farthest you've ever been from Mackenzie, Laura?"

212

Laura thought for a moment before she answered. "Winnipeg, I guess. That was before the doctor hired me."

"Have you ever wanted to travel?"

"I've never thought about it, really."

Of course she hadn't. Laura had grown up on one of the local farms and married a farmer at eighteen. He'd died in an accident a couple of years later, and Laura had worked out for one family or another ever since. If the thought of travelling had ever occurred to her, she wouldn't have had the money.

Naomi rarely remembered that Laura had been married. She never spoke of her husband, and she certainly never invited pity. Naomi looked at her with new eyes. If Laura could face the future with courage, she'd have to try to do the same.

"Well, you're going to now, if you'll stay with me."

Laura nodded. "Of course I will, child. It's what the doctor wanted, and you're all the family I have. We'll stick together, you and I."

Like family. The only family Naomi had. She asked Laura something she'd always wondered, but never dared to ask before.

"Laura, you've spent a long time here. Tell me if I'm out of line, but did you ever wish that there could have been...something more...between you and Dad?"

Laura put her arm around Naomi's shoulders. "No. Your mother was the only woman in the world for the doctor, and Andrew was the only man in the world for me."

"And you only had two years with him. Laura, I'm going to take whatever happiness I can find, wherever I can find it." With or without Carl. "Maybe we'll go to the East Coast. Do you think you'd like to see the ocean?"

Laura mustered a smile. "I think I would, now that you mention it. Now drink your tea, Naomi, and don't worry about work today. Get some rest first."

Naomi drank her tea and went up to her room, longing for a few hours of sleep and forgetfulness. She paused before the open spare room door, then stepped inside. She hadn't been in there since the night she'd spent with Carl. She lay on the bed, sank into the mattress and imagined his weight pressing her down, his dark head pillowed on her breast.

Tomorrow. She'd be stronger tomorrow, and perhaps someday there'd be someone who would make her feel alive again. Like Carl had.

Carl winced as the afternoon sunlight stabbed him in the eyes. He rolled over to face away from the window, sat up and stared at the clock on the bedside table. Just after two. Time he was up and moving.

His roommate worked at an insurance office, so Carl had the flat to himself during the day. He didn't have to leave for the dockyard until eight. He'd already adjusted to the night shift. Working through the night was a hell of a lot easier than lying awake thinking of Naomi, or falling asleep to be awakened in the dark by one of his terrors.

Most evenings, Rick grabbed something to eat at a tavern after leaving work, then headed across town to visit his girl. He and Carl only connected for an hour here and there during the week. An easy roommate to live with, and Rick was glad enough to have someone to share expenses that he didn't ask questions about Carl's past. Carl had slipped back into being Ben MacNeil without a ripple.

On the weekends, Rick liked to party with friends. He'd asked Carl to join him, but Carl wouldn't go down that road. He'd made up a story about lingering stomach problems from dysentery he'd caught overseas. A few careless words while his brain was fogged with liquor, and he might have to run again. But that wasn't why Carl hadn't fallen over the edge and into a bottle of whiskey – yet.

He'd promised Naomi that he'd try to live up to her love. So far, Carl had managed to cling to that promise, though sometimes the craving for a drink grew bone deep, as deep as his craving for Naomi. Now it was just a matter of hanging on until he worked her out of his system.

He washed, dressed and made a pot of coffee and a sandwich in the flat's cubbyhole of a kitchen. While he ate, his mind took him back to the Foley farm, where Barry and Corinne's happiness had filled the house with as much warmth as the old wood range. He missed them more than he ever expected he would.

When he'd finished his sandwich, Carl pushed his plate aside and picked up the Regina paper he'd bought on his way home from work. He read the front page headlines, then flipped through the back pages on his way to the employment ads. He froze when a familiar face caught his eye.

Doctor Franklin's face. On the obituary page.

'A sudden illness,' the obituary said. That usually meant a heart attack. Carl dropped the newspaper, sprang up from the sofa and headed for the kitchen. He needed to call Naomi, hear her voice, tell her how sorry he was. Tell her how much Doctor Franklin had come to mean to him in the short time they'd known each other.

But Carl stopped with his hand on the receiver. If he called her, he wouldn't know what to say. Better write instead. He returned to the living room for writing supplies and knelt by the coffee table.

Dear Naomi,
I saw your father's obituary in the paper this morning. I'm so sorry. If there's anything I can do –

His vision blurred with tears. Of course there was nothing he could do, nothing he could offer Naomi except empty words.

Carl wadded up the paper and threw it across the room as hard as he could, then rose and stalked back into the kitchen.

Just as in Halifax, getting bootleg liquor in Vancouver wasn't much of a problem. Prohibition was less than two months old here, but it hadn't taken long for alternative sources to appear. Rick had a bottle of rye in one of the cupboards. Carl poured himself a double, then followed it with another.

The next thing he knew, he opened his eyes to lamplight. The sky outside the window was dark. Carl lay on the sofa with Rick standing over him, the empty whiskey bottle in his hand.

"What are you doing home? You should have left for work an hour ago."

Carl sat up. The room spun. The bottle had been half full. "Shit. What time is it?"

"It's almost nine. What's going on, Ben? You told me you couldn't drink."

"I guess I was right. I'd better call in sick." Carl got to his feet. Thank God they had a phone. He didn't think he could make it to the phone booth on the street corner.

He made his call, poured a glass of water, returned to the living room and dropped onto the sofa again. Rick was still waiting for an explanation. Carl rinsed the taste of stale whiskey from his mouth and took a deep breath. The truth? Why not?

"I didn't come here directly from New Brunswick, Rick. I took sick on the train, and they put me off in this little town in the middle of Saskatchewan. I stayed at the local doctor's place. He and his daughter looked after me. Naomi. She and I... It wasn't easy to leave her behind."

Rick sat in the armchair and set the bottle on the floor. "So why did you?"

Carl shrugged. "You're in love, so I guess you're immune to common sense, but I'm not. I had to leave. No work for me there. Anyway, her father's obituary's in the paper today. Her mother died years ago, and she's an only child. Tough."

"So that's what set you off? If she means that much to you, why not send for her and marry her? You've got a decent job now."

"Yeah, if I don't lose it for calling in sick in my third week. I'm not ready for a family, Rick. Look, I'm sorry about the bottle. I'll pay for it or replace it. I'm going to bed."

In his room, Carl undressed and crawled under the covers. So damn familiar, right down to the hangover he'd wake up with tomorrow. Only this time, he wouldn't have to face his family in the morning. He wouldn't have to face anyone but himself.

Was Naomi crying now?

It's no good, O'Neill. It's just no good. It isn't going to get easier, at least not fast enough. So what are you going to do?

He could go back to Mackenzie and ask Naomi to marry him under his real name, ask her to go with him to some place where neither of them were known, where the chance of him being discovered by the Army would be almost nil. In her grief and loneliness, she'd probably say 'yes.' She'd said she loved him, and Carl believed her. As for the Mounties, it wasn't their job to track down deserters.

But wouldn't Naomi's love always be tinged with disappointment? And what about later? When their kids started asking questions about the war, and about his family? His parents would be their only living grandparents, his sisters their only aunts. He might never have thought family mattered much, but Naomi would want her kids to have aunts and uncles, cousins and grandparents, even if they were far away. Would her regret eventually turn to resentment?

While his mind spun out of control with whiskey and questions, Carl fell asleep. He woke halfway through the morning with a dry mouth and an aching head – but with his options narrowed down to one. He put coffee on the hotplate to perk, then brought writing supplies to the kitchen table.

Dear Naomi,

I saw your father's obituary in the paper this morning. I'm so sorry. I can only imagine how much you're missing him. I knew him such a short time, but I miss him, too.

Naomi, I'd made up my mind that the best thing I could do for you was to leave you alone, but now I know that I can't. Since I arrived here, I haven't been able to stop thinking about you. I hold you in my arms in my mind when I go to sleep at night, and I wake up imagining you lying beside me. You're the reason I keep putting one foot in front of the other every day. I told you that you made me wish I could be the kind of man you deserve. I still don't know if I can be that person, but I know now that I have to try, and that has to start with taking care of unfinished business.

I'm going to go home, talk to my family and report to the Army. If they sentence me to prison time, so be it. If they send me back overseas, I'll deal with that as best I can and pray that I come home. If I don't, know that you've already saved me in every way that matters.

As soon as I know what it's going to be, I'll write, and when I can, I'll come back to Mackenzie. If you aren't there, I'll find you. If you tell me I've blown my chance, that you aren't interested in a life with me, I'll live with that, but I'll have to hear it from you face to face, because there's nothing I want more than to spend my life with you.

All my love,

Carl

He dressed and took his letter down to the mailbox on the corner. Dropping it in felt like taking a plunge into cold water. If it was too late, if he'd blown his chance with Naomi, what then?

Then he'd wait. He'd do whatever he had to do to prove himself to her, and he'd try again. Because losing her wasn't an option.

Laura stepped into the back porch to meet Naomi as she came in from the barn. "Naomi, Mrs. Anderson just called from the store. She said there's a letter for you from Halifax. She thought it might be important."

Naomi took off her father's old barn coat, hung it up and came into the welcome light and warmth of the kitchen. The sun had just disappeared behind a bank of dour-looking grey clouds. November was almost over. She'd always liked winter, but this year it seemed as if spring would never come again.

Halifax. Could the letter possibly be from Carl?

No, it was time she accepted that she wasn't going to hear from Carl. The letter must be about the job at the veteran's hospital. Would it be a 'yes' or a 'no'?

"Thanks, Laura. I'll go pick it up before she closes." Naomi washed her hands, changed her boots and put on her town coat and gloves. At the store, Mrs. Anderson handed over the letter with her usual curiosity.

"Job offer, Naomi?"

"An offer or a 'no.'" When Naomi didn't open the letter right away, Mrs. Anderson sighed and leaned on the counter.

"It's going to be a hard winter here, with you away and the doctor gone."

Naomi tucked the envelope in her pocket. The people who'd gossiped about her, who'd given her disapproving looks on the street after that piece in the paper, had shown up at her father's funeral with long faces and condolences. When she left, they'd throw her a farewell reception and see her off at the train station with the same long faces. Mrs. Anderson wasn't one of the hypocrites, but Naomi wanted none of it. When the time came, she'd go as quickly and with as little fanfare as possible.

"I don't have much choice, Mrs. Anderson. I've been talking to Doctor Brantley, and he's found a doctor willing to come here whenever I leave. Doctor MacDonald sold his practice last year, but he's agreed to come out of retirement to fill in for a few months, until someone comes along to buy the practice."

"Well, at least he's not a kid fresh out of medical school."

"They're all overseas." Naomi paused, looked out the window at the familiar street. Would the awful ache deep inside her ever go away? If she was offered this job and had to leave soon, she'd need to rush to wind up her father's affairs, but Barry and Corinne would help her, and what point was there in waiting? It might be weeks or months before something else came along.

She opened her letter in the kitchen as soon as she got home and sat at the table to read it, with Laura looking over her shoulder.

Dear Miss Franklin,

We are pleased to offer you a position on our staff. As you know, our hospital is new and we are still determining staff requirements, but our increasing patient numbers leave us short of nurses, particularly nurses with your training and experience. Will you please wire us with your earliest availability?

They didn't just want her, they wanted her as soon as possible. Naomi folded the letter and slid it back into the envelope. "I guess we're going to see the ocean, Laura."

Laura's hand settled on Naomi's shoulder. "So we are. Now we've got some work to do."

Naomi stood. "There's no way we can do it all now. I'll take the train to Yorkton tomorrow to meet with the lawyer, like I'd planned. I'll leave all of Dad's papers with him for safekeeping. What can't be done in his office can be done later by mail or wire. We'll close up the house and get the Andersons to keep an eye on it for us. Barry and Corinne will check on it once in a while, too, and they'll take Hannah."

She heard her voice as if from a distance. Better get the arrangements made, say goodbye to Barry and Corinne – to life as Naomi had known it – before the numbness wore off. If it ever would.

Chapter 19

Halifax, Nova Scotia
December 6, 1917

"Good morning, Private Henderson. Did you get some sleep last night?"

The fair-haired young man in the bed wouldn't meet Naomi's gaze. "Yeah, some." But there were tired lines around his eyes and mouth. Two weeks ago today he'd had his right foot amputated, and he was still in a lot of pain.

Naomi took his pulse and temperature and fought a temptation to sit for a moment in his bedside chair. A week into her new job, she was tired, too. She'd thrown herself into learning the hospital's routine and getting to know her patients – a luxury she'd never had overseas.

She didn't think she'd ever learn to like Halifax. What she'd seen of downtown looked grim and forbidding, though the stores were full of goods for the upcoming holiday season. Warehouses and chandleries of brick and stone crowded the waterfront, overlaid with the reek of salt water, seaweed and sewage. Sailors and soldiers from all over the world filled the streets. Even if Laura would let her, Naomi wouldn't have ventured to explore downtown on her own. The short hours of daylight didn't leave her much time for that, anyway.

But she'd spent a few hours in Point Pleasant Park, with its graceful stands of old pines, and she'd walked the streets near the hospital, in the city's South End. This was the affluent part of town, near Dalhousie University, a neighbourhood of dignified homes and streets lined with mature elms and maples. And one day, in a weak moment, she'd given in to temptation and looked up Carl's medical records.

He'd told her he'd been hospitalized at Camp Hill when his ribs were broken. So, coming off shift late one night, she'd snuck into the records office while the clerk was on coffee break and found Carl's file. She hadn't dared stay long enough to see more than his name and address. His family lived at 45 Russell Street in Richmond.

Richmond was the name given to Halifax's North End, on the other side of Citadel Hill. One of the other nurses, a local girl, had explained that the 'Hill' divided Halifax socially as well as geographically. To the south of the old fort on the hilltop were the homes of professors, businessmen, doctors and lawyers, with paved streets and city amenities. To the north were dirt roads, the bulk of the city's factories, and the homes of their employees, humble or otherwise depending on the home owner's position.

On her first day off, Naomi had taken a tram to Richmond and walked down Russell Street, past Carl's home, a white Victorian with black shutters and trim. One of the largest on the street, it fit his story that his father had a management position. At the sugar refinery, perhaps? Or was it the printing company?

Naomi liked the neighbourhood better than the South End. It felt more approachable. Here and there, hens clucked and strutted in back yards, and the occasional back yard had a cowshed. More like home.

Russell Street sloped down to a grey ribbon of water, the Narrows, a slender channel that connected the two parts of the hourglass-shaped harbour. Carl must have gone to the red brick Catholic church further up the hill. His sisters had probably attended the convent school next to the church. He would have played in the street here as a boy. Naomi had no intention of making another visit. The temptation to knock on his family's door and speak to his mother might grow too strong.

Meanwhile, work kept her from dwelling on her regrets. In the field hospital, they'd focused on giving the patients a fighting chance at survival. Here, Naomi saw where that chance led. The men too badly injured to ever lead a normal life, the men with no one to help them through the pain of recovery, made dents in her heart. But Private Henderson was one of the lucky ones, though he couldn't see that yet. Not quite a man, this boy from a small fishing village outside of Halifax was convinced that without his foot, his life was over.

Naomi checked her watch. Henderson was the last patient on her morning rounds. She could afford to spend a little time with him.

"Your pain will start to lessen soon. It'll get better, Michael. I promise."

She wasn't supposed to call patients by their first names, but she bent the rules once in a while. Caught up in his own problems, Michael didn't appear to notice. He avoided her gaze and shrugged.

"How much better can it get? You know, Nurse, I never got any further than seventh grade in school. Dad needed me on his boat. Now I'm not going to be of any use to him or anyone else."

Naomi held back a sigh. Part of her wanted to scold Michael, and part of her wanted to hold him as if he were her younger brother. "I met your parents when they were in to see you yesterday. They're beyond proud of you, and they're thrilled that you've come home alive. They also told me you have a girl at home who's been in to see you, though I haven't met her yet. How long do you think she'll put up with you moping and feeling sorry for yourself?"

That got under Michael's skin. He met her gaze with a glare. "Sophie loves me. I'd marry her if I had any way to support a family, and I've told her so."

"Then don't let Sophie down. Right now, your job is to heal. When you're ready, you'll have an artificial foot, and I think you'll be surprised at how well you'll be able to get around. You have a younger brother. He looks about sixteen. Is he helping your father now?"

"Charlie's seventeen. He left school to help Dad when I enlisted two years ago."

"Does your father need both of you on his boat?"

Michael looked down again. "No."

"Then only one of you can fish. If you hadn't lost your foot, it would have been you. Now it's going to be your brother. Do you begrudge him that?"

His voice dwindled, sounded young and scared. "Of course not, but I don't know anything else."

"Then you'll have to learn to do something else. You've lost a foot, but there's nothing the matter with your brain. Count your blessings, Michael. Now let's have a look at your leg."

Naomi changed his dressing and left him waiting for his breakfast. Strange how the future could frighten a person so much. Michael and Carl had that in common. Not that she blamed them. Didn't the future scare her, too?

Michael would be all right. His family would rally around him, he'd find something to do and marry his Sophie, and he'd be spared the harshness of the fishing life – the arthritis, the early aging she'd seen in his father, just as she'd seen it in the farmers at home.

By the time she left Michael's room, the sun had risen. Naomi's stomach started to rumble. It had been three hours since she'd eaten breakfast, so she headed to the nurse's locker room for her break, ate the sandwich she'd brought and poured a cup of coffee from the pot that always waited on the hot plate.

The window of the locker room faced the Halifax Common. Naomi looked out over rooftops to the square of brown grass ringed by leafless trees. In Halifax there was always something to stop the eye, unlike the endless views of home. Here, hills, trees and buildings closed off the sky, making her feel hemmed in. She'd felt the same way overseas, but she'd known that was only temporary. Here, she avoided thinking beyond today.

The clock over the door read nine. She could take a few more minutes. Naomi stood by the window and sipped her coffee. So far, she'd held her own here. Her father would have been proud.

That thought brought on a wave of homesickness. She drained her cup, set it in the small sink and put her lunch bag back in her locker. In the next instant, an unseen force knocked her off her feet. Before she hit the floor, an explosive roar filled the air. Then there was only eerie silence.

Naomi caught her breath and picked herself up. Shards of glass from the broken window littered the floor. If she hadn't moved to the sink when she did, she would have been lacerated. A bomb? If the rumours she'd heard were true, if Germany had developed planes that could take off from the decks of ships and bomb North America, Halifax would be one of their first targets. Was the city under attack?

Her ears rang, but otherwise she didn't seem to be hurt. Naomi stepped out into the hall to find it full of shocked, wondering people – doctors, nurses, patients. Ten minutes later Doctor Gregg, one of the senior physicians on staff, appeared from the stairwell.

"Everyone, I need your attention. I don't know the details yet, but there's been a very serious accident. An explosion on the Harbour. We're going to have casualties – a lot of them. You men go back to your rooms and stay out of the way. Doctor Jensen, put in a call to the Dalhousie Medical School and tell them we're going to need their final year students. Nurses, report to your head nurse immediately. We need to make sure every available space in the building – and I mean every space – is clean and ready for patients. Nurse Franklin, I need to speak to you."

Casualties. Doctor Gregg's voice barely reached Naomi through the torrent of remembered sights and sounds and smells that filled her mind.

"Nurse, are you all right?"

"I...I think..."

"Nurse Franklin, you're one of the few staff members here with triage experience. We're going to need you to keep it together."

Naomi dragged herself back to the moment. Doctor Gregg's face was the colour of ashes. Naomi had assisted him with surgeries and thought him an excellent doctor, but he hadn't been overseas, hadn't treated men straight from the trenches, nor had most of the staff. He was right. She couldn't give in to those memories now. She'd have to draw on the strength those experiences had given her instead.

"I'll be fine, Doctor."

"Good. Go down to the lobby and find Doctor Crowe. He's going to be in charge of incoming patients."

The next few minutes went by in a blur. First in a trickle, then a stream, then a flood, soot-blackened, bloodied people arrived, some walking, some carried by loved ones, others pushed in carts or wheelbarrows. With them, the details of the disaster trickled in.

A ship full of explosives had caught fire and detonated at Pier 6 in the North End. Carl's old neighbourhood no longer existed.

People watching from windows had been lacerated with glass, their eyes destroyed. Limbs had been severed. Most of the injured were women and children, caught at home or at school by the explosion. Many would be permanently blinded or disfigured. Naomi shut off her feelings as she had learned to do in the field hospital and assisted while eyes were removed and cuts stitched. She found a spot in a side corridor for a little girl with a crushed ribcage, so she could die in relative peace in her mother's arms. The sky darkened, then lightened again, with no end in sight. Numb, Naomi worked on.

Carl rose from his seat and stretched as the train pulled into the Winnipeg station. There'd be a twenty-minute wait before it pulled out. He sat again and exhaled slowly, trying to let go of his impatience.

Maybe he should have left Vancouver as soon as he'd made up his mind to go home, but he'd waited a few days. He hadn't wanted to leave them in a lurch at the yard, and in the back of his mind he'd hoped that Naomi would wire a response to his letter. She should have it by now, but he'd heard nothing. He hadn't managed to work up the nerve to call her when the train stopped in Mackenzie. He'd been too afraid that if he spoke to her, his longing to see her would grow too strong to resist.

Foolish to expect to hear from her. He hadn't asked her to wire or write, and he'd told her he was leaving Vancouver. If she cared, she'd probably assumed he was already gone. He'd wire her when his own affairs were in order.

But what if she just had nothing to say to him?

Then it would be up to Carl to change that. Someday, somehow. However long it took.

Right now, he needed a distraction. He headed into the station to buy a newspaper and found a knot of people gathered around the newsstand.

"Something else, isn't it?"

"It sure is. Gotta be the Huns, don't you think?"

Carl rolled his eyes. One of those recruitment gambits in the form of a mock newspaper describing an enemy attack on a Canadian city, or else another far-fetched sabotage story. He shouldered past the speakers, dropped his coins on the end of the counter and grabbed a local daily.

Halifax Wrecked. Disastrous Explosion in Harbour leaves City in Ruins.

Jesus, Mary and Joseph. It wasn't a recruitment gambit. Yesterday morning, a munitions ship had exploded at Pier 6 and blown the North End of Halifax away. Richmond – *home* – had been obliterated.

The train whistled. Carl turned and ran. He made it back on board just in time, stumbled to his seat and leaned back, tears trickling down his cheeks.

Too late. That should be your epitaph, O'Neill. Too late to be a son and brother, too late to grow up and go home. Too late to ever give Naomi the extended family she'd want for her children.

After a few minutes, Carl pulled himself together enough to read the rest of the newspaper article. He thanked God he had a seat to himself as the horror of the news sank in. Details were sketchy, but roughly a thousand people had been killed instantly, with thousands more injured. To make things worse, a snowstorm had followed the explosion. Civilians and the military were scrambling to dig survivors out of ruined buildings before they froze, while others had been burned alive in the fires that swept Richmond after the blast. If Carl hadn't run away like a miserable coward, he'd be there now, using his training to save lives.

God, Mother, I'm sorry. Alice, Georgie...
Dad...

Slowly, one hand clinging to the railing, Naomi descended the hospital's slippery front steps. She paused at the bottom to catch her breath, then went on down the walk, moving like an old woman. Never, even in the field hospital, had she been so exhausted in body and mind, but a fresh medical team had arrived from Boston this afternoon and she could go home for a rest.

Forty-eight hours on her feet, and patients still waited in the corridors. Naomi understood shock, but still it amazed her that no one complained. Dazed and silent, they waited their turn and did what they could for others. And yesterday afternoon, when she'd stepped into a patient lounge, she'd found it full of military patients, Michael Henderson among them.

"Private Henderson, what are you men doing here?"

"Don't worry about us, Nurse. There's others that need beds more than we do. We'll be fine right here."

She'd seen human nature at its worst overseas. Here, she'd seen it at its best.

Carl must know about the disaster by now. Was he on his way home? Was there anyone left for him to come home to? Perhaps – Naomi's empty stomach churned at another thought – perhaps he'd come home before the explosion and died along with so many others. She'd had no time to check casualty lists.

Don't, Naomi. You're ready to collapse. Go home, eat and go to bed.

When she'd arrived in Halifax, she'd taken an upstairs flat in an older home down on Morris Street, a twenty-minute walk away. There'd been nothing to let that was affordable and closer to the hospital. That far south of the explosion site, almost all of the buildings remained intact, but nearly every window was broken. As blackout regulations had already required windows to be covered at night anyway, the dark streets felt familiar. Naomi put one foot in front of the other and let her mind shut down. Heaven knew what she'd find at home. The house had no phone, so she hadn't been able to call Laura. If Laura had come to the hospital, chances were she wouldn't have found Naomi. She'd been in surgery most of the time.

Laura had been busy since she and Naomi had arrived in Halifax. She complained that keeping the flat tidy and cooking for herself and Naomi wasn't enough to fill her time, so she'd joined the Red Cross and a sewing circle, and helped the young mother downstairs whose husband was overseas. Now, unless she'd been injured, she'd probably be out helping with the relief effort. Her years in a doctor's household would make her very useful, but Naomi was selfish enough to hope Laura would be home.

A weight lifted from her heart when she found their building whole. Now, if only Laura were there and safe. As Naomi climbed the porch stairs, the front door opened and a pool of light spilled out.

"Child, you're home. Bless you! Come here."

Thank God. Naomi walked into Laura's arms. Ten minutes later, she sat with her aching feet up on the arm of the sitting room sofa, a bowl of steaming soup at hand and a hot bath running.

"Laura, you weren't hurt at all?"

Laura perched on the sofa's other arm. "Not a scratch. I was out in the yard, getting the linens off the line when it happened. I was knocked down, but I wasn't hurt."

Naomi glanced around the sitting room. The flat didn't go far to ease her homesickness, but she'd brought her steamer trunk full of things from home to make the place comfortable. The curtains from her father's room hung at the broken window, hiding the plywood Laura must have scavenged to nail over the opening. Naomi's favourite floor lamp with the green glass shade stood in one corner, and a couple of pictures from her old room hung on the walls – or should have.

"Both knocked from the walls and smashed, but never mind," Laura said. "We'll have the glass replaced when there's glass to be had."

"Speaking of glass, how did the lamp survive?"

"It fell on the sofa. The lamps in both our bedrooms got broken, and everything fell out of the kitchen cupboards. Most of the dishes are broken. I doubt I've got all the glass cleaned up yet so don't walk around without your shoes on. I haven't been here much. I've been out and about helping the neighbours. Left you a note in case you came home – I didn't want you to think the worst. So you've been working since it happened?"

"Yes. Laura, I never saw anything like this overseas. So many children…" She could never tell Laura, could never tell anyone some of the things she'd seen and had to do in the last two days.

Laura gave her a searching look. "Anyone by the name of O'Neill?"

"I don't know. I didn't have time to ask people's last names or check the lists. Anyway, I'm sure it's a common enough name here." At first, Naomi had searched for faces that resembled Carl's, but she'd soon been too overwhelmed to do that. Perhaps it was selfish to voice her fears, but she couldn't help it. "Laura, you know Carl's family lived in Richmond. That whole area was destroyed. Perhaps none of them survived."

Laura shook her head. "Perhaps not, but let's hope for the best. Either way, I think he'll be coming back here now, if he isn't here already. I expect we haven't seen the last of Ben – I mean Carl. Remember what I told you about trust, Naomi?"

Naomi's raw nerves sparked her temper. "Trust? If Carl comes home and finds his family gone, what do you think he'll do?"

Laura held her gaze. "Perhaps he'll be thinking of you."

"Bedford Station. I'd suggest you folks get out here if you can. They don't need more people in the city."

Carl forced his numb mind to think. There was no point in going into Halifax tonight. Bedford was only half an hour away from the city and he had an aunt here, his mother's sister. If any of his family had survived the explosion uninjured, they'd likely be with her.

He got off the train in the chilly dark, slung his duffle bag over his shoulder and walked up the steep hill to Aunt Sarah's. Carl stood for a moment on the sidewalk, gathering his nerve. He hadn't seen Aunt Sarah since a year or so before he enlisted. That felt like a lifetime ago. As he started up the path to her door, Carl's legs started to shake. Who, if anyone, was left?

He mustered his courage and knocked. Women's voices sounded in the hall. Aunt Sarah wasn't alone. The next moment, the door opened and he looked into Georgie's astonished eyes.

"Carl! Of all the... Where have you come from?"

He stepped inside. The front hall smelled of Aunt Sarah's lavender perfume. Carl had always disliked this house, his mother's childhood home, but didn't know why. It came to him now. The place reminded him of everything his mother was. Ladylike. Cultured. Soft. Too soft to hold her own with her husband. As if the house was responsible for her weakness.

"Hello, Georgie. I've been out West. I started for home when I got the news." He reached out to pull her into a hug, then put his hands on her shoulders instead. She might be hurt, and he'd always been a bit shy with her, anyway. Georgie had a sharpness about her that did that to people. Alice was the one they walked over. "You're still standing."

Aunt Sarah bustled into the hall. "Merciful heavens! Carl, you're back!"

"Hello, Aunty. I just got off the train." Carl couldn't spare more thought than that for Aunt Sarah at the moment.

Georgie stepped forward and hugged him. Held him close, something she rarely did with anyone. It warmed Carl's heart and scared him at the same time. Then she backed off and shook back her cloud of short, soft chestnut curls. "I'll be all right. I was on the tram when it happened, going to work. I got thrown from my seat and took a knock on the head, but the headaches are already getting better. Dad's staying with Uncle David over in Dartmouth. He has a badly cut arm, but it'll heal. Alice got off with just some scrapes and bruises. She's staying with Liam at his cousin's in Prospect."

That news distracted Carl from the sadness in Georgie's green eyes. When Carl left Halifax, Liam Cochrane had been casually going out with Georgie. It was Liam Carl had fought at the St. Joseph's fundraising social, and they'd fought again the day Carl hit Alice. Liam had dropped by the house, and tried to protect her. He and Carl had never liked each other.

"Alice and Liam? That's a twist."

Georgie's mouth quirked in a characteristic wry smile. "You might say so. It turns out that Alice had a thing for Liam for years, and never let on to anyone. When she finally let him know, they didn't waste any time. They're engaged."

"They're *what?*"

"Engaged."

Carl's head spun. After he'd gotten his ribs broken, he'd been hospitalized at Camp Hill along with Liam, who'd had surgery on the leg wound he'd picked up overseas, and they'd talked – or shouted back and forth – a bit. They'd even argued about Alice, but Carl hadn't guessed there was anything between his younger sister and Liam.

Maybe he hadn't really listened.

"So they're engaged. Why is she staying with him?"

"Because he needs help looking after his son."

"His—" Carl's voice failed him. Quiet little Alice, taking on a ready-made family. "What son?"

"Turns out Liam fathered a war baby. His English girl appeared here with the kid not long after he and Alice got together. Now the mother is missing. You've missed some interesting times, Carl."

While he stood there speechless, Aunt Sarah broke in. "Carl, you'd better come in and sit down." She and Georgie exchanged a significant look. Carl's gut clenched. He followed them into the parlour, a prim room he'd always associated with long Sunday afternoons of stifling boredom. Heartbreak showed clearly in Georgie's eyes as she sat beside him on the sofa. Carl only managed one word.

"Mother...?"

Georgie shook her head. "All the houses on Russell Street were blown apart. Mother didn't make it out." She paused to steady her voice. "We buried her at Mount Olivet the day before yesterday."

Punched breathless by grief and regret, Carl hid his face in his hands. "God, Georgie, I treated her so badly. Now she'll never know—"

He heard tears in Georgie's voice. Tough, self-sufficient Georgie, whom he hadn't seen cry since childhood. "She never stopped believing in you, Carl. Even after you disappeared. She told Alice so. And you gave her reason to feel that way."

Carl dropped his hands and held her gaze. "What do you mean?" What reason had he ever given his family to believe in him? Georgie's mouth curved in a sad smile.

"After you disappeared, Alice found your Military Cross. Then the notice came out in the paper, telling how you'd earned it. We got the official notification after that. Alice and Mother were both so proud of you. Mother told Dad that you'd come home one day, and when you did, she'd welcome you whether he did or not. I don't think she'd ever spoken to him like that before. You were always her pride and joy, you know."

Carl struggled to breathe around his pain. "My medal. When they gave it to me, just before I left England, I almost threw it away. How did the newspaper say I earned it?"

"They said you put yourself at risk to get your men out of a bad situation at Guillemont. You got wounded and captured in the process. They dressed the story up a little, but the military report said pretty much the same thing."

"A bad situation? You might call it that. I saw a chance to harass the enemy and took it, only there were more of them than I thought. We got pinned down by enemy fire. It was stay where we were and wait for help, or try to get the hell out of there. I decided not to wait. Well, we got out – or half of the men did. So they gave me a medal. I didn't care if I ever saw it again."

Exasperation gave crispness to Georgie's voice. "You were in charge and you made a decision. Then you stuck by it. So they gave you a medal. As for seeing it again, you will. We found it in the house. Alice has it. Maybe it doesn't mean anything to you, but it does to her, and it did to Mother. And it does to me."

She held Carl's gaze. Georgie had never been one for sentiment, but what he saw in her eyes broke something loose in his heart, something that had been tangled for years with anger and spite. It ached and burned, but it was free.

"I need to see Alice, and I need to see Mother. Tomorrow. Then I'm going to report to base." At the moment, Carl couldn't think any further. "Aunty, do you have a bed for me? It's been a long trip."

Aunt Sarah's eyes held an unusual softness that gave her a passing resemblance to his mother, though they'd really never looked anything alike. "Of course. Georgie's in your mother's old room. You take the other spare room."

Utterly spent, Carl climbed the stairs to bed. The room was the one he'd always slept in on childhood visits here. Memories of his mother surrounded him. Naomi and Mackenzie seemed so far away, they might have been a dream.

So his mother had finally found the courage to stand up to his father, for her son. And Georgie wasn't too disgusted with him to care. Alice had found and kept his medal. He hadn't come too late for everything. There might be something to salvage here after all.

Chapter 20

Carl followed a winding path of churned-up mud and snow to the fresh grave under a young maple, marked with an unpainted wooden cross. He brushed snow from a nearby bench, sat and let the waves of sadness wash over him. He'd brought nothing with him, no flowers. He'd come too late to give his mother anything that mattered.

You can give her your future. He heard the words in Naomi's voice. God, if only she really were here beside him, to give him the backbone to face his future.

People came and went, visiting other fresh graves. The Catholic families from the old neighbourhood had often buried their loved ones here. There was every chance that someone who knew Carl would come by, but it didn't matter anymore if he was recognized. An odd sense of freedom came over him, even though he'd likely be behind bars by the next night.

What would he remember about his mother? He'd remember the good times when he and the girls were small, before they grew away from each other. Hearing the piano from the front walk when he came home from school. He'd remember accepting her love like all little kids did, without a second thought for the way she gave it.

The grave marker had tilted forward a little. Carl rose, straightened it and pushed it more firmly into the partially frozen soil. Then he squatted down beside the grave.

"Georgie said you were playing the piano when you... Wherever you are now, I hope there's music there." He traced the horizontal part of the cross with a finger while he struggled to control his voice. "She said you didn't give up on me. That you were proud of me. Thank you for that."

The cold began to find its way through Carl's jacket. He stood and crossed his arms to keep it out. What more was there to say?

"I love you. I hope you know that now, even though I never told you. Now I have to go. I need to see Alice. At least it isn't too late to tell her."

An older man walked by, wearing a black boiled wool coat that reminded him of the one his father always wore. "I'll go see Dad, too. It probably won't change anything, but I'll try. Goodbye, Mother."

Carl couldn't stay longer if he wanted to get to Prospect and back that night. Aunt Sarah had managed to borrow a horse and sleigh from a neighbour for him. Carl started back down the hill. The place where Alice was staying didn't have a phone, so she was in for a surprise.

A few hours later, Carl stood outside Our Lady of Mount Carmel Church, with the wind off Prospect Bay whipping at his pant legs. The village sat at the foot of a long hill, a cluster of fishermen's houses dominated by the Catholic church's tall steeple. Not far from Halifax in distance, but a world away in lifestyle. Hard to imagine a city girl like Alice being happy here, but according to Georgie, she was.

If Naomi could see the place, she'd love it. Only a few copses of stunted spruce clung to the rocky soil. A stretch of rugged, empty land sloped from the top of the hill down to the water, ending in a black tumble of boulders. Naomi's winds would find her here.

Carl didn't know which house belonged to Liam's cousin, but morning mass had just ended and the first worshippers had just come out of the church and hurried off to their Sunday dinners. Carl waited by the church steps to see if Alice would appear.

And there she was, her long golden-brown hair loose around the shoulders of her navy coat. She'd never bobbed her hair like Georgie. Alice had always been a little old-fashioned. Carl had forgotten how pretty she was.

A blond, broad-shouldered man walked by her side. Liam. By the way he moved, his leg must have healed well after his surgery. He had only a slight limp now. Carl struggled with the old dislike. It had no place here.

Alice and Liam spoke to the priest, then joined hands and continued down the church steps. Carl's heart started to race. As Alice got closer, he saw it all on her face – love, grief, a new maturity and confidence. Everything he hadn't been able to see before he left. Alice, the one he'd considered slow. The one he'd always treated with contempt.

Of course, so had the rest of the family. As a kid, Alice had missed a year of school after a bad bout of measles, and she'd never caught up. In fact, she'd never learned to read, but very few people knew that.

Carl had never stopped to think how smart Alice must really be to cope so well. Since she couldn't follow recipes, she cooked by instinct, and cooked well. She had an amazing memory, and she'd inherited their mother's musical talent. No wonder Liam had said what he did in the hospital. 'I hope when Alice marries, she tells the lot of you to go to Hell.' And now she was going to marry Liam.

Watch your mouth, O'Neill. You're here to mend fences, not break them.

Carl stepped forward and caught Alice's attention. Her mouth opened wide with shock. Liam followed her glance and stiffened, eyes flashing danger signals. Hand in hand, they came toward him. Carl met them halfway.

"Alice. Georgie told me you were here. I wanted to see for myself that you were all right.. You're looking well." He turned to the man at her side. "Hello, Liam."

Liam didn't reply. Alice held Carl's gaze for a moment. It seemed she saw something that reassured her, because she gave him a tentative smile.

"Carl, I always knew you'd be back someday."

"Yeah. I arrived at Aunt Sarah's last night. I'm sorry to surprise you like this, but I had no way to let you know I was coming." Carl exhaled slowly. At least Alice and Liam hadn't walked away. "There are a lot of things I need to take care of here. I'm too late for some of them, but not for all. Is there someplace we can talk? You, too, Liam. I owe both of you an explanation and an apology."

Alice and Liam exchanged glances. Liam squeezed her hand, then gave Carl a curt nod.

"Come along. We're staying with my cousin Jess. His wife will have dinner ready. There'll be room for one more at the table."

No one spoke as they walked to a grey, shingled house at the edge of the bay, with a workshop across the yard. Carl's galloping heart slowed a little. At least Liam hadn't forbidden Alice to talk to him. Now, he'd damn well better come up with the right words.

They stopped in the bustling kitchen for a brief introduction to Liam's cousin Jess and his family. Their faces barely registered. Carl followed Alice and Liam into the sitting room. They sat together on the sofa, waiting while he took a chair and fumbled for a beginning.

"I don't know where to start, except to say I'm sorry. For the way I treated Mother, for the way I treated both of you. For all of it."

Alice held his gaze, her hand still tucked into Liam's. No wonder she remained aloof, uncertain. Those last few weeks at home, Carl had kept the family in turmoil with his drinking and his temper. Now he was back, just when she'd found some happiness. She'd expect him to try and ruin it like he'd ruined so many other things for her when they were kids.

"Where have you been, Carl?"

"Out West. Vancouver. Far enough away that I could never hurt you again."

She shook her head. "Carl, I told you... I know you didn't know what you were doing that day."

Truth was, all Carl remembered of that morning was waking up from one of his terrors, coming downstairs and finding Alice in the kitchen with Liam, who'd dropped by to see Georgie. He didn't know why, but somehow, the sight of them together had touched off Carl's powder-keg temper. That was it, except for the shame after his rage passed and he saw what he'd done.

"No, I didn't, but that doesn't excuse what I did."

Regret and a little doubt showed on Alice's face, but no anger. "What's past is past. Did Aunt Sarah and Georgie tell you Mother's at Mount Olivet?"

"Yes. I went to see her this morning before coming out here."

Alice's eyes misted over in a moment of raw grief. Liam stepped into the breach. "So you left to keep from hurting your family, and to stay out of the Army. Why did you come back? What's changed?"

His words goaded.

His skepticism grated.

Carl paused to choose his words and prayed they'd ring true. "I'd made up my mind to stay out there under an assumed name and leave the family in peace. I thought it was the best thing I could do for everyone, and I couldn't face the thought of going back overseas, but I found I couldn't live with myself. I was halfway home when I found out about the explosion from a newspaper. I was so afraid there'd be no one left when I got here."

"Were you working out there?"

"Not at first. As you know, I wasn't in the best of shape when I left Halifax. Well, I got sick. They put me off the train in a small town in Saskatchewan." Carl turned to face Alice. "Something happened to me out there. I don't know if I can explain it. Those people didn't know me from Adam, but they saved my life and asked for nothing in return, just because I was stranded and needed help." He looked into Alice's eyes. Did she believe him? "I did a lot of thinking while I was getting well. Then I moved on to the West Coast and found a job at the dockyard, but I decided I didn't want to be looking over my shoulder for the rest of my life. I'm going to report tomorrow."

While Carl told his story, Liam's expression had changed from hostility to grudging respect. Perhaps the most telling thing was that he released Alice's hand.

"I said before that you have guts, Carl."

"Yeah. Liam, what's happened to your family?" Liam's parents and his older brother's family lived on Kaye Street, only a stone's throw from Russell. Carl wasn't sure he should ask, but when Alice and Liam married, his family would be hers, too.

"Plenty. Mum lost an eye and Dad was badly cut, but they'll both heal. Nolan's lucky to be alive. After the explosion, there was a huge wave. It swept him off the deck of a ship, then dropped him back on it again. He's got a broken leg and a bad concussion. Ruth has a broken arm. Drew got away with just some cuts…but they lost Emily."

"Christ." Of course Liam's brother, a ship's pilot, would have been on the Harbour that morning. Carl recalled seeing Nolan with his daughter, a dark-eyed, black-curled little thing as cute as a button. Nolan and his wife must be heartbroken. "She was only three or four, wasn't she?"

"She was almost five. They've moved Mother and Nolan to the hospital in Truro, and everyone else is staying with Ruth's family there."

Alice took Liam's hand again and changed the subject. "Carl, who were the people who took you in?"

Carl told them about Naomi and her father. He guessed he said more than he'd intended, because Alice smiled and her eyes took on a soft light.

"Do you understand that you've fallen in love? Because you have."

He smiled back. "You're right. I have."

"I think you really have changed. Before you left, you could never have recognized that or admitted it." Alice rose. "I have to go upstairs and get Nicholas, and I have something to give to you."

244

"My medal? Georgie told me you had it. Keep it for me for now, Alice. There'll be time enough for that once I've straightened things out with the Army, and with Naomi." Besides, Alice had already given him far more than he'd dared to hope for.

"All right. Now it sounds like dinner is ready."

At the table, Carl was grateful for the constant chatter of Jess and Fanny's three children. It meant that he didn't have to talk, and he'd said enough for today. While he ate, he stole glances at Alice and Liam. They sat together, with Liam's little boy, Nicholas, in a high chair at Alice's side.

She fed the baby, who looked close to a year old, like an experienced mother. Liam's gaze never left them for long. He watched Alice with an intensity that bordered on desperation, as if she were a piece of driftwood keeping him afloat in stormy waters. Carl knew the feeling. Whatever his worries and regrets, it looked like Alice wouldn't be one of them. She'd done just fine on her own, in spite of her family.

Carl had to leave right after dinner to get back to Bedford before dark. Alice walked out to his horse with him and wrapped her arms around him. Then she stepped back, hugging herself against the cold sea breeze.

"I'm looking forward to meeting your Naomi someday, Carl. She must be special."

"She is." Carl laid his hands on her shoulders. In her crimson wool dress, with roses in her cheeks, she looked so young and glowing that it was no wonder Liam couldn't take his eyes off her. "So are you. Don't ever forget it. And Liam had better not forget it, either. Alice, can you really forgive me for selling you short all these years? You deserved so much better from all of us."

Alice smiled, then her gaze turned thoughtful. "I can. You followed Dad's lead, Carl, like children do. As for me, I think Liam's changed me as much as Naomi has changed you. You and I were always afraid of life, weren't we? Afraid of trying, afraid of failing."

"I suppose so."

She stepped back, squared her shoulders. A tall girl, Alice had always slumped a bit to hide her height, but now she stood straight as a young birch. "I'm not afraid anymore. I'm learning to read music, and when I've learned a little more I'm going to start giving lessons. Liam's apprenticing with Jess, learning to build and repair boats. He's going to be a shipwright, and we're going to be happy. We've *chosen* to be happy. Because it is a choice, you know."

Her voice rang with determination. Could this be Carl's shy, hesitant sister, who'd never talked back, never put herself forward? It looked like he was going to have to get to know her all over again. If he didn't get shipped out before he had the chance.

"You look very comfortable with the baby."

"We're still getting used to each other, but I love him."

"What about his mother?"

Alice's chin lifted. "She was downtown when the explosion happened. A lot of people down there just disappeared. She might turn up yet, but if she does, Liam's going to ask her to let us keep Nicholas. If she says no and takes him back to England, then we'll have to accept that as her choice and get to know Nicholas later, when he's older."

Carl shook his head in wonder. "Alice, I don't think Liam has changed you. I think you've changed yourself."

Her gaze softened. "Carl, I think I understand a little more now about what you went through overseas. I see every day what being over there did to Liam, even though he hasn't said much." She hesitated, her breath steaming in the frosty air. "Do you really think you'll have to go back?"

Carl didn't think of trying to soothe her. Not this new Alice. "I expect when I report, I'll be arrested. Then it will all depend on who ends up handling my case. I'll be more of a problem than anything else to the Army right now. That could work in my favour, or not."

Alice's voice trembled a little. "If you have to go, you won't go without saying goodbye this time, will you?"

"No. Never again."

She hugged him again, tighter this time. "Welcome home, Carl."

Carl climbed into the sleigh and drove off, with Alice watching from the yard. He stopped at the top of the hill and looked over his shoulder for one last glimpse of her. She waved, then returned to the house.

What she'd said about being afraid resonated deeply inside Carl. He'd always thought he was more like Georgie. Always in control, not needing anyone, able to give as good as he got. *Yeah, right.* Naomi had proven him wrong, and Alice had seen through him, right to his shaky core. As for Georgie, maybe she wasn't as tough as she pretended to be, either.

Carl let the horse go at an easy pace along the winding coastal road, so it was dusk by the time he got close to Halifax. A painful mixture of relief and regret tore through him. So much lost, and so much found. He clung to the warmth of Alice's and Georgie's acceptance as he gathered his courage to face tomorrow.

Chapter 21

Carl caught the morning train to Dartmouth, a smaller city that faced Halifax across the Harbour. The damage there wasn't quite as severe. At Uncle David's house a few blocks up from the waterfront, Carl knocked and waited, spine tingling with déjà vu. Another relative he hadn't seen in years. Like Aunt Sarah, his father's brother had never been a significant part of Carl's life.

When he'd called earlier and spoken to Aunt Bets, he didn't ask if his father wanted to see him. He just said he was back in town and on his way. Let the chips fall where they may.

What have you got to lose, O'Neill? Things can't get much worse between you than they were when you left.

Footsteps sounded in the hall. Carl's pulse thundered in his ears. *Shit.* He'd promised himself he'd keep control, expect nothing, not let his father get under his skin, but that wasn't easy when he felt so damned guilty for waiting too long to come home.

The door opened. His father stood there, his right arm in a sling, his blue eyes – so like Carl's – as cool and uncompromising as ever.

"Carl."

In spite of himself, Carl's mouth went dry. His father's face showed no shock, but it also showed no welcome. Wasn't that what Carl deserved?

"Dad. I guess Bets told you I was coming. Can I come in?"

His father nodded, turned away and started down the hall. Carl followed and caught a quick glimpse of Uncle David and Aunt Bets in the sitting room as he passed. In the kitchen, his father leaned against the counter.

"You've got some nerve, showing yourself here now."

Carl's grip on his temper slipped. His father had reason enough to be angry now, and Carl had given him reason enough in the past, but that didn't mean his tone didn't hurt. "You might recall I had some unfinished business with the Army."

"You had some unfinished business with your family." His father tried to stare him down, but Carl refused to look away.

"That's the other reason I came."

"Too bad you weren't in time for your mother's funeral."

That drove a knife into Carl's gut. He caught his breath and took a seat at the table. Doctor Franklin's words came back to him. 'Keep in mind that one day it will be too late.'

"Yes, it is. I went to see her yesterday, then out to Prospect to see Alice. It really threw me when Georgie told me Liam and Alice were engaged, but she's happy."

His father stepped away from the counter. His hands curled into fists. "Alice should know better. Liam fathered a child with some girl overseas. Then he came home and took up with Georgie. Now it's Alice. He doesn't know what he wants, and she's too blind to see it."

If it hadn't been for the scorn in his father's tone, Carl would have thought that fair enough. His father hadn't seen Liam and Alice together lately, and even if he had, he wouldn't have noticed the feeling Carl had seen between them yesterday. Before Naomi, he wouldn't have noticed it himself.

"Georgie told me a different story last night. She said she knew all along that Liam wasn't serious about her. She also said his English girl married someone else while he was in hospital over there. I guess that gives a man the right to look elsewhere. After seeing him and Alice together yesterday, I think they're good for each other. Georgie thinks so, too." Carl paused, remembering the determination on Alice's face, and her words. 'We've chosen to be happy.' "I don't think any of us have ever given Alice the credit she deserves. I apologized to her for that yesterday."

His father turned away, shoulders stiff. Hiding his grief, the way he'd always hidden any sign of vulnerability. "It's too bad you can't apologize to your mother for breaking her heart."

"I know. Mother deserved a lot better from me. For the rest of my life I'll wish I'd had the chance to tell her so." Carl stopped before his voice could break, swallowed and went on. "Georgie said Mother never gave up on me."

His father turned to face him again. "Helen never was able to see you as you really are, Carl."

"Thank God for that. Dad, when I leave here I'm going to report and let the Army figure out what to do with me. What do you think Mother would want from us now? I don't think she'd want us to fight."

His father's anger faded, leaving him looking lost and sad and old, though he was only forty-five. "No, she wouldn't. What do we have to fight about, anyway? We've always been strangers. As far as I'm concerned, we always will be."

"Yeah." Carl got to his feet. Maybe he'd only make things worse, but he couldn't help himself. "That's something we have in common, isn't it? We're both good at being strangers. With each other, with the world. But I'm tired of it. I met a few people out West who made me see that."

His father shrugged. "Then maybe that's where you belong."

"Maybe it is."

Carl struggled to speak around the lump in his throat. Had he really expected this to turn out any other way? Apparently he had. "I guess I'd better go. I'll be in touch with the girls. I promised Alice that I wouldn't leave again without saying goodbye."

"Goodbye, Carl." His father walked out of the kitchen. A few seconds later, his footsteps sounded on the hall stairs. Carl stayed where he was for a moment until the mist in his eyes cleared.

Mother, I tried.

Carl spent a few minutes with Uncle David and Aunt Bets before leaving. "Don't take your father too much to heart," Uncle David said. "Your mother was the love of his life, you know. She just never knew how to handle him."

No, she hadn't, but Carl knew his father had been the love of her life, too. That was the hardest thing of all to understand.

Carl caught the ferry across the Harbour to Halifax. The ride gave him his first clear view of Richmond. He'd seen nothing worse overseas. Almost nothing recognizable remained, but he picked out the heap of brick that had once been the Acadia Sugar Refinery, where his father worked. He'd lost his livelihood as well as his wife. What would he do now?

Financially, he'd be all right. The house had been insured, and Carl's father had always been smart with money. He could afford to take some time to look for another job, but he wasn't the type of man who'd be content doing nothing. And he'd be alone.

Alice would be marrying and moving away, and her father disapproved of her husband. Georgie had worked at the Halifax Herald office for the last two years, and said she liked it. She'd never been domestically inclined. 'Dad's going to need a housekeeper, but it isn't going to be me,' she'd said last night. So there their father was, alienated from Alice and Carl and at arm's length from Georgie. Strangers.

His choice, but that didn't ease Carl's sadness in the least.

Wellington Barracks, where he'd intended to report, had been badly damaged according to Georgie, so Carl headed up from the waterfront toward the Halifax Common, where a makeshift compound had been set up months ago to accommodate the overflow of military personnel in the city. The downtown streets were full of people repairing buildings, picking up relief supplies and checking casualty lists for the names of missing loved ones. Just over a week since the explosion, and the city was still staggering to its feet.

No thanks to you, O'Neill. Carl trained his gaze straight ahead and hurried on. Even if he'd been here earlier, he wouldn't have been of much use in the stockade.

He reached the edge of the Common and looked south across the open space, toward the white-stucco bulk of Camp Hill Hospital. He'd never forget his few painful days there. The building was supposed to be torn down when peace returned, but Carl expected it would be there for good. Too many of the patients would need care for the rest of their lives.

The military compound sat on the north side of the Common, a collection of long wooden huts covered with grey roofing paper. Carl had left his ID tags behind when he left Halifax, so he told the sentry at the gate that he was reporting after extended leave and had lost his tags and uniforms in the explosion.

"Go see Major Murphy, sir. He's second in command here." The sentry pointed. "His office is over there."

Major Murphy looked to be in his forties, with salt and pepper hair, glasses and a harassed expression. He took in Carl's civilian clothes and put on a formidable frown.

"What's your business here?"

"Lieutenant Carl O'Neill reporting, sir. I have a problem."

By dusk, the problem wasn't any closer to solution. Instead of having him marched back downtown to the stockade, the major had confined Carl to a storage hut full of barrels and boxes, with two MPs standing guard at the door. The place smelled of sawdust, motor oil and dampness. He alternated between sitting on a packing crate and pacing in a vain attempt to keep warm. Busy as everyone was, it might be three or four days before anyone found time to deal with him.

At least they'd let him call Georgie. Carl started pacing the hut again, stamping his feet to get his blood running and ease his frustration. Georgie and Alice had been through more than enough lately without more trouble from him.

Naomi. God, how he wanted Naomi. Just to see her, to hear her voice, something warm and bright in a cold, dark world. How long would it be? By the time he was free to go back to her, would it be too late? Her life was changing, too. Would time push them too far apart?

Just after dark, someone spoke to the guards at the door. Expecting supper, Carl stood. He snapped to attention when Major Murphy walked in, carrying a file folder under his arm. He must have had Carl's personnel file brought up from downtown.

"Sir."

Murphy looked just as harassed as before. He glared from behind his glasses. "Where have you been, O'Neill? We sure as hell could have used you here lately."

"I know, sir."

Carl didn't know what to make of Murphy. He might be a strictly by-the-book type or he might not, but one thing he was for sure, was annoyed. He pulled a sheet from the file, read it and shoved it back in the folder with disgust.

"Suspected bootlegging. Fighting. Failure to check in while on leave. You were right, you have one hell of a problem, and now so do I."

Carl had been involved in enough disciplinary situations to know he'd better say as little as possible. He settled for, "Yes, sir."

Major Murphy pulled out another paper and paced the floor while he read it. "Wounded and captured at Guillemont. Escaped from a reprisal camp." He stopped and held Carl's gaze over the top of the sheet. "I'd like to hear how you managed that."

Still at attention, Carl felt the ropes that had bound him in the camp yard closing around him again. "I was part of a detail sent to get water. We were close to the French lines, and we came under fire. The guards pulled us back, but I made a break and ran toward the guns. I was lucky. I got through. As far as I could tell, the enemy thought I'd been killed. They didn't come looking for me."

The major removed his glasses, put them in his pocket and laid his paper and the file on a barrel. He looked Carl up and down as if seeing him for the first time. "A bit reckless, don't you think?"

"Perhaps, sir. The object of that camp was for us to die slowly. I decided I'd rather die fast. If I'd escaped any other way, if they hadn't thought I was dead, they would have shot another prisoner as a warning to the rest." No. Surely the guards hadn't done that. Surely they'd reported him killed to avoid getting into trouble themselves. Carl wouldn't allow himself to believe anything else.

Major Murphy took a moment to consider that. By now, he looked more curious than angry. "And you brought home a Military Cross. You've had quite a war, Lieutenant, I'll give you that. So, were you buying or selling liquor the night you got beaten up?"

"Neither, sir. Let's just say I was in the wrong place at the wrong time. As for the fight, that was self defense."

Murphy nodded. "It hardly seems likely that you'd start a fight with three men." He picked up the file again. "Disappearing while on leave is another matter entirely."

"Yes, sir."

Was that a glimmer of sympathy in the major's eyes? It came and went so quickly Carl couldn't be sure. Murphy studied him for another long moment, then sighed.

"At ease, Lieutenant."

"Thank you, sir."

Murphy tapped the folder. "I have a report here from the doctor who treated you at Camp Hill. It was his opinion that you're no longer fit for active duty. If you hadn't run off half-cocked, there's a good chance you'd have an honourable discharge by now."

Yes, that was sympathy in Murphy's eyes. Perhaps luck was with Carl after all, but it wouldn't be the major who decided his fate. "It wasn't the best decision I've ever made, sir."

But it had led Carl to Naomi.

It was getting too dark in the hut to see. Major Murphy switched on the light – a single light bulb hanging on a cord from the ceiling – and sat on the edge of a barrel. "Sit, Lieutenant." Carl returned to his crate. The major put on his glasses again, held Carl's gaze. "You're from Richmond. Where's your family?"

"My father and sisters are staying with relatives. My mother was killed in the explosion, sir."

"My condolences."

"Thank you, sir."

With another sigh, Murphy rose. "It's not up to me to hand you a sentence, Lieutenant. That will have to wait for a court-martial, and that's going to take a while. I have to decide what to do with you in the meantime."

"Yes, sir."

The major lowered his voice as if he didn't want the guards outside to hear him. "Given your service record, the fact that you've turned yourself in, and the fact that you're bereaved, I think I have some choices. Here's one of them. If you'll give your word that you won't disappear again, I can have you put in charge of a work detail until your trial comes up. Do your job and stay out of trouble, and it will only help your case."

A work detail. So Carl wouldn't have to wait in jail for his fate to be decided. He hadn't realized how much he'd been dreading being locked up again until that moment. "Yes, sir."

"Do you have a uniform?"

"Not at present, sir."

"Report to stores, three buildings down from here, and get one. Then go back to wherever you're staying and get whatever personal items you need. I'll expect you to report to me tomorrow morning at nine hundred hours for your assignment. When you aren't working, you will be confined to this compound until your trial. That will be all." Murphy started for the door, stopped and looked over his shoulder. "Oh, and Lieutenant..."

"Sir?"

"Welcome home."

Chapter 22

Three days later, Carl stood at the corner of Russell and Gottingen, by the ruins of St. Joseph's, looking downhill toward home. The detail had just started removing shattered timbers and knocking down the unstable remains of the church's brick walls. They'd been doing similar jobs in other parts of Richmond since Carl was put in command, but this was their first day here.

The heavy work of clearing the neighbourhood would have to wait until spring. The whole hillside looked like it had been shelled. The remains of the homes Carl remembered still lay where they'd fallen. The only sounds were those of the men working. No wind swirled up from the Narrows, no familiar voices broke the ghostly stillness.

It had been rough dealing with the men at first. They knew he was awaiting discipline, and they knew why, but Major Murphy had made sure they knew about Carl's imprisonment and his medal, too. Some of the men had come home from overseas wounded themselves, and were more than thankful not to be going back. Once they'd seen that Carl wasn't too proud to work alongside them, they'd given him their respect.

At lunch time, Carl beckoned to the corporal in charge of the team working at the walls. "Bryant, you're in command. I'll be back in fifteen minutes." Bryant nodded and went back to his meal without asking questions. He knew Carl was from this neighbourhood.

Carl started down the hill, snow squeaking under his stiff new boots. When he reached home, he followed the partially filled prints his father and the girls had left when they went through the remains of the house for personal items, up the front walk to the sitting room window. That was where his mother had been when the explosion happened – at her piano.

Shards of polished wood reflected the afternoon sun...bits and pieces of the piano and the rest of the furniture. Everything else was covered by the collapsed upper floor. The remains of Carl's bedroom dresser lay on top of the pile, partially covered by a piece of the roof.

They hadn't found much that belonged to him. He'd never been one to accumulate things, never put much of himself into any place. When he'd gone overseas and again when he headed west, he'd left nothing behind but a couple of books and some clothes. And his medal.

He closed his eyes and saw himself sitting on the prairie behind the Franklins' home, with Naomi beside him. *'Overseas, some of the men used to talk about home the way you do. I never knew if I envied them or not.'* He still didn't know. Was it easier to grieve for something you'd lost than to regret something you'd never had?

By the time the leaves came out all the debris would be gone, leaving no trace of the old neighbourhood except for empty cellars and the new boys' school up on the corner. There'd be no reason for Carl to come back here again. If he wanted a home, he'd have to make one for himself.

And now he could offer Naomi his name. He'd almost done just that in the letter he'd written yesterday, but he'd stopped short of proposing. He wanted to wait until he could ask her in person. Still, he thought he'd made his feelings clear.

Naomi, as soon as I can I'm coming west again. I don't belong here now. I don't feel like I belong anywhere, except where you are.

He spent another minute or two with his memories, then walked back up to the church, joined the men and worked with them until sweat ran down his back under his thick greatcoat. At dusk, they marched back to the Common to mess. Afterward, Carl found himself at loose ends.

He ached all over. He'd worked hard today, but it had helped to keep his mind away from the past, and the future. The thought of spending the rest of the evening by the stove in his hut, with nothing to do, didn't appeal at all, but he didn't feel like spending the evening in the Officers' Mess either.

Might as well call Georgie. He hadn't talked to her for a couple of days. In the office a couple of huts down the row, the clerk looked up from his newspaper at Carl's request to use the phone. "I'll ask you to keep it short, please, Lieutenant." He retreated to the back room to give Carl some privacy.

Georgie's voice on the other end of the line went a long way to ease Carl's loneliness. He told her about seeing home. "Georgie, I don't think I could live here now. I felt more at home in Mackenzie than I ever did here. Dad said maybe I belonged out there, and I think he might be right."

Silence. "Georgie, are you still there?"

"Yes. Carl, maybe it isn't really that you can't live here anymore. Maybe it's something else. You really miss Naomi, don't you?"

"Of course I do."

"I thought so, so I did something today... Maybe it was interfering, but it's done."

Carl couldn't remember her ever sounding guilty like that. He got a firm hold on his temper. "What did you do, Georgie?"

"I wired that couple you mentioned, the ones you stayed with for awhile. The Foleys. I asked them where Naomi was, and I told them you were here."

Jesus, Mary and Joseph. He could hear from Naomi tomorrow...or he could hear that she wanted nothing to do with him. "Georgie, I..." He'd intended to say that he wished she hadn't done that, but he couldn't. Truth was he wished he'd had the nerve to wire Barry and Corinne himself, but he'd wanted to wait until he could offer Naomi more than words, until he could tell her he'd faced his problems here.

"Carl?"

He dragged himself back to earth. *Don't get your hopes up, O'Neill.* But his pulse wouldn't stop racing. "Yeah, guess I should thank you. Georgie, let me know as soon as you get an answer, will you?"

He didn't have to wait long. The next evening, he called Georgie again.

"Have you heard anything?"

"Yes. Guess where she is?"

Her teasing tone made Carl want to reach through the receiver and shake her. "Georgie, don't do this to me."

"All right, all right. I'll take pity on you. Are you sitting down?"

Standing in the same office where he'd used the phone before, Carl glanced into the back room where the clerk was working, then dropped into the desk chair. "Okay, I'm sitting. Now tell me. I'm going to get chased out of here in a minute."

"All right. She's in Halifax, working at Camp Hill."

Carl nearly dropped the phone. *Christ.* Here he was, perhaps only a few city blocks instead of half a continent away from Naomi, and he couldn't leave the compound. How difficult would it be to sneak out of here and— *Think, O'Neill. Getting yourself thrown into the stockade isn't going to make seeing her any easier.* For once in his life, for Naomi's sake, he'd try to play by the rules first. If that didn't work, then all bets were off. "Look, Georgie, I need you to help me out with this."

Naomi shrugged into her coat as she walked through the quiet hospital lobby. Over the last several days, work had slipped back into its normal routine. The injured from the explosion had all been sent home or transferred elsewhere, leaving only the military patients to care for.

At this hour, most of them were having supper. Other than the receptionist and Naomi, the only person in the lobby was a petite, rather pretty young woman with bobbed chestnut hair that framed her face in soft curls. When she saw Naomi, she rose from her chair and hurried toward her.

"Excuse me, are you Naomi Franklin?"

"Yes. I don't believe we've met."

"We haven't. My name is Georgie O'Neill. I think you know my brother, Carl."

The family resemblance was slight, but telling. Georgie had a feminine version of Carl's chin, and her eyes were the same shape, though they were green instead of blue. Blood rushed to Naomi's face. Carl couldn't know she was here, but he must have told Georgie about her. By letter, or in person? "Yes...yes, I do. Where is he?"

Georgie's grin bore more than a passing resemblance to Carl's, especially with that touch of self-satisfaction. "He's here in Halifax, and he's fine. Are you on your way home?"

"Yes. I mean, yes, I'm on my way home." So much for dignity. Then again, Georgie was probably used to girls making fools of themselves over her brother. She appeared to take Naomi's confusion as a matter of course.

"If you don't mind, I'll walk with you for a few minutes."

They started along Robie Street. Naomi was reeling with the news, and still hadn't caught her breath, but Georgie answered her most pressing questions without being asked.

"Carl's at the compound over on the North Common. You probably know he was absent without leave. They've put him to work instead of locking him up for now, but he's going to face discipline eventually. He's confined to the compound when he's not working, otherwise he'd have come to see you himself. He's written to you, but of course you haven't gotten his letters."

"No. I left Mackenzie sooner than I expected. This opportunity came up, and I took it."

Georgie's voice softened with sympathy. "Carl told me about your father. I'm sorry."

"Thank you. How did Carl find out I was here?"

Another self-satisfied grin. "I found out for him. He didn't want to contact you until he knew what was going to happen to him, but I knew how badly he missed you, so I decided to meddle. Was I wrong?"

"Wrong? Oh, Georgie... No. You weren't wrong. The explosion... Was anyone in your family hurt?" Naomi scolded herself for waiting this long to ask. She felt even worse when Georgie winced.

"My father was badly cut, and we lost Mother...before Carl arrived home."

His mother. How sad. Carl had wanted so badly to make amends to her. Naomi's regret cut almost as deep as his must. "What a shame. Carl told me things were difficult between him and his family. He wanted to change that, especially with your mother."

"I know. Carl and I have had a couple of long talks, and he's been to see Alice. I think things are going to be different between us from now on."

"I'm glad. Do you think Carl will be allowed to see me?"

"I don't know about his being allowed, but I know my brother. He always finds a way to get what he wants, and he wants to see you. Go to the compound and ask. The worst they can do is say 'no,' and if they do, you can write to him or phone him." Georgie pulled a slip of paper from her purse. "Here's the mailing address and phone number. Mine are there as well. I'm staying with my aunt in Bedford. Give me yours and I'll pass them on."

In her smart chocolate-coloured suit and coat, Georgie looked very much the stylish city girl. Naomi doubted they had much in common, but she didn't doubt they'd find things to laugh about once they got to know each other. She found a pencil and tore a corner from the note. "Georgie, we don't have a phone, but here's my address. I don't know how to thank you."

"I don't know exactly where things stand between you and Carl, but I know he's a different man than he was when he left here. For that, I don't know how to thank *you*." Georgie gave Naomi a quick hug. "Now I have to hurry if I'm going to catch my train back to Bedford. Good night."

With a squeeze of Naomi's hand, Georgie hurried off, a herald angel wearing the latest winter hat from Bon Marché. Naomi turned and ran in the other direction, toward the Common. Toward Carl.

A raw, sore place deep inside her closed over. The things he'd said in his farewell note weren't empty words. In the end, he hadn't chosen life under someone else's name over a life that could include her. For the first time since he'd left and her father passed away, Naomi saw life in colour again.

When she got within sight of the compound, she stopped to catch her breath and gather her thoughts. It wouldn't do to arrive at the gate looking like some kind of wild creature. She wasn't some girl Carl had met downtown. She was a professional nurse inquiring after a friend and former patient.

A chain-link fence surrounded the compound. The sentries at the gate smirked at each other when she approached them.

"Can we help you, miss?"

Naomi sized them up. Both around twenty at a guess, waiting to be shipped overseas and desperate to prove themselves. She'd put dozens of boys like these two in their place, but for Carl's sake, she'd give them the chance to act like gentlemen.

"I hope so. My name is Naomi Franklin, and I'm a nurse at Camp Hill. I've been told that a former patient of mine, Lieutenant Carl O'Neill, is assigned here. I'd like to see him if he's available."

One of the sentries, a tall, good-looking kid who seemed to see himself as quite a ladies' man, smirked again as he looked her slowly up and down. "Miss, we don't allow ladies in here."

The way he said 'ladies' made Naomi's cheeks heat. It would be a satisfaction to find a telephone, call the compound and report the boor, but Carl was too close for her to give up that easily. "All right, I'll give you a message for him."

"Can't do that, miss. We aren't messenger boys."

Enough. Naomi gave the boy a vicious glare along with her most charming smile. "Fine. I'll phone instead, and I'll tell Lieutenant O'Neill that you refused to take a message or take me to him. Good evening, gentlemen."

She turned to walk away, counting off the seconds under her breath. Before she got to five, the other sentry called out.

"Wait a minute, miss. There's something you don't understand."

Naomi turned back and favoured them both with another smile. It seemed neither of these boys cared to find themselves in Carl's bad books. In trouble he might be, but he was still their superior and would no doubt enjoy making their lives hell.

"What's that?"

"Lieutenant O'Neill's not allowed to leave the compound except for work. He's got trouble, and you'll only make it worse."

Naomi took a moment to enjoy the boys' discomfort before replying. "I know exactly what Lieutenant O'Neill's trouble is, and I have no intention of making it worse. Will you please just tell him I'm here?"

The sentries exchanged another glance, then the good-looking one nodded. "All right, I'll go and tell him. You stay right here."

Carl picked up the book he'd brought from Aunt Sarah's, riffled through the pages and then threw it on his bed. Jesus, Mary and Joseph, this was killing him. Georgie had said she'd find a way to speak to Naomi today, but what if she'd failed? What if Naomi didn't happen to be working? What if Georgie had left a note and it hadn't gotten delivered? He was going to Hell on a road of 'what ifs.'

To think Naomi had been here in Halifax while he'd been longing to be back in Mackenzie with her. Had she been hurt? Georgie said she'd been here for the explosion, so she hadn't stayed at home long after her father's death. Now here she was, grieving and alone at the other end of the country.

No, she wouldn't be alone. She'd have Laura. Naomi would never leave her behind. She couldn't have gotten Carl's letter before she left home, and there hadn't been time for it to have reached her here. Did she think he'd given up on her? That he didn't care enough to risk coming home for her sake?

Patience. She had a job here. She wouldn't be leaving any time soon. Eventually, Georgie would contact her.

But Carl could find himself in jail or shipping out before that happened.

Working in the old neighbourhood was difficult enough, but confinement and boredom in the evenings was ten times worse. He started swearing, then stopped mid-stream when he heard footsteps outside.

Whoever it was knocked on his door. Carl opened it to Private Driscoll, one of the night's sentries. The smile on the kid's face made Carl's hands curl into fists. "What is it, Driscoll?"

"There's a young lady at the gate asking for you, Lieutenant."

Carl's heart threatened to burst out of his chest. *Calm down, O'Neill. It's probably Georgie stopping to tell you she had to leave a message for Naomi.* "Did she give you her name?"

"It's Naomi Franklin, sir."

Driscoll watched him closely, looking for a reaction. Carl refused to give him one, just as he'd refused to react in the reprisal camp. If not for that experience, he'd probably have made a complete idiot of himself. "Thank you, Private. Go and tell her I'll be right there."

He shut the door, waited a few seconds and started swearing again, with a fierce joy too deep for prayer. She wanted to see him. After weeks of feeling like the only person on the planet, the joy and relief of finding her so near brought tears to Carl's eyes.

Christ, O'Neill, pull yourself together. She's out there waiting for you. Carl glanced in his mirror to make sure his uniform looked respectable and his face showed no traces of tears, then he picked up his greatcoat and stuck his arms in the sleeves while he ran across the compound to Major Murphy's quarters. Thank all the powers that be, the major was there.

"What is it, Lieutenant?"

Carl hadn't had a chance to speak to Murphy since reporting for assignment. He might earn himself a black mark by asking for what would look like special treatment now, but it was that or walk out of camp without permission. Not seeing Naomi wasn't an option.

"Major, I have a favour to ask." In a few quick sentences, Carl told Murphy about Naomi. "I had no idea she was in Halifax, but she's standing out at the gate now."

Murphy frowned, clearly annoyed at being faced with another judgement call. "Lieutenant, I thought I made it clear that you're confined to this compound after work."

Carl's stomach sank. Writing to Naomi or talking to her on the phone with others nearby wouldn't be enough to save his sanity.

"You did. Sir, I came back here and turned myself in for two reasons – my family, and this young lady. You've been more than fair to me and I respect your orders, but I need to talk to her. Alone." He paused to breathe, expecting his tongue to trip. "I want to ask her to marry me, sir, and I want to do it in person. If you'll give me permission to leave the compound, I give you my word of honour I'll be back here within two hours."

Murphy took off his glasses and held Carl's gaze. After a long, agonizing moment, the major nodded.

"From what I've been hearing, you're doing your work well and staying out of trouble. Now you've come to me instead of sneaking off, which makes me think you've learned a thing or two about acting on impulse. I think I can trust you for a couple of hours. I'll write you a pass."

"Thank you, sir."

Major Murphy signed the pass and handed it to Carl. Dizzy with relief, Carl tucked it in his coat pocket. "I'd better hurry, sir."

He snapped off a salute. Murphy returned it with a smile. "Good luck, Lieutenant."

Carl jogged to the gate, showed Driscoll his pass, hurried out and there stood Naomi, as beautiful as he remembered. So beautiful it knocked the breath from him. The cold air had put roses in her cheeks, just as it had the day he'd first gotten out of bed after his pneumonia and gone outside to see her. Only this time, instead of looking fearful, she glowed with excitement.

But he was in uniform, and the sentries were watching. Damned if he'd give them more than they already had to gossip about. He only allowed himself to take her hand, but that was enough to alert every nerve in his body.

"Naomi. I wasn't sure you'd want to see me."

She held his gaze, a challenging spark in her clear grey eyes. "Why wouldn't I? I told you I loved you."

"Yes, you did. And I hurt you."

"You did what you thought you had to do. You were wrong. Most people are now and then. How long do you have?"

That was like Naomi. After all, she hadn't judged him before. Maybe someday, Carl would find the words to tell her what she'd taught him about generosity.

"I have two hours. Where can we go?"

"To my place. It's not too far. Come on."

She dropped his hand and started running, slipping and sliding along the path across the Common. Carl jogged after her, thinking he could catch up easily, but the little vixen could run. He sped up, heart hammering, snow flying up to sting his face. Like being ten years old again.

Naomi didn't stop until she reached the sidewalk at the south end of the broad field. As Carl came up behind her, she turned so that he ran into her arms. He lifted her off the ground and buried his face against her neck.

She smelled like heaven. He didn't give a damn who saw them now. He knocked her hat off, kissed her hair. "God, Naomi, I've missed you."

She giggled. His mouth found, captured, claimed hers, and she responded with all the ardour of the night they'd spent together. The memory blended with the reality to set Carl on fire. He kissed her again, hard and deep, before he set her down. Naomi pulled off a glove and ran her thumb down his cheek, brushed her fingers over his wet lips.

"Carl, if I'm dreaming, I don't want to ever wake up."

Carl settled his hands at her waist. "I can't believe you're here. Half of me has been back in Mackenzie with you ever since I left. Naomi, I saw your father's obituary in the paper. I made up my mind then that I had to go back to you, but I needed to deal with things here first."

Naomi ran her hand over his back. "I think that deep down I knew you'd go home. But let's go. I don't want to waste a minute."

God bless you forever, Georgie. Naomi almost said the words aloud as she and Carl hurried along Robie Street. If it hadn't been for Georgie's interference, they might not have found each other for weeks. Maybe years – if Carl had to ship out again – maybe never.

How long would it be before he was tried and his sentence handed down? Naomi shook off the thought of what could come, refused to let it spoil this moment. She couldn't wait to be in his arms again.

It took them half an hour to get to Naomi's flat. It felt like a lifetime. They clattered up the stairs and into the narrow hall, gasping for breath, to be met by an astonished Laura.

"Ben – Carl, by all that's holy! Naomi, I was starting to wonder what was keeping you. Now I know."

Carl shrugged out of his greatcoat and gave Laura a quick hug. "Hello. You didn't really think you'd seen the last of me, did you?"

She looked him over, shook her head. "No, I can't say I did."

Carl sobered. "I'm sorry for sneaking away the way I did, Laura. I knew I had to go, and I was afraid that if I tried to say goodbye, I wouldn't be able to manage it."

Naomi kept her gaze on Carl while she took off her coat and hung it up. She just couldn't stop staring at him. She'd been so afraid she'd never see him again.

Beneath his excitement, Carl looked tired and strained. No wonder. He'd lost his mother and his home, and his future still hung in the balance. If only he could stay here, get some rest and let Naomi enjoy spoiling him for a while, but their two hours were ticking by.

"Laura, Carl's only free for a couple of hours and—"

"Say no more, child. I was on my way downstairs anyway. Mrs. Thompson asked me to come down for the evening, as her children are both out with relatives."

Of course Laura understood. She always had. Naomi hugged her. "Laura, I am so lucky to have you."

After Laura closed the hall door behind her, Naomi began undoing the buttons of Carl's uniform jacket, not an easy task when he kept distracting her with kisses wherever he could reach her. His teasing nibbles on her neck and ears did outrageous things to her nervous system, while some cool, logical part of her mind protested.

She'd never been so forward. *Forward?* Make that shameless. She trembled with haste to get beneath Carl's clothes to his warm skin. She slipped his jacket off his shoulders, hung it on the doorknob and undid the first few buttons on his shirt, then she burrowed into his arms and pressed her lips to the hollow of his throat, gathering his taste on her tongue before carrying it to his mouth. He let out a shuddering breath and molded her to him.

"Sweetheart, we should slow down."

"Do you think so?" She kissed him again, drew his tongue deep into her mouth while she slid her hand beneath his shirt. His muscles contracted at her touch and his heart raced in time with hers. Then Carl pulled away.

"Naomi, I don't know what's going to happen to me. It might be a long while before we can really be together."

"I know that."

"Then there's something I need to say." He put his hands on her shoulders. "I want to marry you. Life is short and fragile, and I want to spend whatever time I have with you. That's why I decided to come home. I want us to have children, and I want them to know my family, to have aunts and uncles and cousins. And I want them to know their father's not a deserter."

To hear him talk about family like that set a dozen imprisoned hopes free in Naomi's heart. Her family had always been so small, just her and her parents, and then Laura. Now she looked into the deep blue of Carl's eyes and saw sisters in Georgie and Alice, brothers in their husbands. Nieces and nephews. And of course, children of her own, including a dark-haired little boy like the one she'd dreamed of that night back home. A boy with Carl's face, free of shadows.

"There's nothing I want more."

Carl smiled, an amazed, vulnerable smile. "I know it sounds ridiculous, even disrespectful to ask you now, with your father gone such a short time and my mother..." His voice died away. Naomi ached for him, for the regret he'd carry for the rest of his life.

"Georgie told me about your mother. I'm so sorry you didn't get to talk to her. I know how badly you wanted to."

Carl blew out a breath. "I'm sorry, too, but Georgie said some things that have made it easier. I've made peace with her and Alice, at least." He paused, gathered himself. "What's done is done. Alice says she's choosing to be happy, and I want to do the same. With you. If I'm sentenced to jail, we'll marry as soon as I get out. If they send me overseas, we'll marry before I go – unless you'd rather wait."

Naomi took a moment, basked in the love written on Carl's face. "I don't want to wait. These last few weeks without you and Dad have been the loneliest of my life. I'd marry you tomorrow if we could manage it. I don't want to waste a minute of whatever time we have. Starting now."

She moved into his arms, pressed another kiss over his racing heart. With a hiss of breath, Carl pulled her against him and slid his fingers into her hair. "Oh, love. If you're sure this is what you want, I'm yours."

Naomi looked up at him, let everything she was feeling show. "I'm sure."

Carl bent his head and began teasing her lips, tracing them with his tongue. Wrapped up in the pleasure of it, Naomi didn't notice him undoing her blouse buttons until he reached inside to cup her breast through the silk of her slip. She pressed into his hand and opened her mouth against his in invitation, but he shifted to nip her chin.

"Not yet, love." He scooped her up in his arms, held her snug against his chest. "Where's your room?"

Naomi pointed to the door, then gave herself over to the thrill of being cradled in Carl's arms. He carried her into her bedroom, nudged the door shut with his foot and set her on her feet.

His mouth covered hers in the passionate kiss she craved. They had so little time, but they didn't rush. Instead, they savoured each other like two starving people savouring a meal. Clothing came off piece by piece, between kisses and caresses. His thumb stroking the hollow between her breasts made her sigh. Her fingertips following the line of his oblique under his trousers made him shiver. Skin sliding against smooth skin left them both breathless.

At last there was nothing between them. Carl backed Naomi toward the bed and followed her down.

Lying beneath him, cradling his weight, she took his face in her hands. Not so hard a face now, but still the face of a fighter. A man who wouldn't back up or back down, even when it might be smarter to do so. Naomi prized that deeply ingrained streak of stubborn defiance. Without it, Carl would never have survived to come back from overseas. He would never have gone west and landed on her doorstep, and he wouldn't have returned home to be here with her now.

Carl looked into her eyes, long and deep. "This is for keeps, Naomi. If we do this, there'll be no turning back."

"No turning back." How could there be when her muscles melted under his weight, while her heart lifted to the skies with certainty?

Her blood ran thick and hot with anticipation as she brought Carl down to her for a long, slow kiss. Then they lost themselves in other touching, tasting, teasing. Naomi rediscovered the long lines and hard curves of Carl's body, relearned the thrill of giving him pleasure, revelled in the pleasure he gave her.

There was one moment, just as Carl was about to join his body to hers, when Randall Clark's face flashed into Naomi's mind. Her body froze. Tears of shame came to her eyes. *Oh, God, I'm not going to be able to do this.* Carl lifted himself away from her, stroked her hair with a feather-light touch. "Naomi, sweetheart, this is me. I'd die before I'd hurt you."

"I know." And in that moment, her body knew, too. Carl kissed her tears away, and then took her with him to a peak of pleasure that brought new tears to her eyes, this time of sheer joy.

Chapter 23

Perfection. With nothing but that one word floating in his mind, Carl wrapped Naomi in his arms. Smoothly, warmly naked, her breasts pressed to his chest, her heart beating in time with his. Sheer perfection.

He'd discovered before that Naomi's body offered more in the way of generous curves and firm flesh than a man would suspect at first glance. A fairly tall girl like Alice, Naomi had a more substantial frame, a less willowy shape. Carl liked that, just as he liked the toughness hidden behind her natural grace.

The memory of the night she'd pulled her gun on him rose up to make him chuckle. Naomi lifted her head, peered at him through a cloud of tousled hair.

"What's funny?"

"I was just wondering if you brought your revolver to Halifax."

"I did. It'll go with me wherever I go."

"Why?"

"Because it will always remind me of you."

Carl rose up on his elbows to kiss her. The lightness inside him didn't feel quite warm enough for happiness, so what was it?

Hope, O'Neill. It must be hope.

"I really was in danger that night."

Naomi grinned. "Do you think I might really have shot you?"

"Yes, if I'd made a wrong move, but that's not what I meant. I meant that was when I fell in love with you, though I didn't know it then."

She nibbled his lips. "Hmmm. I'd never have thought of threatening a man with a pistol as a way to capture his heart."

Carl drew Naomi's head down to his shoulder. Maybe she hadn't captured his heart that night, but she'd opened it. "I'd never wanted to comfort a woman before, but I wanted to comfort you. I think that scared me as much as I scared you."

Naomi smiled against his skin. "I think I fell in love with you that night, too. And until then, I was convinced I'd never want a man to touch me again."

He ran his hand down her side, over the curve of her hip. If he'd known then what Randall Clark had done to Naomi, Carl would never have dared go into her room. If Naomi hadn't been raped, she wouldn't have felt so vulnerable, and what had happened between them might never have happened. A riddle he'd never be able to solve.

"Naomi, back in Mackenzie I agreed to respect your privacy, and I still will, if that's what you want. But if you want to tell me what happened to you, if it will help you put it behind you, I'll listen."

Naomi lifted her head and looked into his eyes. "While you were in Vancouver, I was subpoenaed to testify at Clark's trial. He was convicted. He'll never hurt anyone again."

Jesus, Mary and Joseph. She'd had to go through that without him. "And I wasn't there for you. God, Naomi, I—"

She placed a finger over his lips. "You were there for me, Carl. You'd already given back the part of me he stole. If you hadn't, I'd never have been able to face him in the courtroom that day. And yes, I do want to tell you now."

She settled into his arms again. Carl held her close and stroked her hair while she told him what had happened that day out on the prairie, and about the trial. It hurt as much to hear as it did to tell.

"Naomi, I'm so proud of you. I only wish I could have dealt with Clark myself. Hanging was far too good for him. And I deserve a whipping for not being there with you."

Naomi pressed a kiss to his chest. "It's over. Let's talk about the future, not the past."

The future. How was it that he, who'd never spared a thought for tomorrow, had been led to such a rich one? "Naomi, when I'm free I want to go back to Saskatchewan."

Naomi lifted her head and looked into Carl's eyes. "Really?"

"Yeah. I don't have a home here now, and the girls will be going their own ways. Alice is going to be married, Georgie has her job at the Herald, and there are too many of my old friends here that I don't care to see again." And he wanted to see Naomi look like she had that first day he walked with her. He wanted her to have that look of belonging, of being home. From the way her face lit up, she liked the idea, though she didn't say so.

"Is Georgie a reporter? She looks the part."

"No, she's a copy editor, but I'm sure she'd make a fine reporter. She's not afraid to stick her nose into anything."

The glow faded from Naomi's eyes. "I'd hate to take you so far away from her and Alice."

"No guilt, Naomi. I know it's far enough away, but there are these things called trains. We'll visit as often as we can, and we'll write. Don't you miss home and Barry and Corinne?"

Naomi's eyes misted over. "Miss them? There have been days when I've almost died of homesickness."

Carl gathered her close again and told her the plans that had taken root in his mind during the quiet hours in his quarters. "It turns out that my mother left a will. There's some money that was left her by her father, that's to be divided amongst Alice and Georgie and me. It's not a fortune, but it'll be enough to help us build a home. We'll find a place not too far from Mackenzie, but large enough for us both to find work. I've been thinking a lot about that. Most of the jobs I had before I enlisted were in construction, and the Army has taught me something about managing people. I think I'd like to have a contracting company someday. Of course, I'd have to learn some things first." The clock on the nightstand caught Carl's eye. He had only a little more than half an hour left. Reality settled in, cold and relentless.

"It's time for me to go. God, I hate to leave you."

Naomi sighed, kissed his shoulder. "I'll walk back with you."

They washed, dressed and headed back to the Common, making plans as they went – the kind of plans Carl had never expected to make. "I'll talk to Major Murphy tonight about getting permission to be married. I think he'll give permission, but we might have to do it without any real ceremony. We can have a proper wedding later. What I'd really like is to marry you in the church out in Prospect, where Alice is staying."

Naomi's smile held a trace of sadness. "Since it can't be at home, with Dad to walk me down the aisle, it doesn't matter to me where we have the ceremony. I just want to be your wife, but of course I want Laura and your family to be there."

Carl took her hand. "I wish your father could be there, too, but you'd love Prospect. It's beautiful out there, but even if I can get permission, there's the problem that you aren't Catholic." Not a small problem, especially considering the fact that Carl hadn't been to mass or confession in years. "Leave that up to me. You get busy choosing a wedding dress."

They said their real goodbye before they came within clear sight of the compound. When they reached the gate, Carl pecked Naomi on the cheek. The sentries couldn't see the wicked smile she gave him.

If only she had a telephone – but she didn't. "I'll write tonight and tell you how my talk with Major Murphy goes. I'll write every day."

"So will I. Goodnight." Another quick kiss, and she hurried away. Carl watched her until she reached the other side of the Common before entering the compound. The gate closed behind him – a hollow, lonely sound.

Pull yourself together, O'Neill. You've got a lot to do, and not much time to do it.

Carl checked his watch. Just past eight-thirty. Not too late to try to see Major Murphy.

When he knocked on the major's door, Murphy answered immediately. "Come in, Lieutenant. I thought I might be seeing you. I take it you have something to tell me."

Carl saluted, removed his cap and stepped inside. "Yes, sir. I came to ask your permission to be married, sir."

Murphy smiled and clapped him on the shoulder. "So she said 'yes.' Congratulations, Lieutenant. Once your court-martial is behind you, I'll be pleased to give you permission."

"Yes, sir." Carl swallowed and took a deep breath. Just what he'd expected. Now for the dicey part.

"Is there something else, O'Neill?"

"We... I hoped we could be married at Christmas, sir. Here, if necessary. Whatever my sentence turns out to be, it would be easier for both of us that way."

Major Murphy's smile turned to a frown. "You aren't making sense, Lieutenant. What if you end up shipping out and your bride ends up expecting a child?"

Carl's stomach dropped. It looked like he'd found the limit to the major's tolerance. He tried desperately not to stammer and failed.

"I'm – I... That's already a possibility, sir."

Murphy had an Irish temper of his own. He gave it free rein. "For God's sake, O'Neill, I thought you'd learned something about self-control! You could be sitting in a cell when your first child is born. You could be in a trench overseas, or you could be dead."

The man knew how to deal out a tongue-lashing, and he'd likely never given one better deserved. Of course they should have waited, but remembering Naomi's touch, Carl couldn't be sorry.

"That's why we don't want to wait to be married, sir."

Murphy threw up his hands in disgust. The brick red of his face reminded Carl of his father in a temper. "You're hopeless, O'Neill. Get out of my sight."

"Sir—"

"Get out of here before I have you sent down to the stockade. Go!"

Carl went. So much for the easy way. He'd just have to find another.

Back in his hut, Carl threw himself on his bed. All the arguments he'd had at home about going to church – maybe he should have listened after all. If he had, he might have a friend at court now.

Carl hadn't thought to ask Georgie whether Father MacManus from St. Joseph's had survived the explosion or not, but if he had, he'd be too preoccupied with his decimated parish to have time to help Carl, who'd never been anything but a thorn in the good father's side. No, a priest who didn't know him would be a better bet. Tomorrow was Friday, and a Catholic chaplain would be coming to the compound to hear confessions. Carl hadn't met Father Norris, but it was time to make his acquaintance.

Carl halted in the doorway of the makeshift chapel, a hut like all the others in the compound. Nothing here but the altar and a few rows of chairs. No confessional, no anonymity. Only the thought of Naomi kept him from turning on his heel and walking away.

Seated on a chair near the altar, Father Norris gestured to the chair beside him. "Come in, Lieutenant." Even though Carl knew that Father Norris had served as a chaplain overseas, the lack of formality surprised him. He removed his cap, crossed himself and walked in.

"Bless me, Father, for I have sinned. It's been over three years since my last confession. I was overseas for most of those three years. It would take a lot less time to tell you the sins I haven't committed than the ones I have."

Father Norris echoed what Father MacManus had always said. "It's best to start with the sins that are hardest to confess."

Now there was a choice. "Of course I killed in battle, but I also killed when I could have avoided it. I committed all the usual sins when I had leave. I was captured, and I broke my sworn word as an officer. When I came home, I didn't honour my parents or treat my sisters with respect. I ran away to avoid being sent back overseas, and I let my family think I was dead. I don't know how many lies I've told, how much profane language I've used or how many times I've been drunk. But none of that is the real reason I'm here. I'm here because of a woman."

Heat raced up Carl's neck and flooded his face. He hadn't meant to say so much so bluntly. He sat there, mortified, while Father Norris studied him.

"When you say because of a woman, what do you mean?"

Only that? In response to a confession of what amounted to murder? Yeah, Father Norris must have pretty much heard and seen it all. Carl breathed a little easier. Apparently he hadn't wrecked his chances of getting the priest's help yet.

"I mean that I'm in love with her and I want to marry her."

"And she insists on being married in the Church?"

Careful, O'Neill. The man's no fool. You could win or lose right here. "No, Father. She isn't Catholic. I want us to be married in the Church."

No lie, but it felt like one. Father Norris' eyes narrowed a little. "And she's willing to do that, and to raise your children as Catholics?"

Carl had planned to answer 'yes' to that question, but with Father Norris' eyes on him, the word stuck in his throat. Maybe it was the setting. Maybe that much of his upbringing still clung to him, or it might be because he'd already been too honest, but he couldn't lie to Father Norris any more than he could lie to Naomi.

"We haven't discussed that, Father. We haven't had chance, but she says she'll marry me anywhere."

"And you wish to return to the Church yourself?"

Tongue-tied, Carl stared down at his feet. So much for his glib story. Of all days, his conscience would choose today to raise its voice.

"Father, I never really belonged to the Church. Oh, I was baptized and confirmed, but I stopped believing in God a long time ago, if I ever did believe. Then I met this woman, and I'm not so sure anymore."

"How did you meet her?"

Father Norris leaned forward, his gaze intent, as if he really wanted to know. Maybe Carl hadn't blown his chances yet after all. "I got sick, and she looked after me. She made me see that I couldn't keep running for the rest of my life. So, I came home and turned myself in to the Army. Yesterday I found out that she's here in Halifax, and I asked her to marry me." Carl stopped, unsure of his ground. Father Norris' views were probably stricter than Major Murphy's when it came to these things. "Then I sinned with her, too. I love her so much, Father."

After a moment, Father Norris nodded. "I can see that you do. It shows on your face. Lieutenant, you came here today looking for my help, not reconciliation with God, didn't you?"

Yes, only somehow it had turned into more than that. The acceptance Carl had found in the last few days, from Naomi, from Alice and Georgie, and now Father Norris, added up to more than the sum of its parts.

"I didn't think there could be any forgiveness for some of the things I've done."

The look in Father Norris' dark eyes reminded Carl of Barry, the night Carl had told him about the young German gunner. "If that were true, I don't think you would have been led to this young woman as I believe you have been. As for your sinning with her, perhaps God is using that sin to His advantage. Have you asked permission to marry?"

"Yes, I have, and it was informally granted, but when I told Major Murphy what happened yesterday he wasn't impressed. I'm still going to be disciplined for being absent without leave, Father. If I don't marry before that happens, I might not be able to marry for months. I don't want to do that to her."

For a few seconds that felt like an eternity, Carl waited. Then Father Norris rose. "You haven't said you want to return to the Church, but with this woman's influence, I believe you will. I can't promise you anything, but I'll speak to Major Murphy. As for penance, I'd say you've already done enough."

Knees weak, Carl got to his feet. "Thank you, Father."

"Give thanks to the Lord, for He is good."

Carl's mind went blank, unable to remember the response he'd unwillingly repeated so many times. In the end, Father Norris supplied it. "For His mercy endures forever. Think about that, Lieutenant."

The next evening after mess, in the middle of Carl's daily letter to Naomi, Major Murphy knocked on his door. Carl's full stomach turned over as he came to attention. Maybe Murphy had decided to transfer him to the stockade after all, or perhaps the date for Carl's court-martial had been set.

"Sir."

Murphy set his cap on Carl's desk and nodded toward the chair. "As you were, Lieutenant."

Pulse drumming in his ears, Carl sat. If Murphy took back his permission to marry Naomi, there'd be no option but to sneak out and do it secretly. No way was Carl going to leave her completely unprotected.

The major looked down at him, frowning. "I had a visit from Father Norris before he left yesterday. He wanted to talk to me about your case."

"He told me he was going to speak to you, sir."

"It seems you made an impression on him. That was your intention, no doubt."

Carl didn't answer. Murphy went on, his frown a touch less severe. "I was furious with you the other night, and I'm still angry, but what's done is done. I gave you a pass, so I have to take some of the responsibility for the consequences."

"I want to do what's right for Naomi, sir."

"The right thing would have been for you to wait, but since you didn't, I can see Father Norris' point that it might prove very embarrassing for your young lady if you have to wait for months. Of course, you both should have thought of that."

"Yes, sir."

Major Murphy sighed and sat on the edge of Carl's bed. "Father Norris thinks this girl is a good influence on you. I certainly agree that you could use one."

"Yes, sir." Carl struggled to keep the hope blossoming in his chest from showing on his face. Murphy had no reason to come here if he weren't considering changing his mind.

"I also suspect that if you aren't permitted to marry her, you'll do something to make more trouble for me and for yourself."

Smart man. On pins and needles, Carl waited while the major took off his glasses, polished them and put them back on. When he spoke, he sounded less grudging than Carl knew he intended. "So, though it sticks in my throat, I'm going to give you permission to marry as soon as you can arrange it. Father Norris is coming back over here tomorrow afternoon to discuss that with you."

Bless you, Father. Carl gripped the arms of his chair to keep from jumping to his feet.

"Sir, I—"

"Do you have any idea what you're getting into?"

A grin started somewhere deep inside Carl and spread across his face. "No sir, but I know Naomi is the one to teach me."

For the next few days, Carl rode a rollercoaster of anticipation and frustration. Father Norris agreed to speak to the local bishop about getting the permission required for marriage to a non-Catholic, but this close to Christmas, in a city full of grieving citizens and damaged churches, getting his attention seemed hopeless. When Father Norris finally managed it, the bishop wanted to speak to Father McManus, Carl's parish priest, who was frantically busy himself. Carl wrote to Naomi in despair. The next evening, she wrote back.

I don't think we should have any more problems. I called Georgie from the hospital and got Father McManus' address. Then I went to see him. He remembered you, of course. I told him how we met, and how you'd decided to come home. Then I told him that we'd already been together, and that if we couldn't be married by a priest we'd be married by a judge, you'd probably never darken a church doorway again and I would bring our children up Presbyterian. He saw my point. I expect you'll get a letter from the bishop very soon.

That's my girl. The letter still in his hand, Carl fell back on his bed laughing, picturing the look on Naomi's face when she marched up to Father McManus' door, almost hearing her crisp tone. Still chuckling, he rose and grabbed a piece of writing paper.

Dear Naomi,

I love, love, love you. If only I could have been there. I'm sure Father MacManus does remember me, and I doubt that he'll ever forget you, either.

Now things had to be arranged with the priest in Prospect. Carl wrote a note to Alice, and she promised to do what she could. In the end, Father O'Brien agreed to perform the ceremony. By that time, Christmas was only three days away. Carl called Camp Hill to speak to Naomi, to find out if she'd been able to get out of her Christmas Day shift.

"Yes. Connie is going to trade shifts with me. Her husband's at sea on a merchant ship and she's not expecting him back until after Christmas, so I'm going to work New Year's Eve for her."

Carl's heart lifted at the excitement in her voice. "I've got leave, too, but just for the day and night. I'll hire some kind of a rig to get us out to Prospect in the morning."

Naomi's tone turned crisp. "You'll hire a rig to get yourself out there. Laura and I will go on our own. You aren't going to see me before the wedding."

"Naomi, you don't—"

"No buts. Do you think I haven't driven a horse as many miles as you have?"

She had him there. Carl smiled at the memory of the day she'd come across him on Barry's mare, but she was a long way from home. "Not on that road, you haven't."

In the pause that followed, he pictured Naomi rolling her eyes. "I've written to Alice myself, and she's sent me directions. She and Georgie are also going to stand up with me, and Liam said he'd stand up with you, if you want him. I gather the two of you haven't always been the best of friends, but he made the offer."

"He did? Alice must have bewitched him."

"Probably."

Carl thought it over, liked the idea. The man was going to be family, after all, and Carl hadn't forgotten the things Liam had said to him in the hospital. Things that had played a part in sending Carl west, and in bringing him home again. "I'll write and tell him I'd be pleased."

Naomi's voice softened. "I've got something else to tell you. The letter you wrote me from Vancouver – I got it yesterday. Barry and Corinne sent it on."

Good. She had proof now that the things he'd said to her weren't just talk, that he really had been thinking of her while he was out there. She deserved that.

"I'm glad. I wanted you to have it before we were married. Now you know I never stopped thinking of you."

Naomi's voice trembled a little. "I already knew, Carl. I always did."

Chapter 24

Naomi reined her rented horse to a stop on the hill above Prospect and turned to Laura. "What do you think?"

In the distance, the choppy Atlantic frothed and gleamed in the snatches of sunlight that came through the odd gap in the clouds. A cold, grey day, but thank heavens, it wasn't snowing. After all that Naomi and Carl and Georgie and Alice had gone through to arrange the wedding, it would have been awful if a storm had blown in to ruin it. And Naomi didn't need sunshine to lift her heart. It was above the clouds already.

Laura looked out at the bay, watching the surf that sent up plumes of spray from the boulders along the shore. "It's a little like watching a fire, isn't it? Always changing. It kind of holds you, but it looks so cold."

"Someday we'll see it in the summer." Naomi checked her watch. "Ten-thirty already. I hope Carl made it here all right." Alice and Liam had arranged for Carl to wait at a neighbour's house until Liam came to get him. Naomi was to go to Liam's cousin's house to change into her dress, then walk over to the church with Alice and Georgie.

Carl couldn't have chosen a better place for the wedding. Damaged, war-obsessed Halifax might have been a thousand miles away from this picture-postcard fishing village, with its cluster of weathered houses ringing the bay and the graceful spire of Our Lady of Mount Carmel reaching upward. This harsh, rock-strewn landscape bore no resemblance to home, but it had space and calm. Naomi didn't feel claustrophobic here.

Alice's description made Liam's cousin's house easy to find. As Naomi and Laura pulled into the yard, a tall, slender young woman in a yellow print dress and a rust-coloured sweater stepped out, a fair-haired baby of about a year old in her arms. A welcoming smile curved her lips and warmed her amber eyes.

"Hello. You must be Naomi and Laura."

The young woman bore no resemblance to Carl, but she fit his description of his youngest sister. Alice lacked Georgie's sparkle, but she had a quiet beauty of her own.

"And you're Alice. Hello."

A boy of about fourteen came out behind Alice, nodded shyly and began unhitching the horse. Naomi and Laura followed Alice inside. In seconds, the low-roofed kitchen filled with people. Liam shook hands, took his son from Alice and made way for others. Liam's cousin Jess and his wife Fanny introduced themselves, their two black-haired, rosy-cheeked daughters, Clara and Maud, and their son Everett, who came in from seeing to the horse.

Georgie had come out the previous night. Carl's father wasn't there. Naomi couldn't help a twinge of disappointment. If her father were alive, he'd have become the true father Carl had missed, but she wouldn't think of that. Her father would want any tears today to be happy ones.

When the hubbub died down, Jess, a burly man as dark as his wife and children, took Naomi aside. "I understand that your father passed away not long ago. I know we've just met, but Liam and Alice are family, and that makes Carl and you family in a way. I'd be proud to walk down the aisle with you and give you away, if you'd like."

Misty-eyed, Naomi smiled. The village, the church, her bridesmaids, were all new to her. Why not have this kind stranger walk her toward her new life?

"I'd like that very much, Jess."

Georgie appeared and took Naomi's arm. "Time's flying, Naomi. We'd better go upstairs and get ready." She pulled Laura along with them.

There'd been no question of coordinating dresses. There hadn't been time. Georgie and Alice had both lost most of their clothes in the explosion, but Alice had salvaged a dress of navy blue crepe de chine with a lace collar. With her long, golden brown hair pinned up under a soft-brimmed black hat, she looked a little old-fashioned, but that suited her. Georgie wore a simple but stylish dress of blue wool, made elegant with a brown velvet hat and a string of pearls above the middy collar.

Like Alice's, Naomi's dress looked a little bit quaint. A lace overskirt covered the straight skirt of white crepe, drawn in at the waist with a strip of satin embroidered with rosebuds. The top bloused just slightly, with a V-neck and elbow-cuffed lace sleeves. She wore a garnet necklace to fill in the neckline. It had belonged to her mother, and the garnet was set in delicate gold filigree that matched her gold hoop earrings. She'd chosen a simple, short lace veil to cover her hair, which she'd brushed and left loose, as she had the night of the dance in Mackenzie.

She stood in front of the small oval mirror in Liam and Alice's room, longing for her full-length mirror at home. "Alice, Georgie, Laura, am I put together properly? Are there any ends sticking out anywhere?"

Georgie ran a critical eye over Naomi's dress, then gave her waistband a slight tug to straighten it. "There. You look perfect. It's no surprise that Carl fell in love with you."

Naomi turned from the mirror to face Carl's sisters. "I want to thank both of you for being so understanding and welcoming in such a difficult time." Then she turned to the woman who had been like a mother to her. "And thank you, Laura, for coming east with me and being a part of my wedding – and my life."

Laura hugged her. "I've looked forward to this day for a long time, Naomi."

Alice came to stand at Naomi's other side and put an arm around her waist. "You've brought out the best in Carl. That's something no one in the family has been able to do. Mother would be pleased."

A niggling fear at Naomi's heart disappeared. Georgie and Alice didn't resent her for taking Carl away from them. "I've always wanted sisters. Now I have them."

Georgie dabbed at her eyes with her lace handkerchief, careful not to smudge her makeup. "Yes, you do. Now we'd better go down. Carl will be waiting."

While they dressed, the house had gone silent. Everyone had already left for the church. The girls and Laura got into coats and boots and hurried along the frozen road to the church, carrying their shoes. Laura went down a side isle and took a seat near the front. Jess was waiting for Naomi in the vestibule.

As she took his arm, Naomi closed her eyes and pictured her father's face, smiling, approving. Jess tucked her arm more firmly under his.

"Are you ready?"

She looked to the girls for moral support and found Alice gone. Before Naomi could ask where she was, the strains of Schubert's *Ave Maria* floated from the organ. Georgie grinned.

"That's Alice. Wedding gift for you."

"Oh, Georgie. Carl said Alice was going to see to the music, but I never thought she'd play herself."

"That was one of Mother's favourite pieces."

"Carl told me Alice was talented, and he's right. Jess, I'm ready."

Everett and Clara propped open the doors and slipped into their seats. And there was Carl beside Liam at the altar, in his dress uniform, jaw set, eyes glowing with love and pride, focused only on her.

Her wanderer come home.

When the time came, Carl slid a worn gold band with a small but sparkling diamond onto her finger. Lost in his eyes, Naomi barely noticed it. Carl's voice trembled when he promised to love, honour and cherish her for the rest of her life, but hers rang with certainty when she made the same promise to him. Then the ceremony was over, the certificate signed and they were back in Fanny's warm kitchen, where the smells of roasting turkey, gingerbread and balsam fir set everyone's stomach growling.

Sugar was in short supply, so to tide them over, Laura and Fanny set plates of spicy War Cake on the table, along with a pot of tea and molasses brown bread. Once everyone was busy eating, Alice disappeared. She returned in a few minutes with something closed up in her hand, and crossed the room to where Naomi and Carl stood by the window. She looked from Carl to Naomi and back again, her gaze soft with emotion.

"Carl, I think Naomi should keep this for you now."

He nodded. Alice faced Naomi and held out her hand. "I'll let him tell you about this, if he hasn't already."

She opened her hand. A silver Maltese Cross, threaded on a blue and red ribbon, lay in her palm. Naomi took it, examined it.

A Military Cross. One of the highest honours a soldier could earn on the battlefield. Naomi wasn't the only one who considered Carl a hero.

"Carl, is this yours?"

"Yeah."

"You've never said a word."

"I never thought there was any point, before I came back to Halifax."

Everett must have caught the glint of sunlight off silver as Naomi lifted the medal from Alice's hand. Wide-eyed, the boy joined them. "I've only seen pictures of those. Put it on, Carl."

He shook his head. "Not today, Everett. Today's about the future, not the past."

"I know, but just for a minute, while you're in uniform."

Naomi held Carl's gaze, laid her free hand on his chest. "I'd like to see it on you, too. Just for a minute."

He took a deep breath and nodded. Naomi lifted the ribbon over his head, settled the medal against his chest and watched the emotions mingling behind those deep blue eyes. Sadness, pride, hope. Mostly hope.

"You wear it well, Carl."

It took her a moment to notice that everyone in the kitchen had gone silent, even Nicholas, now in his father's arms. Liam looked down at his son, then his gaze connected with Carl's. The unspoken message that passed between them tugged at Naomi's heartstrings. Carl, Liam, her patients at Camp Hill, the ones in the field hospital – if fate were kind, because of them, Everett and little Nicholas would never truly understand the meaning of that piece of silver lying against Carl's chest.

Dear Lord, never again.

Carl took the medal off and gave it back to Naomi. "Put it away for me." Alice handed her a small velvet box that looked like something she'd probably used for her own jewellery. Naomi laid the medal inside and put the box in her purse. Then, while everyone was still quiet, Carl took Naomi's left hand.

"Naomi, your ring was Mother's wedding ring. Somehow, Georgie convinced Dad to let her keep it." He lifted Naomi's hand to his lips. "Mother wore it for better, for worse. I know what that means now, thanks to you and your father and Barry and Corinne. Can you trust me enough to do the same?"

The mist in Naomi's eyes turned to tears that spilled down her cheeks. "It's beautiful... Yes. Yes, yes, yes." With each 'yes,' she placed a soft kiss on his mouth. The last time, he wrapped her against his chest and kissed her soundly. Laughter broke out as he let her go. Naomi wiped her eyes with the back of her hand and laughed with the rest. Liam raised his teacup.

"Guess Fanny's saving the blueberry wine for dinner, so this will have to do. To the bride and groom."

Carl raised his cup in return. "To the future bride and groom. Be happy, Alice. If you aren't, I'll only be a week's train ride away."

Liam held Carl's gaze in a friendly trial of strength. "I'll remember that."

Naomi believed him. Liam reminded her of Carl more than either man would probably care to know. Irish to the core, with enough loyalty to outweigh all his faults put together, and scarred inside and out. But if love could heal, it would heal Liam, too. The way he and Alice looked at each other left no doubt of that.

Laura cleared her throat and turned to Carl. "And you... Take care of my girl. Not that I think you won't, but she's the only family I have."

He grinned. "If I don't, I know it won't take you a week to find me." His grin softened. "Laura, my mother is gone. I'm going to adopt you as my mother from now on. Can you live with that?"

Laura's voice shook just a little. "I suppose I can."

Naomi hugged her. "I adopted you as my mother a long time ago, Laura. Thank you for...for everything."

After dinner, the time came to head back to Halifax. Laura insisted on driving the sleigh she and Naomi had come in, so Naomi could ride with Carl. She said goodbye to Jess and Fanny with hugs.

"You both made our wedding day beautiful. I'll never forget you for that."

Fanny hugged her again. "You're more than welcome, my dear. We won't forget you, either. We'll see you again, the next time you and Carl come home."

Home. Naomi's conscience pricked her as they drove away in Carl's sleigh, with Laura following "Carl, I feel so selfish, taking you away from your family when you've really just found them."

He wrapped his arm around her, looked into her eyes. "You aren't taking me away from them. I told you that before, remember? And settling everything here will take some time. Time for them to know us. We're going to write and visit. They'll have a reason to come west and see a part of the country they've never seen. And anyway, I would never have really found them again, if not for you."

She leaned against him, rested her head on his shoulder. The sleigh bells jingled, and the strains of Alice's music blended in harmony with the song in Naomi's heart. "I'll do my best to make sure you never regret it. Always."

Carl bent his head and kissed her, a kiss that tasted of Christmas dinner and frosty air and a lifetime of promise. "I'll do the same, Naomi. Always."

Carl's stomach tightened with nerves as he unlocked the door to the room he'd booked at a quiet, old-fashioned inn in Bedford. Aunt Sarah had recommended it, but no one she knew had stayed there for quite some time, and he hadn't been able to go see the place himself. Since he and Naomi only had this one night, he wanted it to be perfect.

He switched on the light and breathed a sigh of relief. A snapping fire, bright homemade quilts on the bed, a fragrant Christmas wreath over the mantel and a vase of red roses on the bedside table – as he'd ordered. He hung their coats in the closet and took Naomi in his arms.

"What do you think?"

She pressed herself against him and looked up with a smile that set his heart racing with anticipation. "I think it's far too warm in here for you to have so many clothes on."

She nibbled at his lips while she unbuttoned his uniform jacket. Then her hand delved under his shirt to play over his chest, and the room no longer mattered.

They couldn't get close enough, fast enough. They hadn't been intimate like this since that first evening at Naomi's flat, and their need for each other had only grown stronger since then. Open-mouthed kisses and teasing caresses. Naomi's gasp of pleasure as he plunged deep inside her, joining his soul to hers. Her body tightening around him as she came.

When Carl reached his own shuddering release and called her name, it sounded like a prayer of thanks – the only truly honest prayer he'd ever offered, even before battle.

After all, she was his heart's deliverance.

EPILOGUE

November 11, 1920

Carl finished pinning his medal to his dress uniform and checked his reflection in the bedroom mirror. Naomi came up behind him, looked over his shoulder, smiling. "You still wear it well."

"Thanks." He put on his cap and turned around. Naomi twirled in front of him.

"What do you think?"

Her dark brown dress might be somber, but the warm glow in Naomi's eyes and the bloom of pregnancy on her skin overcame it. Carl took her in his arms. "You're beautiful." More beautiful every day, the way only a happy woman could be. For their first two years here in Yorkton, they'd been glad Naomi didn't get pregnant. She'd been busy training as a midwife while Carl had thrown himself into his job with a local contracting company – and he'd needed time with her alone. Time to get used to everything Naomi had brought into his life.

Three years. Long enough for hope to turn to happiness. Through his court-martial, through his month-long jail sentence afterward, through the bad days and the good, he'd had Naomi to lean on. Now, with an honourable discharge behind him, their new home finished, his fledgling construction company growing and Naomi settled in her work, the time was right for a family. They'd banked the money from the sale of her father's practice for their children's future.

They were dressing for the Armistice Day Ceremony at the cenotaph downtown. At eleven o'clock – the eleventh hour of the eleventh day of the eleventh month – Carl would stand with his fellow veterans to remember all the ones who hadn't returned from overseas. Ben MacNeil. The young German gunner. Never an easy obligation to fulfill, but afterward there would be a warm fire in the fireplace, a hot dinner and Naomi.

Laura would eat with them, then return to her apartment at the back of the house, or go out to visit one of her new friends. Laura loved Yorkton, and Barry and Corinne were only an hour's train ride away.

Three years.

Alice wrote that she and Liam were happy in their new home in Lunenburg, with Nicholas and their baby daughter Katie. "Liam still has bad days, like I'm sure you do, but the good ones make up for it."

Yes. There were bad days, and nights when Carl's bad dreams woke him, but when that happened Naomi was there, and that made all the difference.

Carl took her hand and led her to the bedroom window. It looked out over open prairie, brown and dry under a grey sky like it had been the first day he'd seen it in Mackenzie. The view was why they'd chosen this lot at the edge of town, that and the room it offered for a couple of horses. Naomi even condescended to tell him he rode well now.

Carl drew her in front of him, facing the window, and rested his hands on her shoulders. Alice was right. The good days were more than worth it.

"What do you see?"

Naomi leaned against him and looked up, love shining from her eyes. "I see years. A lot of years. Good ones."

So did he.

Historical Note

The Halifax Explosion of 1917 remains the largest non-natural, non-atomic explosion in recorded history. It was used as a case study for the Manhattan Project. It occurred on the morning of December 6, when the *Imo*, a Belgian relief vessel, collided in The Narrows with the French vessel *Mont Blanc*, bound for Europe with a cargo of explosives and airplane fuel. The collision started a fire on the *Mont Blanc* that touched off the volatile cargo. Blame was never clearly established.

The community of Richmond in Halifax's North End was obliterated. Approximately 2000 people were killed and thousands more injured, many blinded by flying glass as they stood at windows watching the *Mont Blanc* burn. The tragedy lent impetus to the development of safety glass. The Catholic parish of St. Joseph's, in the heart of Richmond, lost half its members that day, along with the church itself and the girls' school next door. Rebuilding took decades.

In the aftermath of the Explosion, one saving grace was the presence of the military in the city. Crew members of the Royal Navy flagship HMS *Highflyer* sacrificed their lives trying to prevent the *Mont Blanc* from exploding. Soldiers and sailors rescued countless people from collapsed buildings, kept order, and helped oversee the distribution of the relief supplies that quickly poured in from far and wide.

One of the first responders was the state of Massachusetts, where so many Nova Scotians had family ties. To this day, the Christmas tree that glitters each year in Boston's Prudential Square is a gift from the people of Nova Scotia in remembrance of help provided in time of need.

Stories of the Explosion are woven into the fabric of Halifax's culture. We remember 'Ashpan Annie', a toddler who was found in the rubble of her home days after the blast, lying in the ashpan of the kitchen stove. The warm ashes had kept her from freezing. She died last year. We remember the recuperating soldiers at Camp Hill Veterans' Hospital who gave up their beds to those more seriously injured. We remember Vince Coleman, a telegraph operator who, when he realized the *Mont Blanc* was likely to explode, stayed at his post to send a warning message to an incoming train. Coleman's bravery saved dozens of lives, but cost him his own. His message ended with a simple 'goodbye.'

Needless to say, ghost stories of the Explosion abound. A friend of mine who lives in the North End told me that one day she arrived home from work, glanced in her kitchen window and saw a man in old-fashioned clothes sitting at her table. While she was looking at him, he vanished. Her 'visitor' became my inspiration for Liam Cochrane.

I taught for ten years in one of the few North End buildings to survive the Explosion, the school directly across Russell Street from St. Joseph's Church. Originally a Catholic boys' school, the building was still under construction in December, 1917. Climbing the main stairs in the dark early on winter mornings, I often felt that if I listened carefully enough, I'd hear echoes of children's laughter from ninety years ago.

About the Author

Jennie Marsland is a teacher and an amateur musician as well as a writer. She fell in love with words at a very early age and the affair has been life-long.

Jennie has always been fascinated by history. Glimpses of the past spark her imagination. She finds her inspiration in the beauty of Nova Scotia's landscape and in family stories about earlier times, passed down from her parents and grandparents.

With a background in Biology and a degree in Agriculture, animals have always been a big part of Jennie's life. Her household includes her husband and two Nova Scotia Duck-Tolling Retrievers, Chance and Echo, who are without a doubt the most spoiled creatures on the planet. When she isn't writing, she gardens, plays guitar, dabbles in watercolours and caters to the needs of the four-footed tyrants of the house.